Intimate Kill

Margaret Yorke

Intimate Kill

St. Martin's Press
New York

MYSTERY
Yorke
M.

Library of Congress Cataloging in Publication Data

Yorke, Margaret.
  Intimate kill.

  I. Title.
PR6075.0715   1985   823'.914   85-1754
ISBN 0-312-42536-8

First published in Great Britain by Hutchinson & Co. Ltd.

First U.S. Edition

10 9 8 7 6 5 4 3 2 1

All the characters and events, and most of the places in this story, are fictional. Resemblance to real people is coincidental.

Part One

1

Now that it was happening, it felt unreal, like a dream.

He had been outside before, of course. At the open prison where he had finished his sentence he had undergone a carefully planned resettlement programme, beginning with escorted expeditions into the nearby town. For the last six months, after completing a course in computer studies, he had worked there, travelling daily on the bus.

Stephen Dawes had served ten years of a life sentence, and today he had been released on licence, for authority was sure he would not kill again. He had carried no gun; his was a domestic murder.

This morning he had been apprehensive, as well as eager, for this was real freedom, though he was on parole and must report regularly to his probation officer. He sat in the train gazing out of the window at the passing scene – first houses backing the railway line, then open countryside with the autumn leaves turning to copper, and sombre, blackened fields where stubble fires had burned. He had seen the plumes of black smoke and the leaping flames from the prison, a cluster of wartime buildings set in tranquil rural isolation.

Because he had no family, and there were tenants still in his house, he had spent his terminal leave in approved lodgings. He was going there now, for the lease was not up until Monday.

In a way, it was a relief to postpone the moment of true independence. Prison had been home, and he understood the recidivists who committed fresh offences in order to return to a life where the regime was preordained and where they were sure to find, if not friends, at least acquaintances, and where they would have no struggle for physical survival.

Stephen held a newspaper on his knee. He glanced at the headlines. There was trouble in Ireland and the Middle

East, just as there had been at the time of his arrest. After the first stunned months of his imprisonment, he had followed home and world news with concentration. One day he would be released, and he must keep in touch with what was going on.

The train stopped at a small station and two brisk-looking middle-aged women got into the carriage. They moved past Stephen and settled down across the aisle. He wondered how they would react if they knew who he was. Women like them had screamed, jeered, and cursed obscenely when he was bundled out of court and taken off to begin his long sentence.

He sighed, picking up the paper again and turning to the sporting page. There was a report of a golf tournament. It would be pleasant to play golf again, he thought. On a golf course there would be space, acres of ground unimpeded by humans, and no watching eyes, just the pairs and foursomes walking over the turf in the damp, autumnal weather. He rehearsed in his mind how it would feel: the air moist against one's face; the ground springy under one's feet.

He would never again take for granted the freedom to breathe fresh air.

Stephen's train was not very full. The two women who had just got on were talking about the daughter of one of them who was soon to be married. Stephen could pick out only a part of their conversation above the noise of the train. The daughter of the second woman had just had a baby. It went on: life, marriage, birth – and death. People in prison had died – not many; a few convicts, and one warder from a heart attack. His own life must continue, and he must direct it, take over responsibility for himself.

Odd, now, to think how he had dreaded going to the open prison, although it was a necessary step to his ultimate release. Until then, in each of the different prisons where he had been held, he had had a cell to himself and so a degree of privacy. He had known that at the open prison he would have to sleep in a dormitory until it was his turn to be given a room. The experience had been a real shock, the long months of waiting a further test of endurance. But gradually the rest of the programme had begun to take effect; he had responded to the new routine and to the environment;

slowly, the man buried inside the docile prisoner had begun to come alive.

And next week he would have a home.

Ivy Lodge, at Fairbridge, had been his widowed mother's house. When, more than seven years ago, she was killed in a car accident after visiting Stephen in Wormwood Scrubs, he had wanted Frank Jeffries, his solicitor and friend, to sell it. At that time, Stephen had felt that he would never again live anywhere but in a cell.

'We can't tell how long you'll be inside,' Frank had said. So much would depend on reports and assessments, on how Stephen weathered his incarceration, and ultimately on the opinions of review boards. 'Property will appreciate. Eventually, you'll want somewhere to live and that will be the time to sell it, when you've decided where you want to go, and what you're going to do. Meanwhile, you'll be getting the rent and your capital will be protected.'

Frank had been proved right. While Stephen was detained at Her Majesty's pleasure, house prices soared, and now he had no immediate financial worries. His probation officer had accepted his wish to spend the first weeks attending to what must be done to put the house straight after its years of occupation by tenants. Then he intended to set up on his own, he had said. Before his arrest, Stephen had been a management consultant, and he had used a lot of his time in prison to study. He had improved his French and learned German, and had added a degree from the Open University to his other qualifications. He might start an export business, he thought, or go in for computer systems. But he need not decide just yet. There was something else he had to do first.

Frank had not approved of his plan to live in Ivy Lodge as soon as it was empty.

'You could have a hard time,' Frank had warned, recommending selling it at once. It needed only one chance word to bring the case to mind. He imagined broken windows, obscene telephone calls, anonymous letters – all the things that had happened after Marcia's disappearance and before Stephen's arrest. Society had grown more violent since then; Stephen might be physically attacked.

'I've learned to live without friends,' Stephen had said. 'I'll manage.'

The tenants would be out on Monday at midday. Then, using it as a base, Stephen could begin his search for Ruth and the child.

Frank had visited Stephen regularly over the years, the only person to do so after the death of his mother. On his earlier leave, Frank had driven him to Rawhampton, where Mr and Mrs Collins, his hosts, lived in a semi-detached house in a pleasant suburb. Frank had been unhappy because Stephen was not spending his leave with him and his wife.

'I understand,' Stephen had said, aware that Frank's wife, Val, whom he had met and married after the trial, would not wish a convicted murderer to cross her threshold.

Frank had wanted to pick him up today and drive him over, but Stephen had refused to let him.

'I'm quite used to things, now,' he had said. 'I must stand on my own feet.'

There was still a great deal he must adjust to in the everyday world, Stephen knew, and he had better begin at once.

He caught the bus from the station, uncertain of the exact fare and holding several coins in his hand. You dealt only in very small sums in prison, and he knew he would have some shocks at the actual cost of living; he had seen that when, escorted by a prison officer, he had shopped for some clothes for his job. A worse shock had been the green hair and shaved heads of the first punks he had seen, much more vivid in the flesh than in newspaper shots or on television.

As he sat in the bus, Stephen thought about Ruth. She would certainly not have told the child who her father was. She would want to protect her; that was why he had never heard from her since it had happened. A cheque he had sent her before his arrest had not been presented, and after the trial, when, through Frank, he had attempted, again, to send her money, she had moved. He had left it then. In reports of the case, she was referred to as 'the Unknown Mistress' and cited as the motive for the murder. Naturally, she wanted to have nothing more to do with him.

12

He meant to find her.

Mrs Collins must have been watching for him, for as he walked up the short path between bright dahlias and dwarf Michaelmas daisies, the front door opened.

'Ah, there you are, Stephen,' she said, plump and smiling, but brawny too, and, he knew, trained in the art of self-defence; Mr Collins had taken care to tell him that on his first visit. To Stephen, it seemed a wise precaution, since their guests had led chequered lives. When they were younger, the Collinses had fostered a number of children sent into care. Now, they hoped to rehabilitate some of those considered not too far gone for redemption, and were sometimes successful. 'Come along in – the kettle's on and you'd like some tea,' Mrs Collins told him.

She took Stephen into the kitchen and asked him about the journey while he drank his tea. He wished that she had thought of coffee.

Stephen mentioned the golf course.

'You should have a game,' said Mrs Collins. 'But who with? Reg doesn't play.'

'I could play alone,' said Stephen. 'You don't need a partner. But it'll have to wait until I can get at my clubs.'

Mrs Collins frowned.

'Surely it's better with a friend?' she said. That was part of the problem for these people whom she tried to help: their isolation.

'Maybe,' said Stephen, already losing interest in the subject.

'Well, there's a letter for you in your room,' Mrs Collins said. 'You'll want to read it and get settled in. Lunch will be ready at one. It's steak and kidney pie.' She smiled encouragingly at him. He'd enjoyed her cooking on his other visit.

The last released murderer to stay at 33 The Grove had also been a refined sort of man; he had eased his aged mother on her way with sleeping pills: a mercy killing, the newspapers had called it, and his sentence had been a light one. In between, Mrs Collins had housed boys guilty of breaking and entering, and several older thieves whom she'd tried to set on the right path. It was always worth the effort, and launching Stephen Dawes back into society would be worthwhile, too. His had been one of those *crimes passionels* that the French were so lenient about; no doubt, in his case, there had been provocation, though that was no excuse for murder.

Accepting her gentle dismissal, Stephen went upstairs. His room overlooked the churchyard, and on his previous visit the sound of the clock on the belfry tower tolling the hours had been comforting when, disoriented and apprehensive, he had lain wakeful in the night. He had known, then, that adjustment to release would not be easy.

Frank had kept hoping that Val would relent and let him invite Stephen to Dove House, but as the time came nearer he evaded the subject, and Stephen had let him off the hook.

'You can't blame her, Frank,' he'd said, and remembered his mother's funeral, to which he had been allowed to go. He had no brothers or sisters to be embarrassed by his presence, but his aunt and uncle had not seemed eager to speak to him after the service. He'd been almost glad to return to prison with his escort, who had been quite sympathetic.

There was a glass vase holding three late roses on the table in his room. That was unexpected. It was something his mother would have thought of, and Stephen cleared his throat, swallowing. He had shed no tears since his arrest, not even at her death; in order to survive his time in gaol, he had tried to drain himself of all emotion.

The letter Mrs Collins had mentioned was propped up beside the vase. It contained a short note from Frank wishing him luck and promising to get in touch as soon as he could. In other words, thought Stephen without rancour, as soon as he can slip the leash. Enclosed with Frank's note was another envelope addressed to Stephen; on the back was the address of his mother's solicitors.

Stephen turned the envelope around in his hand. His mother had left him everything she owned. Apart from the house, he had expected very little; his father had been killed during the war, and she had worked as a physiotherapist to support them both. It had turned out, after his mother's death, that she had taken out a life insurance policy which she had increased after he was sentenced. The premiums were high and must have made things very hard for her.

He slit open the solicitor's envelope. Inside was a smaller

one, the Basildon Bond Azure that his mother always used, addressed to him in her rounded, rather girlish hand.

A surge of emotion filled Stephen. He turned the envelope over, running his fingers along it where the flap was gummed. She had been dead for so long. It took him several minutes to calm down enough to slit it open.

The letter was written on two sheets of paper and was dated six months after he had been sentenced.

My dear son, Stephen read,

You will read this only if I should die or be rendered senseless through illness or accident before your release. My solicitor has been instructed to see that you receive it, in those circumstances, when you are free.

Looking backward is not always helpful. Looking forward is a wiser, positive course, and now you must try to put the past behind you, but I am sure you will be concerned about the child and her mother. Forgive me, Stephen, if I say that it seems to me that Ruth would have stood by you if she had truly loved you. Had that happened, I would have met her and we would have supported one another. I would have known my grandchild.

Susannah is my granddaughter, my only grandchild, and I, too, am concerned for her. I am sure that when you are free, you will want to find her to make sure that she is not in want, and because I think you may find it difficult, after the passage of years, to trace Ruth Watson, I have done it for you. My plan is to check, from time to time, that she is still where last heard of, and if I find she is in need, I will, in the meantime, help her. Then this letter will be updated or rewritten. I have employed a reliable private detective, a man recommended by my solicitor.

After your arrest, Ruth Watson took a job in Cumbria as a housekeeper. She was able to have Susannah there, but she left after a year and went to Oxford. She lives there now, at 79 Blossom Road, and works in the health department. Susannah goes to a day nursery and at other times is cared for by another mother. Ruth has a good job with a regularly rising salary and has made adequate arrangements for the care of Susannah while she is at work. There seems no cause for worry about either of them.

By the terms of my will, if you should predecease me, Susannah will inherit what I leave. I tell you this in case I become senile and you read it while I am in a geriatric ward.

Stephen looked up from the letter. He had known about that, of course; he had seen a copy of his mother's will. They treated you humanely over matters such as that, in HM Prisons; you were allowed to conduct your personal affairs if you applied in the proper manner.

He read on.

You will be curious about Susannah. You may seek her out. But I beg you, when you have satisfied yourself as to her welfare, let the past bury itself. Lay your ghosts and then go forward.

The letter was signed simply, *Your loving mother.*

Still holding it, Stephen stood up and crossed to the window, his vision of the churchyard below misted by tears.

His mother had given him the lead he needed.

2

On that first day of his freedom, Stephen went out after lunch. At the bank, using his new card, he cashed a cheque. He felt anxious, passing the cheque and the card across the counter under the defensive glass partition which made communication distant but was such a vital safeguard: he had met perpetrators of violent bank robberies during the past decade. The teller seemed to find him no different from any other customer; giving him only a cursory glance, she stamped the chequebook, handing over twenty pounds. He fought down a wild impulse to tell her that he had been released from prison that morning. What would she do? Yell for help?

But all the teller saw was a man who looked, to her, rather old, with thick grey hair cut short, a neatly trimmed grey beard and a soft moustache. The only thing she might have remarked about him was that he wanted his money in single notes, not fives or tens. A pound went nowhere today.

Stephen had been cleanshaven at the time of Marcia's death. He had grown the beard and moustache in the last months when his release looked probable. To disguise himself properly while he looked for Ruth and the child would be foolish and theatrical, but small differences might help him avoid recognition until he was ready for it. Eleven years ago Stephen had been thirty-seven years old, with dark hair that perpetually flopped across his forehead. He was already making a good income, and he and Marcia had lived in a large white house with a mellow tiled roof, set in over an acre of land and approached by a private road on the edge of Hagbourne Green. The prosecution had made much of the house's position. Four others shared the unmade approach road, but the Dawes's house was the last. All were screened from each other by trees; you could come and go unseen, and often unheard, as Stephen, it was alleged, had done that Wednesday night when he used his car to dispose of Marcia's body.

Some days after her disappearance, her handbag had been found by a woman exercising her dog along the beach at Birling Gap, near Beachy Head. It was an expensive bag, and the woman took it to the police, who, from sodden papers found inside, established ownership. They expected Marcia's body to come ashore too, but it didn't. Now, however, they knew what to ask the forensic scientists to look for, and the laboratory produced evidence from Stephen's car which was enough to convict him. The winds were strong at the time of Marcia's disappearance; bodies known to be in the water had been washed out to sea before and never seen again. A formidable circumstantial case existed and there were precedents where murder had been proved in the absence of a body. The prosecution's case was that Stephen had killed his wife because she would not agree to a divorce; an added motive was her money. He had rigged the evidence to make it look as though their house had been broken into and she had been abducted by an intruder.

Men in prison talked incessantly about their crimes and sentences, but not Stephen, except when forced to by psychologists and prison officers, all wanting him to acknowledge guilt. He was responsible for Marcia's death; he had accepted that; without doing so, there would have been no parole; but he did not want to talk about it. He thought about the past, however, and about his life with Marcia, which, at first, had seemed to be so good. Certainly, he had worshipped her, uncritically, for years. Then he had begun to realize that their bond was hollow. For relief, when Stephen's memories grew too painful to be borne, he had turned his mind towards Susannah, the infant he had seen only once.

Now she was eleven. What would she be like?

Restlessly pacing the streets that afternoon, Stephen knew he must begin his search for her.

Tomorrow he would hire a car; buying one would be too much of an undertaking at the moment, but he bought some motor magazines to modernize his knowledge, and a small notebook. He also bought a paperback about a recent natural-history television series. Then he went to Boots and bought a new toothbrush. This burst of initiative exhausted him; he felt as though eyes bored into his back as people watched his actions. On his leave he had experienced the same sense of being always under observation. He went back to the haven of his lodgings, where Mrs Collins was watching television. She invited Stephen to join her, and he sat there till her husband came home from his work as janitor at a local school. Whilst the set was on, there was no need for conversation.

After the evening meal, taken at much the same time as he was used to eating in the prison, but very early by the standards of Hagbourne Green, Stephen went up to his room. He spent a long time lying on his bed. Convicts did that, too.

But he was not a convict now.

He went downstairs and asked Mrs Collins if he might have a bath.

'Yes,' she said at once, and added that he could have another in the morning if he wanted. She'd remembered what he'd most enjoyed about his leave.

He woke as the clock in the church tower struck four. It was cold in the room, but his bed was comfortable and he pulled the covers round his shoulders. Would he ever sleep with a woman again? Stephen thrust the thought from his mind.

Staring into the darkness, he resolved to move his life onwards that very day.

After breakfast, he went to a hire-car firm in the town and rented a Mini. Marcia had had a Mini; it was familiar, small, and economical. He gave his address as Ivy Lodge, Fairbridge, and arranged that he could return the car to another branch of the hirers if he wished. Then, saying he would pick it up later, he went to the public library, where he looked up hotels in Oxford. That was where Ruth had last been heard of; that was where his search must start. With a list of hotels, he went to the post office and telephoned to one of them. It had a room free, and he booked in, saying he would arrive the following afternoon. Then, finding that stamped postcards were no longer available, he bought two stamped envelopes and looked about in vain for somewhere to sit and write. Post offices used to have tables where you might write out telegrams, but now there weren't any telegrams either.

Stephen stood at the counter and, using paper from his new notebook, wrote two letters, one to Frank and one to his probation officer, giving each of them the address of the hotel and saying he would be there until he moved to Ivy Lodge on Monday. He might be being over-zealous, but it was the sort of zeal he was determined to employ, for he was not going to risk further loss of liberty through any bureaucratic offence. Besides, he was used to obeying orders.

He had lunch in a pub, beer and cottage pie, sitting in a corner, and then he collected the car. There was space to park it outside 33 The Grove.

Stephen had a great sense of something accomplished when he told Mrs Collins that he would be leaving the next day. He had brought her a plant in a pot, and a bottle of whisky for her husband, and he paid his rent to the end of the week. That evening, after the meal, he recorded in his notebook all that he had done since his release. The list was quite long.

He left for Oxford as soon as the worst of the morning's rush hour was over, accepting Mrs Collins's advice not to drive in such heavy traffic. He set off carefully, made uneasy by huge freight lorries that bore down on him. Tensely, Stephen sat behind the wheel, sweating slightly. He hadn't

19

driven Frank's BMW on his leave, though Frank had suggested that he should. He'd felt unequal to the challenge.

North Oxford, when he drove through it, looked little altered, but there were large white lines painted on the road: a bus lane. Stephen realized what it was and moved out of it; there was so much that was new and he must learn it fast, before he made an error.

As he went slowly down St Giles', he saw a parking space and thankfully slid into it. He noticed that there was now a charge, and watched other people to see how the system worked. Fifty pence for a two-hour stay, he read. That should give him time to consult a street directory and find out the whereabouts of Blossom Road.

Well before his time was up, Stephen was sitting in the car outside a terraced house in a side street below Folly Bridge.

Susannah wouldn't be there now; she would be at school. And Ruth would be at work. He could postpone the moment when he would ring the bell and have to think of what to say.

He drove off again, found a long-stay park and left the car, thankful he had chosen one so small and easy to manoeuvre. He had lunch at a pub, sitting quietly reading the paper, his back against the wall so that he would know if anyone was looking at him. Then he walked round the altered town. The busy large new Central Library had, at first, alarmed him when he went there to find out the whereabouts of Blossom Road, but he had soon calmed down, realizing that all the other readers were intent upon their own affairs. He went into Marks and Spencer's – that had moved, too – and bought himself some pale green pyjamas with a dark green collar. The crowds of shoppers on the pavements and the office workers hurrying back from lunch bothered him, making him feel claustrophobic, and he wandered down St Aldate's, into Christ Church Memorial Gardens.

Here, he felt soothed. There were only a few people about, and he strolled through the meadows to the river, where he saw several boats, propelled by husky young men, slicing through the water. The sight made him feel old. He shoved his cold hands into his jacket pockets and turned back.

He would return to Blossom Road and wait there until Ruth came home from work. Perhaps Susannah would arrive back first, from school. At eleven, she might have her own key and let herself in before her mother was due.

The thought worried him.

As he drew up outside the house, two young men in jeans and anoraks entered it. Were they undergraduates? Did Ruth take in lodgers? He got out of the car and walked slowly up the steps to the front door, where he saw a row of bells. The house had been converted into flats, he realized, and read the list of names. He saw no Watson there.

It took Stephen nearly half an hour, spent walking round the nearby streets, to summon enough courage to ring one of the bells and ask the pretty Indian woman who answered it if she knew where Ruth Watson lived now.

She didn't. There had been no Ruth Watson living there in her time, and she'd been a tenant for six years. Sorry.

Of course she'd moved. It was more than nine years since she'd first gone to Oxford. What now?

The telephone directory, he thought. Surely she'd be listed? But she wasn't; none of the Watsons had the right initials.

He told himself that this was only a minor setback. He would check in at the hotel and begin a proper search tomorrow.

Stephen's new room lacked the personal touches with which Mrs Collins had tried to make him feel at home; now he was really on his own, but he had no social obligations. Here, beyond paying his bill, he need make no effort.

He had dinner at a corner table in the hotel restaurant. Several of the other guests were alone; some were business representatives who were tired after a day on the road and all they wanted was a comfortable bed, their own bathroom, a few drinks and television. To Stephen the place seemed like the Ritz as he lay in a deep bath, topping it up with hot water as it cooled.

There would be ways of tracing Ruth. The landlord might know where she was, for instance, or the health department, where she had worked. She might still be employed there.

He tried it the next morning.

References to Health, in the telephone directory, were mostly concerned also with Social Security, Stephen saw.

21

He decided to ring them all in turn and ask for Ruth. If he found her, he need say nothing: just hang up and then decide what to do. If, improbably, she recognized his voice, or if he told her who he was, she might be the one to do the hanging up, but he would have traced her. He could write to her, tell her he only wanted to make sure that all was well with her and with Susannah.

Their romance had begun slowly. Ruth was receptionist to a group of dentists in Guildford. She had been there for some years, and Stephen had grown used to seeing her behind the desk and appointment book. One evening, he noticed her waiting at a bus stop after he had fetched his car from a parking lot, having had the last appointment of the day with Mr Fowler, the senior partner. It was raining, and Stephen stopped to offer Ruth a lift.

Mr Fowler was crowning a tooth for Stephen, and he had to return a few weeks later. He deliberately looked for her this time. Six months after this she had a large parcel to carry; she had been to the sales in her lunch hour and bought a set of saucepans. He carried them up to her attic flat. After that, he began to go round by the bus stop where he had first seen her whenever he left the office at about the right time. Taking her home meant only a minor detour for him.

Marcia was not one of Mr Fowler's patients; she went to a dentist in London.

A whole year passed before Ruth and Stephen began sleeping together. Both were lonely, and the opportunity existed. It had been as simple as that.

Stephen went to a call-box not far from his hotel and lined up a row of tenpence coins. He drew blank at all the numbers he tried. No one had heard of Ruth Watson.

Hospitals, he thought. They belonged to the health authority, surely?

He needed some more coins. He got into his car and drove into the city. This time parking was not easy, and he had to circle round before a space became vacant in St Giles'. Two hours, he thought: he mustn't forget.

He cashed another cheque, this time more confidently. His money was disappearing fast.

The hospitals did not care for his vague inquiry, but, at

one, his call was transferred to the medical social workers' office, and at last someone thought she remembered a Ruth Watson who had worked in the records office of another hospital. He was given a number to ring.

Stephen tried to control his increasing sense of frustration. It could take weeks to find her, and in the end he might be compelled to follow his mother's example and employ a private detective, a thought that filled him with distaste.

But now a female voice was telling him that yes, Ruth had worked in this hospital. She had, however, left years ago.

'Who is it wants her?' the voice inquired.

'A cousin,' said Stephen glibly. 'I've been out of the country and lost touch. The last address I had was Blossom Road.'

'She got married,' said the voice. 'Surely you knew? She's Ruth Mansfield now. Has been for some time. Let's see – Tommy must be six or seven.'

'Tommy?'

'She has another family. Nice, isn't it, after her being widowed like that? They went to live in Winchester.'

Widowed! Of course, that would have been her explanation. But Tommy! Another family! Why had he never thought of that?

'Do you know her address?' Stephen asked faintly.

'No – sorry. Like you, I've lost touch – you know how it is,' said the voice. 'Sorry not to be more help.'

She was busy; she was going to hang up. Stephen spoke quickly.

'Her husband – what do you know about him?' he asked. 'Mansfield, you said. Do you know his first name? Where did he work?'

'I'm not sure,' said the voice. 'William, was it? Or George? Maybe Charles. Something like that. A king, anyway. He worked in a bank.'

She could tell him no more. Stephen thanked her and hung up.

He turned away from the telephone box and slouched off down the road. Why had he never realized that she might marry? He'd supposed that her life would centre on Susannah, but surely it was much better for the child to have a stepfather and a brother than just one parent, as long as the

23

man – this Mansfield – was kind to her? If he worked in a bank, he would have a secure occupation, and Ruth and Susannah would be safe.

Stephen went back to the car, started it up and drove away from the city, not caring which way he went.

They didn't need him, that was certain. But he needed them – or something. He had not anticipated Ruth's marriage because to do so would upset his fantasies.

He drove on, turning away from the town into the country which, after some miles, had its customary soothing effect upon him. The trees still bore clusters of faded leaves; neatly trimmed hedges bordered fields of ploughland and meadows where sheep and cattle grazed.

Stephen had no map, and was not at all sure where he was, but the next signpost indicated Newbury. You went through there to get to Winchester from Oxford.

He turned off.

3

Ruth Mansfield turned in at the gate of Merrydown House, walked round the side of the house, took the key from her pocket and unlocked the back door. She wore smart boots with small heels, and a maroon suede jacket. Round her hopped her two sons, Tommy, aged almost seven, and Bill, aged five, whom she had just collected from the primary school in Melton St Lucy, where they lived.

Today, the boys both carried conkers on strings, and Bill had a further collection in his pockets. They both talked at once, telling her all about their day. Melton St Lucy was an expanding village between Newbury and Winchester, and Merrydown House was one of seven in an exclusive close built on what had once been allotments. The Mansfields had moved in as the builders left, just over three years ago, after spending the first years of their marriage in a much smaller house on a large estate on the edge of Winchester.

Ruth loved her new house. How lucky she was, how well things had turned out for her, she often thought, and would startle Edward, a quiet man, by suddenly hugging him warmly for no apparent reason, or making a favourite pudding of his and saying they were celebrating.

'Celebrating what?' he would ask.

'Just life,' Ruth would reply, and would add, 'I know you think I'm silly.'

He didn't. He was amazed and thrilled by the increasing success of their marriage, which seemed to be developing with no conscious effort from him. The knowledge that Ruth was happy gave him joy. He was grateful because she did not, like so many women, feel irked by the restrictions of family life; she did not resent the demands made by him and the children and showed no wish, herself, to return to work. They did not need a second salary, but he would never oppose her if, later, she wanted to resume her own career.

They both still hoped for another child, although Ruth was nearly forty-two. Plenty of women had late children these days, and Edward would like a daughter of his own. Susannah had taken his name – Ruth's idea, something he would not have dared to suggest himself. She never mentioned the child's natural father, and Edward thought that the blow of his death still haunted her, for occasionally she would sit silent and pensive, seeming to withdraw herself from her surroundings. He wondered if Susannah looked like her father; she was not like Ruth, except about the eyes.

Edward had been married before, but his wife had left him because he was dull. They had had no children. His first wife had later married a property developer, and now had a villa in Portugal as well as a large house with a swimming pool in Beaconsfield. Because of this earlier rejection, Edward knew himself all the more fortunate now.

Ruth loved the accelerating tempo at the end of the day. This afternoon, the boys clamoured for biscuits and a drink, then ran into the garden to play in the last of the daylight. Ruth could hear their high, happy voices as she set out tea on the kitchen table. Susannah would soon be home, delivered to the village by the coach in which she travelled to the comprehensive school in Anderton with the other older

25

children from the district. She was happy at school, showed a talent for mathematics and science, was a good swimmer and was learning the flute. The boys always welcomed her with noisy hugs when she came home and she was devoted to them and to Edward.

Some time later, Edward's key would be heard in the door, and the family would be complete. At this moment, Ruth's heart always lifted.

She had lied to Edward mainly by evasion. When they met, he thought she was a widow for she posed as one. She had intended to maintain this pretence, but, when he wanted to marry her, she saw that she would be unable to keep secret the fact of Susannah's illegitimate birth. Her birth certificate would one day be needed – for a passport, if for no other reason – and no father was named on it. Ruth was terrified of losing Edward and the security he offered, so she told him that her daughter's father had been killed just before their wedding.

Ruth had been so certain that starting a baby would tip Stephen into leaving his wife.

How could she have known what would happen? They must have had some terrible row, and perhaps it was an accident, but Susannah must never learn that her father was a murderer.

They were safe now. Stephen would be in prison for a very long time and when he came out he wouldn't know where they were. During the trial, she had been terrified that someone would discover that she was his mistress. He, at least, had not disclosed her identity, but revealing it would not have helped him at all.

She had fled from the district and severed all links with her former friends. She had not even cashed the cheque Stephen had sent her, though the money would have been useful. She owed him nothing and would accept nothing from him.

The secret must never come out.

Stephen stood in a Winchester call-box with still another pile of tenpence coins in front of him. The box smelled of sweat, tobacco and urine. It was not unlike the odour of prison, he thought, propping the door slightly open while he consulted the tattered telephone directory.

In a way, this curious mission he had embarked on was therapeutic. He was perforce coming to grips with practical aspects of life and he was beginning to shed the defensive tone he had detected in himself when, for instance, he had inquired for Ruth in Blossom Road.

He'd written down the questions he needed to ask now, in case, under pressure, they flew out of his head.

When each bank replied, he asked for Mr Mansfield.

'Mr Mansfield?' Every bank answered in the same questioning manner.

'Yes. Mr George Mansfield,' Stephen said firmly. 'I'm sure he's with your branch.'

'I'm afraid there's been a mistake,' came the response. 'There's no Mr Mansfield here.'

'Ah well – I'll try – ' and Stephen would name the next bank on his list.

A king's Christian name, his informant had said. If the name was not George, the bank would answer, 'We've no Mr George Mansfield here. Do you mean Mr Henry Mansfield?' Or whatever his name was. Wouldn't they?

What would he say when he was connected with Ruth's husband?

'How's your stepdaughter? This is her father speaking,' he said aloud as the telephone rang at one branch of the Midland.

On his fifth call, something happened.

'Mr Mansfield's not with us any longer,' he heard. 'He's moved to our branch in Anderton. Can someone else help you?'

'Ah – ' said Stephen calmly. 'No thank you. It's personal. I'll get hold of him there.'

He put back the receiver with a pounding heart and looked at his watch. Banks closed early. Was it at three? Work went on after that, of course, behind the scenes, balancing up; bank staff kept more or less normal office hours. Why should he not locate the branch in Anderton, even if he couldn't, today, identify Mr Mansfield?

Before going back to the Mini, Stephen bought a road

27

atlas. He couldn't go on driving blindly about the place like this, depending on signposts.

He reached Anderton at three-fifteen. By now he was getting used to the car and felt much more at home on the road, but parking was a major problem. Years ago, when last he drove, it had been possible to park in the main streets of most towns. Now, even in Anderton, a market town of modest size, there were double yellow lines along each side of the High Street. Stephen took a side turning and, some way down it, saw a car pulling out from the kerb. He reversed neatly into the vacant space, and, before walking away, looked carefully about to make sure there were no signs forbidding parking here. He must not risk the slightest infringement of even the remotest by-law; Stephen knew he could never endure re-arrest.

He walked back into the High Street. Banks were usually in the centre of towns, so it shouldn't be difficult to find the one he sought. An islanded Victorian building stood two hundred or so yards away at the end of the market square. It must be the town hall, he thought, walking towards it. The time showed on a clock face on its tower, and as he drew near he saw, just beyond it, the premises of two of the major banks. On the other side of the road, opposite some shops and a café, were two more.

Stephen saw a man walk into the branch at which he had reason to suppose Ruth's husband worked. So it was still open and he could go in, too. With his bank card, he could cash a cheque.

Stephen entered. There was a short queue, neatly cordoned off into a single file. Before he joined it, Stephen sat down at a table to write out his cheque. He could see the names positioned in front of each teller. Only one was a man, and surely he couldn't be married to Ruth, for he was extremely young. His name, Stephen saw, was Mr T. Simpson. He lined up behind the last customer and chance brought him to Mr Simpson's window. The young man smiled pleasantly as he conducted the transaction. In the background, other clerks were at work. Was one of them Mr Mansfield? Did he specialize in Securities, or Foreign Business, as indicated at various windows?

Stephen paused for a last look round before leaving the

building and saw, attached to the wall, a board listing staff members and their functions. At the head were the words *Manager: Mr E. F. Mansfield.*

Blood pounded in Stephen's ears. He felt dizzy, and had to stretch out a hand to the wall to steady himself. One of the other customers, an elderly woman in a brown tweed coat, looked at him with concern.

'Are you all right?' she asked.

'Yes – oh yes, perfectly, thank you,' said Stephen, standing back to let her leave before him.

'You don't look well,' said the woman in a nannying tone.

Stephen followed her to the pavement and breathed deeply, filling his lungs with cold fresh air.

'It was stuffy in there,' he said.

'Ah – well – take care,' said the woman.

The faintness passed as Stephen walked away from her. It would never have done to have passed out in Mr Mansfield's bank. He realized that he had had no lunch. That would explain the faintness: in HM Prisons you were regularly fed. There was a café on the far side of the road and he went into it. It served light meals, and he ordered baked beans and sausages with tea. Quite like old times, he thought, reading down the unimaginative menu. There were salads, however, and sandwiches, and the place was busy.

Was it likely that Ruth could be here? It was opposite her husband's bank, after all. Women sometimes went to these sort of places when they were out shopping, didn't they? Not women like Marcia; they'd want somewhere smarter; but ordinary housewives with limited budgets. He glanced round at the female customers. Would he recognize Ruth now? He found it impossible to visualize her in his mind's eye, so fickle was memory. Her hair had been dark, and reached to her shoulders; she wore it up in a pleat at work. Unpinned, it was soft, and, closing his eyes, he could recall the scent of her skin, and the feel of it, soft and smooth.

'Do you mind if we join you?' said a voice, and Stephen opened his eyes quickly.

The speaker was an elderly woman accompanied by, presumably, her husband: both were white-haired; both looked fit and cheerful.

'Not at all – please do,' said Stephen, half rising.

'Please don't get up. It's busy today,' said the woman, sitting down opposite Stephen.

'It's always the same on market day,' said the man. 'This place must be a little gold mine.'

'Oh – is that so? I haven't been here before,' said Stephen.

'Not local, then?' said the woman.

'No. Just passing through,' Stephen said, guardedly.

'You get value here,' said the woman. 'No fancy dishes and no fancy prices.'

By the time he had finished his meal, Stephen had learned that the pair were pensioners, and one of their weekly treats was a cream tea in Pam's Pantry. Papers and television had bombarded Stephen, while he was in prison, with the plight of the pensioner, yet here, within a few feet of him, were three other elderly couples, all nicely dressed and enjoying themselves. Their cheerfulness was what chiefly struck him. He felt a prickle of interest, and asked his new friends if they went out a great deal.

They did, indeed, he was told. They had bus passes and rail cards which entitled them to cheap travel rates, and they went all over the place, even to Scotland, for next to nothing.

Before they began to be curious about him, Stephen asked for his bill, bade them farewell, and left.

In the telephone directory, he found an entry for *Mansfield, E. F., Merrydown House, Yeats Close*, with a Melton St Lucy telephone number. Stephen returned to his car and consulted his map. Melton St Lucy was about seven miles away.

It was so near. He might as well go there now. Why put it off?

4

Stephen did some shopping on his way back to the car. There was a small branch of Marks and Spencer in Anderton, and he bought himself a sweater and two shirts. In Boots, he bought a large natural sponge and a red flannel. He was much less fussed today. It was obvious that he attracted no attention. There might be other ex-cons moving about these reasonably tranquil streets, he thought. How could one tell who these other people were?

As he drew near to Melton St Lucy, he saw two school buses ahead of him. They groaned up the hill leading into the village and stopped in the main street beside a row of shops. Their load of jostling children spilled forth on to the narrow pavement. Stephen, halted behind the buses, saw the children peel off in varying directions, separating and coalescing like pieces of mercury. Some went into a sweet shop; others stood talking. One boy walked off alone, carrying a violin case. Stephen watched them intently; Susannah might be among them.

Most of the children moved away from the buses in small groups, and on the whole the sexes seemed to divide, but there were some boys and girls in pairs. Stephen was impressed by their obvious good health and high spirits. One or two boys scuffled together, more or less amicably, though he saw one lad clout another quite hard with his school bag. The clouted one kicked out at his attacker, but the conflict did not develop; honour seemed to have been satisfied, and the two set off in opposite directions.

It was the girls, however, who interested Stephen. What did a girl of eleven look like these days? Was she still a little girl? She would be twelve next month.

The girls all wore grey skirts, with varying jackets. Some had on blazers, others raincoats, and some wore anoraks. Some had short hair, some had plaits or Alice bands. There were pony tails and frizzy curls.

Surely one of them had to be Susannah? He thought that she must be at least as old as the smaller among the children now filing off along the village roads.

The coaches had ground into gear and moved away, and some of the children were going in the same direction. For want of a better idea, Stephen followed. He had no idea where Yeats Close was, and it might take some finding since the village seemed quite large; from its name, he had imagined a hamlet. It was odd to think of Ruth being here

31

somewhere, maybe only yards away, unaware that he was near. Would she know that he was due for release? Probably she never gave him a thought now.

The light was fading, so she was unlikely to be out and about in the village where he might run into her by chance. Even so, he didn't want to ask directions. Whoever he spoke to might tell Ruth a stranger had been asking for Yeats Close. Now, in the dusk, he could find the place himself, walking round the streets until he came upon it. This was a safe time, when the lights were on in the houses, the curtains drawn, and mothers would be preparing their children's tea.

He hoped Ruth was at home. He hoped Susannah and Tommy were not left to fend for themselves while she went out to work. She had never been ambitious; all she had seemed to want was to settle down and raise a family. Well, she had done exactly that.

By this time Stephen, in the wake of the coaches, had left the village behind. He went on until he found a side road where he could turn, and then drove back, turning off the main street into a narrower road where, on either side, there were some good-sized houses, mainly old ones built of brick or half-timbered, several with thatched roofs, conforming much more to what he had expected the village to be like. Some cars were parked here and there, and Stephen, pleased at his regained parking skill, put the Mini between two of them. He went on foot along the road, looking for side turnings, and met Cowper Crescent, but not Yeats Close.

In the next hour and a half, Stephen walked round the whole of Melton St Lucy. He found that it consisted of two main streets which crossed where the buses had unloaded the children, and a number of lesser roads which linked up to form a roughly circular, densely populated area. Wherever there was space between old buildings, new ones had been inserted, often wildly out of character with their surroundings. Names were no guide to status, for there was a small brick bungalow called The Grange and a large Tudor house labelled Rose Cottage.

Building development was one of the things that had affected the landscape more than anything else since he went out of circulation, he saw. Even in the country, where there should be space to breathe, it seemed that people were being packed together, hugger-mugger, into bright new hutches. Gardens of even fair-sized raw new houses were minuscule, backing on to one another as tenement yards had done in earlier years.

Stephen wandered down several newly laid residential roads, some of which were dead ends. He walked briskly, not wanting to be suspected of loitering with intent by any passing police patrol, and had almost given up hope of finding where Ruth lived when he came to another new road looping away from a street which led to the village centre. It was lit by a single lamp, and he saw the name at the side: *Yeats Close*.

Stephen walked down it. There were seven houses, all different, and all set back a little from the road behind low fences or shrubs. At the end of the close, where the road ended in a turning circle, was a square brick neo-Georgian house with a short entrance drive and a double garage at the side. A light was on over the porch. Neatly painted on the gatepost were the words *Merrydown House*.

Stephen turned away quickly, in a sudden panic lest he be observed and identified, though such fears were irrational, he knew, for only Ruth would know who he was and she would not be looking at the dark night outside her warm house. He walked rapidly back to the Mini, unlocked it and clambered in, his legs shaking and his teeth chattering. He folded his arms across his chest, bowing over the wheel, trying to regain control of himself.

After a while he calmed down. He must go back to Oxford and reflect on his day's discoveries. He could return to Melton St Lucy any time. Now that he knew where she lived, he should be able to recognize Susannah. He had only to watch for her.

He felt totally drained, exhausted; he couldn't cope with anything more today.

Driving back, he coincided with the rush hour on the ring road round Newbury; traffic pressed about him at the roundabouts and he circled one because he got into the wrong stream and missed his turning. It was a relief to be back in his anonymous hotel room with its pale wood fittings, washing his hands for dinner.

He took a book down with him, and averted his gaze from the other guests. He did not want to be drawn into any form of contact.

Afterwards, he wrote up his notebook. He had a lot to record, and he had accomplished his main aim: he had established that Ruth and Susannah were well provided for, and he knew where they lived.

The knowledge left him feeling oddly flat. For so long, his main purpose for the future was to find them, then to take away their troubles. Now they had been traced, and were unlikely to have the sort of problems he could solve.

But he hadn't seen Susannah.

At eight o'clock the next morning, Stephen was sitting in his Mini at the end of Yeats Close. Already the village was busy; cars sped away, exhausts sending white plumes of pollution into the cold morning air. Stephen sat hunched behind the steering wheel with his coat collar pulled up and his glasses on, apparently reading the paper. He had no hat; the clothes he had owned when he went into prison were all packed up in trunks at Ivy Lodge and locked in the attic, use of which was denied to the tenants.

Stephen waited. From this position he would have a clear view of anyone coming down Yeats Close on foot. If he saw a smallish schoolgirl emerge, she might be Susannah. He dared not risk parking outside her house.

At twenty minutes past eight, two schoolgirls and three schoolboys came from the close towards him. They passed in front of the Mini and headed off towards the spot where the buses had stopped the previous afternoon. Stephen sat up, staring at the girls, who both wore navy gaberdine raincoats. One, taller than the other, had wiry red curls tumbling on to her shoulders; she was well developed, surely much older than eleven? The smaller one was just an ordinary-looking girl, with a pale face and short, thick brown hair falling forward from her parting just as Stephen's hair still fell, and he knew at once that she was his daughter.

Stephen had forgotten the sensation of intense emotion. His heart seemed to flutter in his chest as he looked at her. When the little group had gone some way up the road, he started the car and followed. Because of her red-haired companion, he was easily able to pick out Susannah as the children clustered together waiting for the buses.

Stephen followed the two buses to the big comprehensive school in Anderton. Now he knew where Susannah lived, and where she went to school.

He wondered about her day. There would be assembly, he supposed: hymns, prayers and notices. Did that still go on in schools? Was Susannah clever? Was the red-haired girl a friend or simply a companion because they were neighbours? He was glad Susannah didn't walk alone up the road. Some of the boys might be rough, might tease a lone small girl. He got out of the car and walked all round the perimeter of the school. It consisted of a number of modern structures around the original Victorian building, which had once been a grammar school. Stephen spent a long time outside it. People came and went, in cars and on foot, and suddenly a group of boys in shorts and singlets emerged and set off running up the road towards the open countryside. That surprised Stephen who thought exercise in schools was an afternoon activity.

At last he got into the car and drove into Anderton. He felt curiously peaceful. He could watch her, if he wanted to, quite easily. He could find out a lot about her simply by observation. Some of his companions in recent years had been put behind bars as the result of careful observation by the police.

Stephen went into the library and read the local paper. There were magazines there, too, and he looked at some of those. He had spent a lot of time in prison libraries, but this was different. Here, he could go when he liked, spend all day if he wished.

When he did leave, he found the town swarming with children. Some of them went into W. H. Smith's, and others walked on to a snack bar further down the street.

Stephen stared hungrily at the girls. Quite a lot of them looked rather like Susannah, but he did not see her. He

35

would know her again, surely? That one flash of recognition was enough, wasn't it?

He lacked the nerve to go into the snack bar, whose clientele all seemed very young. It wouldn't do to be thought a lascivious old man, ogling the children. Instead, he went to Pam's Pantry again, where he had sausage and chips. After that he drove into the country and went for a long walk. Then he returned to Yeats Close. He was parked at its entrance by three o'clock, and some time later he saw a woman approach with two small boys. She was a short, smartly dressed woman in boots with small heels, a maroon jacket over a tweed skirt and with a silk scarf tied round her head. Her face was turned away and Stephen did not recognize Ruth as she turned down Yeats Close with her sons.

Later, he saw the red-haired girl coming along, and the three boys, but without Susannah. Where was she? Had she met with an accident? Stephen's heart plummeted. He waited for a long time, thinking she might have gone into a shop, thus falling behind her companions, and he walked up the road to see if he could find her, but by then all the children had disappeared into their homes. Stephen was frantic with worry. He could not know that Susannah was having a flute lesson and would be collected afterwards by her father, as she thought of Edward Mansfield.

That night, Stephen dreamed he was back in prison, a nightmare he would have many times for the rest of his life. He woke sweating and trembling, afraid he might have shouted out and woken other hotel guests. He got up and put on a sweater, the new one he had bought the day before, and made some tea, thankful that the hotel provided guests with a kettle and the necessary equipment.

Drinking it, he fretted about Susannah in preference to other terrors. Reason told him she had stayed at school for some special project or had gone to tea with a friend, but these days he found it difficult to accept a rational explanation for almost anything.

In the morning, he was outside Yeats Close again. She emerged, safe and sound, with the boys and the other girl.

Stephen shivered. He must not let his natural curiosity become an obsession.

36

The days had to be filled, however, and he had another aim, one that, in prison, he had despaired of ever realizing. He wanted to learn the truth about those last hours of Marcia's, all those years ago, for Stephen Dawes was not a murderer. Marcia, bitterly jealous, had killed herself and, while so doing, had engineered the evidence to frame him for her murder. He had been unable to prove his innocence at the time, and it was unlikely that now he would be able to clear his name but, unless he could do so, he could never openly approach Susannah.

If he talked to Lois Carter, Marcia's friend, might not something come up in their conversation which, pursued, would yield a wisp of evidence to offer hope? Lois must have thought about it, in the interval. Lois might remember something.

She was, he thought, his only hope.

5

Lois Carter had lived with her mother at Primrose Cottage in the old part of Hagbourne Green, near the church and the inn. When Stephen and Marcia were househunting, one of the reasons they chose Badger's End, rather than another house five miles away, was because Lois would be a neighbour. She and Marcia had been friends for years.

It was Lois who had revealed, in court, that Marcia had told her Stephen wanted to leave her and marry someone else. The other woman was pregnant, and Marcia had learned of the birth of the baby two days before her death. The prosecution extracted all this hearsay evidence as if by accident.

Lois had testified that she had advised Marcia to agree to a divorce, and thought she would come round in time. The inference was that Stephen would not wait. She knew that they had had a serious quarrel just before Marcia had disappeared.

Stephen had come home one Thursday evening in November to find the house in darkness. This was unusual, for Marcia was almost always in when he returned and, if she were to be out after dark, she would switch on both the porch light and the one outside the garage.

She must have gone somewhere and stayed later than she planned, he had thought as he put the Rover away. Her car was in the garage, so Lois must have collected her. They often went off together, but he couldn't remember Marcia saying anything about such a plan for today. Still, he might have forgotten, weighed down as he was by mingled joy over the birth of his daughter and despair as to how he would sort things out between Ruth and Marcia.

He began turning on lights inside the house. It was a raw evening, though not really cold. The heating was on and the hall felt pleasantly warm. He took off his coat and hung it in the cloakroom, then washed his hands and rubbed his fingers over his chin, which rasped faintly. It didn't matter; he and Marcia no longer exchanged a ritual kiss when he came home.

As he opened the drawing-room door, cold air rushed at him. He put on the lights and saw chaos. The french window was open, a small chair and an occasional table were over-turned, and the doors of Marcia's display cabinet, where she kept her collection of china figures, stood wide. All the pieces had gone. Other ornaments which had stood about the room had also disappeared.

Stephen did not notice, then, the damp place where, forensic scientists later testified, blood of the same group as Marcia's had been shed and mopped up incompletely. He hurried to the dining-room, which was in similar disorder. All the silver had been taken, including the few sporting trophies he had won in his youth.

It seemed obvious that thieves had broken in through the french window. It was lucky that Marcia was out or she would have had a frightening experience, thought Stephen, running upstairs to see what had happened there. But of course, if the house had not been empty, it might not have been robbed.

In the main bedroom, the contents of drawers and cupboards were jumbled in heaps about the room. Marcia's jewellery was missing, and her silver hairbrushes. His bedroom had been turned over, too, and his dress studs and cufflinks had gone.

Before he called the police, Stephen had tried to find Marcia. He had telephoned Lois.

Lois had not seen Marcia all day, nor spoken to her, which was unusual. They met or spoke on the telephone almost every day. Lois had rung early, but there was no reply; she had popped in that afternoon on her way back from fetching some shrubs from a specialist nursery but no one was at home. The house hadn't been broken into then.

Perhaps Marcia was round at one of their immediate neighbours' houses. Stephen tried them on the telephone, but none of them had seen her.

He dialled the local police station, telling the officer who answered his call that his wife was missing and the house had been burgled. A Panda car soon arrived, followed not long afterwards by the CID.

It was the detective sergeant – later a formidable witness – who cleared everyone out of the drawing-room and took another detective to look at the french windows. Broken glass was spattered all over the terrace outside the house. There were only a few tiny slivers in the room.

'I realized that the window had been broken from the inside,' he had stated in court, when it was alleged that Stephen had broken the glass to make it look as though an intruder had done it in order to open the door.

At the time, Stephen did not see the significance of this discovery. He was concerned only with the whereabouts of Marcia, and at last the police began to take this seriously.

Her sheepskin coat and warm boots were in the cupboard, and it looked as if none of her clothes were missing. Her washing things and nightdress were there; she had not packed an overnight bag or larger case. All this was soon established. After a detective inspector arrived, the atmosphere in the house had changed in minutes. The police became icily hostile as they pressed questions at Stephen, who by now was thoroughly alarmed for Marcia's safety. Lois had come up to the house, and she, too, was anxious.

'They've taken her! The thieves must have abducted her!' said Stephen. 'She must have been here when they came. They may have hurt her. We must find her. Where can they have taken her? Where can we start searching?'

It was not until they had taken him to the police station that they began asking Stephen what he had done with Marcia, and where were the things he had taken from the house in his attempt to make her murder look like robbery with violence.

They took his Rover off for testing. It had been parked all day outside his office, and there were witnesses to prove it, but even before the laboratory results came in they were asking him to explain why there were over four hundred miles on the clock since it was serviced on Monday. That was a lucky shot for the police: the service record was in the glove compartment, marked up to date.

Stephen's diary showed no distant business appointments. He had driven to the office each day, a distance of twenty-one miles, making forty-two for both journeys, a hundred and twenty-six including the day of Marcia's disappearance. Allow more than a hundred for running around and there was still a big disparity.

He had been to see Ruth in hospital, which he did not mention, but that would account for only ninety miles. Stephen could not explain it.

Nor could he explain why one of Marcia's shoes was in the Rover's boot, and other factors which the scientists discovered.

'What have you done with her?'

That was what the police kept asking Stephen. The question was put by Detective Inspector Simpson, who had turned so glacial at Badger's End, and then by Detective Superintendent North, a tall thin man with a sallow complexion and pale blue eyes whose gaze never left Stephen's face.

At that stage, Stephen was still unable to believe that this was really happening – that, instead of searching for Marcia, who must have been taken away by the thieves, they were accusing him of killing her.

'Why should I want to do such a thing?' he had demanded.

They knew. Already they knew about Ruth – not her name, but of her existence. They would not tell Stephen how they had found out, but later he concluded that Lois must have told them.

The day after Marcia disappeared, they found a heavy spanner in the pond at Badger's End. At the trial, counsel for the prosecution alleged that Stephen had used it to kill Marcia with a blow or blows to the head. The pond water would have washed away any traces of blood or tissue which might have adhered to it.

It was Stephen's spanner, and he did not deny it. He kept it in a tool box in the garage. It was at this point that he realized he needed a solicitor. Frank Jeffries dropped everything and came straight round to the police station.

'They ought to be out looking for her,' Stephen said to him. 'They're wasting all this time with me – God knows what's happening to her.'

'They are looking for her,' said Frank.

Police search parties had spent the day scouring the woods around Hagbourne Green; men were examining the garden at Badger's End, quartering it off with tapes and inspecting it inch by inch for signs of recent interment.

'What can have happened?' Stephen demanded.

Frank knew that even the mildest individual could be pushed beyond endurance and resort to violence. A knife might be grabbed and used as a weapon, some heavy object lying nearby become a bludgeon. He just could not imagine Stephen going cold-bloodedly out to fetch the spanner and batter Marcia to death, however much she might have provoked him. Frank considered Marcia to be spoiled and shallow, but she was lovely to look at and Stephen had clearly adored her at the time of their wedding, when Frank had been best man. But couples did drift apart; much of his work was connected with divorce, and it was hardly surprising if Stephen had become bored with her and had found a mistress. These things happened, but they rarely led to murder.

'She'll turn up,' Frank had said. Dead or alive, she must.

But she didn't.

After forty-eight hours of helping the police with their inquiries, Stephen was allowed to go home. Meanwhile, the search continued.

Three days after her disappearance, which by now had been widely reported in the press, with her description and the details circulated round police forces throughout the country, word came from Sussex.

Marcia's handbag had been found.

Now the hunt for the body was localized. Coastguards kept watch for it, expecting it to be washed up along the coast, as were so many suicides in that area. A search of the cliff top was made, and the Sussex police, who knew what they were looking for, found a woman's shoe which matched the one already found in Stephen's car. Later, expert evidence proved that they were, in fact, a pair, and had been sold to Marcia several weeks before.

Some of Stephen's clothes were taken away for testing. A pair of his shoes proved to have soil adhering to them which was similar in composition to that found on the Sussex cliffs. Similar soil and wisps of vegetation – mainly grass – were found on the floor beneath the driver's pedals in the Rover. The grass and vegetation matched what grew on the headland at Beachy Head. Two long blonde hairs were found on a rug in the car, together with a tiny wisp of blue wool. Lois testified that a blue wool suit of Marcia's was missing from her wardrobe, but not, as far as she could tell, a top coat of any sort.

After a while, Stephen accepted that Marcia must be dead, sure that she had carried out the threat of suicide which she had made when he had asked her for a divorce. But she had done so in a monstrous manner, contriving a chain of circumstantial evidence which made it look as if he had killed her. He almost began to wonder if he could have done it, driving down to Sussex in the night and back again in a state of amnesia. But what about the robbery? Where were the china figures, the jewellery? He knew he had not turned the house over when he came home on Thursday.

And he had not killed her. He had not wished her dead. He was filled with guilty remorse, however, for obviously he had hurt her so grievously that she had thought her life no longer worth living. How wretched she must have been, quietly plotting this revenge in the months when he had thought her merely remote. How she must have hated him!

He did not understand about the car. How had she taken it to Sussex to acquire the evidence from there? She could have gone on Wednesday night, even the night before; for a long time now, he had been sleeping in the spare room at the back of the house and might not have heard her take the car. But how had she returned to Beachy Head, alone, after he had seen her for the last time on that final Thursday morning? What state of mind had she been in?

Carrying out her fatal plan must have involved Marcia in a greater physical effort than he had ever known her make before, but Stephen knew that she was capable of passion. The fire of hatred, and her desire for revenge, had fuelled her and given her the strength.

Thinking about it made him sick with pity.

He was not charged until four months after Marcia's disappearance, by which time, in spite of the absence of a body, the Director of Public Prosecutions had decided that there was a case. There were precedents.

Neither Frank Jeffries nor Stephen's mother ever believed him guilty, but he seemed to have no defence. He would not disclose Ruth's name, and made Frank swear not to do so either, but it would have made no difference to the outcome if she had come forward. In hospital after the baby's birth, she could provide no alibi.

No one, apart from Stephen, could be found who had seen Marcia on that last Thursday. She was not at home when Mrs Bishop, the cleaning woman, had arrived, nor had she said that she would be going out early. Always, before, she had given prior warning or had left a note.

Defence counsel argued that if Stephen had, as alleged, already murdered Marcia and disposed of her body, he would have given Mrs Bishop a reason for her absence from the house, which he had not done, but the jury seemed to find this omission of no importance. After his return from work that afternoon, the prosecution said, he had staged the break-in, hiding the items taken from the house in some not-yet-discovered place.

'But no one could really believe I'd do such a thing,' Stephen kept saying.

'Most murders are domestic – within the family,' said Frank. 'I'm afraid that's a fact, Stephen.'

'But this was suicide,' protested Stephen.

He could not bear to think of Marcia's state of mind as she drove alone through the night, acquiring evidence of where the car had been; leaving her shoes in position; possibly putting strands of her hair on the rug, though those, and the fibres from her suit, could have got there innocently. Somehow, on that Thursday, she had travelled back to Sussex and, perhaps at night, had stood shrinking on the cliff and jumped. No one had seen her there during the day; no one had seen her on her last journey. Frank made extensive inquiries but with no result. She might have worn a wig or other disguise, dumping such props near her destination, but no such evidence was ever found. No refuse collectors had turned up a wig or spectacles from any bin.

Stephen returned to work in the months before his arrest. At first, he was greeted with reserve, but after a while people seemed to accept him again, though he sensed hostility from some and was moved to an area of operations where he no longer came into direct contact with clients.

'Just until this all dies down,' said the managing director rather doubtfully.

Stephen had spoken to Lois.

'Surely she talked to you about what she intended to do?' Stephen asked her.

Lois denied it. She said that Marcia had been very upset when she heard about Stephen's romantic attachment – that was how Lois described it. Then she became angry, stubbornly determined never to let him go.

'I tried to get her to change her mind,' said Lois. 'After all, she could live happily enough without being married. Marriage isn't everything, by a long chalk. But she was quite conventional in some ways. And you'd let her down. She changed again when she knew about the baby – got quieter – more depressed.'

That was true. Marcia had become very subdued.

None of the pieces missing from Badger's End was ever

found. If any had turned up, the defence would have had some evidence to support the theory of thieves coinciding with Marcia's flight. As it was, Stephen was forced to realize that Marcia had turned the place over herself, after Lois had visited the house and before his own return. She might even have been watching, hiding somewhere in the woods beyond the garden, and had made her own escape when she had seen her plan begin to take effect.

If only he had found her then, he could have saved her. And if her body had been washed ashore, she might have saved him after all, for there would have been no head wound indicating battering by a spanner, unless the rocks had had the same effect.

Stephen was sent to Brixton after his arrest. No part of his later sentence ever seemed more dreadful than the months he spent there on remand. Bail was refused, and he was nearly broken, in those early weeks, by the slopping-out, the smells, the dehumanizing loss of individuality. Frank arranged for meals to be sent in, one benefit allowed to prisoners awaiting trial, but there was no escape from the clanging doors, the sudden spells of false quiet, the total nightmare. There was, however, hope. The prosecution must satisfy the jury that, beyond reasonable doubt, he had committed the crime of which he stood accused.

Then, day by day, in court, the case against him grew.

The local doctor, and a solicitor who had drawn up Marcia's will, both testified that she had expressed fear for her life. Lois, asked if Marcia had mentioned such a fear to her, reluctantly admitted that Marcia had said she was afraid Stephen meant to kill her. Defence counsel, attempting to defuse these revelations, tried to establish that Marcia was in a state of jealous near-hysteria, but the sympathy of the court was now entirely with the dead woman.

If Stephen had murdered Marcia, he would not have disposed of her handbag with the body, defence counsel posited. Prosecution countered that the bag had lain near her body and was bundled up in a tidying operation. Use of the spanner indicated premeditation.

'What other explanation is there for what happened? I ask you that, members of the jury,' declaimed the eminent barrister retained by the Crown. He described how, in the darkness, Marcia's shoe had fallen to the ground, 'Perhaps as he shook the rug, unrolling it from around that poor, wronged woman,' he suggested, after spelling out the reasons Stephen had for wishing to kill his wife. He preferred another woman, and Marcia Dawes was wealthy; he must have expected to inherit all she had, but here he had been foiled, for she had made a recent will.

The jury was out for hours, and had to be put up overnight at a hotel, but they found Stephen guilty and he was sentenced to life. His appeal was dismissed.

Stephen had been sure that he would be acquitted. After the trial, he was numb at first. Amidst all the horror, however, it was Ruth's defection that hurt him most for it must mean that she believed him guilty. He excused her by thinking of the child; Ruth had to protect her little daughter, and would not want her to know that her father had been convicted of murder.

Had she changed the baby's name? They had decided to call her Susannah for no very clear reason; they had both liked it, and it seemed to fit the crumpled little face. They had intended, too, to register her birth with her father's name on the certificate. Ruth would not have done that now.

Sometimes, on visiting days, Stephen would see the children of other prisoners and would ask their ages in order to form an image of the various stages in life through which Susannah would pass. He built fantasies around her, and the wildest of them involved the clearing of his name so that he could take on his natural role in her life, but as the years passed and he felt increasingly distanced from the outside world, he knew that these were only dreams.

Stephen had emerged from prison a much harder man. The clock could never be put back, but he could seek for answers to the puzzles. Lois, sad and angry at her friend's death, might have held back something she could have said at the trial which would have indicated Marcia's plan. She had been hostile then, and no wonder, blaming him for what had happened – and he was to blame, but indirectly.

46

Lois, under the terms of Marcia's will, had inherited everything – the money her father had settled on Marcia and most of the proceeds from the sale of Badger's End; the little that had been Stephen's share had gone in legal fees. Amongst Marcia's papers there might have been a note, or something that would indicate what was in her mind.

Lois probably still lived in Hagbourne Green. He'd go there.

6

In the morning, Stephen decided to drive to Fairbridge first and look at Ivy Lodge. He did not recognize reluctance in himself to postpone a confrontation with Lois, justifying the diversion by deciding that, from the outside appearance of the house, he would know if it needed much repair and whether the garden was neglected. He wondered if Fairbridge itself had changed a great deal in the years of his absence. After his marriage, he had spent only rare weekends there, or occasional days. His mother had always welcomed Marcia, but had found the younger woman's lethargy and lack of interest a trial. Mrs Dawes was still working when she died; Marcia had held no serious job in her life: the two could not have been more different, and each found too much of the other's company a strain.

It was not far off his route to go by way of Melton St Lucy, and Stephen easily yielded to the temptation. It had been in his mind all along.

When he reached the village, Stephen found that cars were parked along both sides of the main road outside the shops, and there was a lot of traffic passing through. He left the Mini in a side road and went into the greengrocer's to buy some apples. As he lined up behind two women in quilted anoraks and three men holding shopping lists and baskets, he felt his pulse rate quicken. Neither of the women was Ruth, however much she might have changed. Did he really hope to see her? He wasn't sure. The men had obviously been dispatched by their wives with careful weekend lists, and Stephen was fascinated by the care with which, advised by the shopkeeper, they made their selection.

Then a fourth man entered. He was slightly bald, with thick eyebrows and a ruddy complexion. Unknown to Stephen, this was Edward Mansfield, sent by Ruth to buy lemons, which she had forgotten.

Stephen bought two bananas as well as a pound of Cox's. He was served by the greengrocer's girl assistant, who smiled at him as she handed him his change. The tiny encounter warmed him, but he knew it would have been different if she had realized that he was a released convict. How could he structure his life afresh under this burden? Yet he did not want to assume a false identity in order to make a new start. Could one live down a past of this sort? If he had really committed the crime, he could have devoted his future to some form of reparation; others had done that successfully.

Prison reform, he thought: that would be a worthwhile task to take on, but not under the assumption of guilt.

He soon saw that Fairbridge had grown, but the first big change he noticed was the bypass. He turned down the new approach road and eventually found Willoughby Lane, at the end of which lay Ivy Lodge. It was a small Victorian house, with a low wall fronting the pavement, and behind that some shrubs. These had grown and concealed much of the house from the onlooker. His mother had liked to look out and had kept them well trimmed, but Stephen thought he might be glad of their protection.

Always, before, his mother had hurried out when she heard the car turn into the drive. She would never do that again, and now strangers were here. Stephen got out of the Mini and walked past the open gate; he saw a large hatchback car of an unfamiliar make outside the garage, and a child's bicycle lay on the ground. It was painful not to be able to go in and claim the house, and yet, in a way, he was still not quite ready for it; life, for Stephen, had been passive for so long.

To divert his thoughts, Stephen decided that since he had

been unable to identify his tenant's car, he would pinpoint as many as he could of those he passed during the day: a childish game, but it would take his mind off more serious matters.

He drove through the town, which was very busy, with pedestrians straggling across the main street among the traffic instead of using the zebra crossing. He noticed another Mini, two Hondas and a Vauxhall Cavalier. Beyond Fairbridge, he stopped for petrol at a filling station. It was a self-service place; he had seen how these proliferated and, whilst he rather welcomed the anonymity they offered, it was not surprising that jobs were scarce with machines doing things once undertaken by humans. The spotty young woman who took his money was bad-tempered and curt, a contrast to the pleasant girl in the greengrocer's earlier, but then she had not been disfigured with acne.

He had no excuse, now, to put off going to Hagbourne Green. It was only forty-five miles away, and once he had known every inch of the road. He used to do it in a little over an hour in the Rover.

It took less time now, with the various bypasses and new stretches of dual carriageway he found had been constructed, but Hagbourne Green itself, as he drove past the church, looked exactly the same. There was the village green, with the pub at one side and Primrose Cottage facing it, a copse beyond. He went slowly by, up the hill and along the lane that led to Badger's End. What had been a rough track was now tarmac, and the house itself had been painted an ugly mustard-yellow colour. Just as the shrubs round Ivy House had grown, so had the trees surrounding Badger's End. A willow which Stephen had planted as a slip and seen grow quite tall was now immense, with great spreading strands of bare branches.

The garage doors were open, revealing a white Porsche and a red Cortina estate car.

From this garage, Marcia must have set off alone in his car, to secure evidence that would condemn him.

Suddenly angry, Stephen drove rather fast through the village down to the George and Dragon. Here, he and Marcia had sometimes gone for a drink on a Saturday morning, though Marcia did not really like pubs. Was it still the same landlord? If so, would he refuse to serve Stephen?

Stephen decided to make the test. He locked the car and walked over to the single entrance that served both bars. The place was very full, and he hesitated before going into the lounge bar; he and Marcia had never used the saloon bar, but that was where, now, Stephen would have preferred to go. There would be less chance of recognition. He glanced round as he entered, but saw no one he remembered.

Come on, he told himself. You've got money in your pocket to pay for your beer. Buy one, and a sandwich too. You need not talk to anyone except whoever serves you.

He made his way over to the bar, where two men moved to make room for him at the counter, meanwhile continuing their discussion about the relative performances of their cars.

Stephen caught the barman's eye, ordered a half of bitter and then changed to a pint. When he asked about sandwiches, he was shown a menu written on a slate by the bar. Things had clearly changed at the George and Dragon, and Stephen ordered braised kidneys. While he waited for them to arrive, he sipped his drink, his back to the room and the customers.

After a while, he relaxed enough to turn half sideways. One of the car enthusiasts nodded in a friendly fashion.

'Good place, this,' said the man. 'These people haven't been here long. Brought it up no end, they have.'

'Oh.' That answered Stephen's question about the landlord.

'They do very good dinners in the restaurant.' The man waved his tankard towards the far end of the room and Stephen saw that it had been extended. Eleven years ago you couldn't get food at the George and Dragon in the evening. 'Quite reasonable, too,' said the man, and went on to tell Stephen what a dinner for two would cost and which were the best wines on the list.

Even with Marcia's extravagant housekeeping, they could have lived for a week, all those years ago, on what such a meal would cost today.

Stephen's braised kidneys arrived, in a small earthenware

dish, with the rice in another. He took them to a corner of the room, where two women had just left a table. His mood had toughened. Why should he fear entering this place, once so familiar to him? What had he done that was so much worse than the sins of other men? Why should he go through the rest of his life apologizing for the past?

Before leaving the pub, he went into the washroom where he met again his friend from the bar.

'See you again, if you're this way,' said the man pleasantly, ready to leave before Stephen, but Stephen barely heard him and did not answer. 'Funny cove, that,' said the man, rejoining his friends, and they all stared as Stephen crossed the lounge bar to the door.

Across the green, Primrose Cottage stood in its small garden, fenced around with yew, its latticed windows sparkling in the sunlight. It had been rethatched recently. Well, these days Lois wouldn't be strapped for the price of some straw, thought Stephen.

He walked across the green towards the cottage, opened the white wicket gate and went up the path to the front door. Standing there, waiting for it to be opened after he had rung the bell, Stephen looked about. The garden was as neat as ever. The small box hedge that bordered the paths was closely trimmed; the cupressus in the centre of the lawn had doubled in height, and a flowering cherry he remembered Lois planting was now a big tree. Were there still goldfish in the lily pond? One winter they'd all died in the frost and he had given Lois four new ones.

Something was missing. He looked about, frowning. What was it that was different? Then he realized that the gnome which had always sat by the stream, apparently fishing, had gone. There had been another one on the small bridge, he remembered, and more scattered about the lawn. Now, there was only close-cropped grass. He could not see a single gnome anywhere. Marcia had mocked at Lois's gnomes but had given her several. Had she now gone off them?

She was taking a long time to answer the door. He was about to ring again when he heard footsteps. Stephen swiftly rehearsed an opening sentence – 'Ah, Lois, you'll be surprised to see me. May I come in?' – when the door opened. A heavily pregnant young woman with straight shoulder-length dark hair stood revealed.

'Yes?' she said.

Stephen, tense for the encounter, was totally disconcerted at seeing a stranger.

'Oh,' he said. 'Excuse me – I thought – is Lois Carter in?'

'I'm afraid you've come to the wrong house,' said the girl. 'I don't know any Lois Carter.'

'She lived here,' said Stephen.

'Well, I live here now. And my husband,' said the girl, moving as if to close the door.

'You bought the cottage from her, then,' said Stephen, rallying.

'No. We bought it from some people called Henshaw.'

'When?' asked Stephen.

'Four years ago.'

Four years! And another family had lived there before that. Where had Lois gone? Who would know? The Henshaws?

'Where do the Henshaws live now?' he asked. 'I want to find Lois Carter, and perhaps they would have her address if she sold the cottage to them.'

The girl shrugged.

'My husband might know.'

A long, lanky young man had appeared at the back of the hall while they talked. He stooped to avoid hitting his head on the beams as he came forward.

'There's someone here asking for a person called Lois Carter,' the girl told him.

'She lived here with her mother,' said Stephen.

'Can't say I know anything about them,' said the young man.

'The people you bought the cottage from – the Henshaws – have you an address for them?' Stephen said.

'I may have,' said the young man. 'I think we sent on a few letters after they moved. I'll look, shall I?'

'Please,' said Stephen.

'Shan't be a tick,' said the young man. 'You'd better come in.' He held the door back for Stephen to enter and muttered something to his wife, who had retreated to the rear as he

52

came forward. Then he went into what had been the Carters' sitting-room, while the girl stood silently watching Stephen as he waited.

They don't trust me, he thought. They think I may be going to rob them, or something. Well, perhaps they were right to be cautious; you read of such dreadful things happening these days, old ladies mugged and raped by layabout youths who broke into their houses in search of cash. Did he look threatening? Stephen caught sight of himself in a mirror that hung on the wall. There were pouches under his eyes, but his thick hair was tidy and he was neatly dressed in a sports shirt with a collar and tie, worn with grey flannel trousers and a tweed jacket. The young man was arrayed in faded blue jeans and a much darned guernsey sweater.

He reappeared with an address book.

'I remember now,' he said. 'Mr Henshaw died and we only saw her once, the old lady. She went to live with her daughter somewhere near Burford. But as I said, that was four years ago. She may be dead too, by now.'

'I hope not,' said Stephen. 'You've found the address?'

The young man read it out and Stephen wrote it down in his notebook. He would rather ask Mrs Henshaw for Lois's address than go round Hagbourne Green looking for someone who might also know it, but who would, perhaps, remember him.

7

Stephen's notebook now contained a number of positive entries recording the several hundred miles he had driven since his release, and the other events of his days.

He had begun to enjoy travelling along in the Mini, with its window open and the autumn air brushing his face, and was adjusting to the heavy traffic and faster roads. He had made a number of mundane purchases, held brief conversations with various people and been smiled at by a greengrocer's assistant. He had visited Hagbourne Green and come to no harm, whilst discovering that Lois had moved.

He had made some human contact, however minimal.

Stephen had got on well enough with the prison warders in charge of him. He had given no trouble and had managed to avoid being drawn into any provoked by others, chiefly by keeping himself as remote from them as possible. He became known as the Professor, because he was always reading, and because of his studies.

After his mother's death, he had asked for a prison visitor. The man who came to see him was a retired schoolmaster who had taken up this work after his retirement because, as he told Stephen, he knew what loss of liberty was like. He had been a prisoner during the war and, being older than many fellow captives, had adapted to the restrictions better than some. He had offered only passive support to escape schemes, and had used his time to read for a degree which, when he came home, had enabled him to choose a new profession. Before the war he was a shop assistant.

'It's the mental discipline of working towards a definite goal which helps you to accept what can't be altered,' he declared.

Stephen was thus impelled towards an educational course early in his prison life, and, as his visitor had foretold, it gave him an anchor. The man came to see him several times; then his visits ceased, and Stephen heard later that he had already been ill when they met. Now he was too frail to make the journey, and he would not recover. Stephen was not interested in having another official prison visitor after that, but, with his positive approach, the man had helped him. The full-time educational course he had been allowed to undertake at his second prison had been of enormous benefit. Then, at the open prison, had come the opportunity to learn about computers.

All the time, he had avoided bridge schools and other cliques, growing a carapace about himself, becoming, in the interests of self-protection, a thorough loner. He was resigned, now, to living with no close form of communication, for to reveal his true identity would destroy any prospect of genuine intimacy. And closeness achieved while it was hidden would be false.

54

As was the case when he met Mrs Henshaw.

The weather was so good the next morning when Stephen drove into the Cotswolds that before he reached the hamlet where she lived, he turned off down a lane, parked the car in a gateway and went for a long walk. He lost all sense of time, striding out with increasing vigour. He breathed the crisp air deep into his lungs and his eyes devoured the landscape, with the mellow stone walls, the pale autumnal grass, the heavy grey ewes pregnant with lambs that would drop while winter was still cruel. He met no one, and by the time he had retraced his steps the morning had gone.

Mrs Henshaw's address was Marsh Farm, Little Chipping. He had found the village on his map, a tiny dot, but he came to Marsh Farm first, seeing the name painted on a white gate as he approached it. There was a cattle grid at the entrance to a long drive which led to a low stone farmhouse with a faded grey roof like so many he had seen that morning. In a paddock beside the drive, two young girls were jumping ponies over some fences.

Stephen parked neatly at the side of the gravel space in front of the house. There were farm buildings beyond it, and sheep grazed in a meadow beside the house. It was so peaceful and lovely; he felt his spirit expand as he walked towards the front door and rang the bell.

It was answered by a woman of much his own age, perhaps younger, with a healthy fresh complexion, brown curly hair and bright blue eyes. She looked at him inquiringly but with a smile.

'Oh – good morning – could you tell me, please, is Mrs Henshaw at home?' Stephen rather gabbled his request.

'She's at church,' said the woman, and then, looking at him more closely, asked, 'Are you a friend of hers, or are you selling something?'

'I'm not selling anything,' said Stephen. 'And I apologize for disturbing you. I want to trace Lois Carter who used to live at Primrose Cottage in Hagbourne Green, and I thought Mrs Henshaw might be able to help me.'

'Well, I don't know about that. She will if she can, I'm sure,' said Rose Wainwright. 'I think Carter was the name of the people she and my father bought Primrose Cottage from, and she might have their address. She won't be long. You'd better come in. What did you say your name was?'

Stephen hadn't. He thought quickly.

'John Baxter,' he said, picking a first name at random and his mother's maiden name.

'Well, Mr Baxter, come in and have some sherry,' said this pleasant woman, opening the door wide and standing aside.

A black Labrador came slowly towards her from the recesses of the house and stood sniffing gently at Stephen as he entered. The dog wagged his tail slowly, seeming to approve, as Stephen hesitantly followed his hostess into a low-ceilinged room with flowered chintz curtains at the latticed windows, and several large, shabby armchairs and a sofa all covered in faded rose-coloured linen. The *Sunday Times*, separated into its various sections, was divided among them. A log fire burned in the huge open hearth.

'Sit down,' said his hostess. 'I won't be a moment.'

She trustingly left him there while she went out of the room, but Stephen remained standing. He gazed around. On a gateleg table were displayed some photographs of children and ponies. Old sporting prints hung on the walls. Through the window he could see a long garden, with rosebeds and flower borders that still contained late-blooming chrysanthemums and dahlias. The lawn, which needed cutting, was spattered with dead leaves from a big weeping willow that hung its bare fronds over the end of the hedged-off cultivated area.

Mrs Wainwright came back with a tray, some glasses and a decanter of sherry.

Stephen plucked at his memory of social usage.

'I'm admiring your garden,' he said.

'It's rather bedraggled, I'm afraid,' said Mrs Wainwright. 'I need to get out there.' She poured two glasses of sherry and handed one to him. 'I'm afraid I've got to go out to the kitchen, if you'll excuse me. May I leave you with the paper?'

'Of course. This is very kind of you – ' Stephen indicated the sherry, which was very dry and very good. 'I'm so sorry – I'm causing a lot of trouble.'

'Not at all,' said Mrs Wainwright. 'People are in and out of here all the time. I was just afraid at first that you might be wanting to con mother into something, or that you were a Jehovah's Witness, but I can spot them pretty fast – they don't ask for people by name and they usually hunt in pairs.'

'Do they?'

'Yes. Haven't you noticed? Awfully sweet, quite often, but so muddled and such timewasters, and one doesn't want to get into an argument. At least, I don't.'

So saying, Rose Wainwright went out of the room, taking with her her own glass of sherry. The Labrador followed.

Stephen sipped his sherry and sat down rather stiffly on the sofa. He put his glass on the small table beside him and let his back rest against the cushions while he gazed at the fire. Slowly, he began to relax. He was still sitting there, looking at the glowing logs, when Rose returned after fifteen minutes. He had not touched the paper, and for a moment did not notice that she had come into the room. She thought at first that he was asleep. He looked rather hollow-eyed, above the beard; perhaps he had been ill.

Then Stephen saw her and sprang to his feet.

'I can't think where mother's got to,' said Rose. 'Or rather, I can. She must be socializing. Gone to drinks with one of her buddies after church, I mean. I'm afraid Dick and I hardly ever go to church.'

'I'd better go,' said Stephen. 'I could call back again, or perhaps telephone.'

'Not at all. Stay to lunch,' said Rose. 'There's plenty.'

'But – but – '

'Or is your wife expecting you?' Rose asked.

'No – no, she's not,' said Stephen, somewhat distractedly. 'I've got no wife. Not now.'

'Oh dear – I'm sorry. Well, then,' Rose swept on, not wanting to hear a tale of marital woe or bereavement, but feeling about this slightly shabby, diffident man as she would about one of her children or an animal on the farm if it needed succouring. 'All the more reason to stay.'

'But you don't know me,' said Stephen.

'You're connected with Primrose Cottage. That's introduction enough,' said Rose, and added, 'You may not know my name. It's Wainwright – Rose Wainwright, and my husband's Dick. Now, sit down again and I'll go and lay an extra place at the table.'

Used to being told what to do, Stephen subsided. To sit in that comfortable room – something he would have taken as a matter of course eleven years ago – was, to him, a small miracle. This time, left alone again, he picked up the *Sunday Times* colour supplement, but he did not look at it.

At one o'clock, Dick Wainwright came into the room, followed by the Labrador and the two girls, still in jodhpurs and smelling faintly of horse. Stephen felt like running away then. The room was suddenly full of bustle and sound, but it was cheerful, happy confusion that now surrounded him: there were no clangs of locking doors, nor loud, hurrying footsteps on concrete, or sudden shouts.

'Hullo. Dick Wainwright,' said the farmer, a sturdy man, not as tall as Stephen, with a shiny, beaming red face and a balding head. 'Here comes Rose's mama.'

'How do you do,' said Mrs Henshaw, making an entry. She held out her hand. She was a pretty woman still, an older, slimmer, more elegant version of her daughter, with neatly waved silver hair.

Stephen timidly shook her proffered hand, releasing it quickly but holding his own extended for seconds. He had been physically touched. He dropped his hand suddenly, afraid that they would all be staring at his strange conduct.

The two girls were introduced as Penelope and Kate. The younger one must be about eleven, thought Stephen, trying not to stare too curiously at her. He was almost rigid with shyness, but the family were chattering so happily together that his silence went unnoticed.

Mrs Henshaw led him to one side.

'Mr Baxter, I hear you're a friend of the Carters,' she said. 'Of course, they left Hagbourne Green a long time ago. It must be ten years, or nearly so. That's when we bought the cottage. My husband was on the point of retiring, and we wanted to settle in before he stopped working – put down roots, you know. So I don't know how much I can help you. I have no recent news of them.'

'I've been away and lost touch,' Stephen said, rallying from being addressed as Mr Baxter.

'Ah yes – well – '

Mrs Henshaw was prevented from asking him where he had been by Rose, who announced that lunch was ready.

The meal was not served in the dining-room, which Stephen noticed across the passage as he followed the women and girls. Its door was open, and he could see a long oak refectory table and a dresser to match, both very old. They ate in the farmhouse kitchen, a big room with low beams and an immense elm table that was capable of seating twelve or more. At the further end of the room was an Aga cooker and, at the side, a big double sink with twin drainers. Below this was, as he later realized, a plumbed-in dishwasher. He and Marcia had had a dishwasher, but he had forgotten about such things.

He had forgotten about domesticity. Perhaps he had never really known it, once he grew up and left home.

Rose had roasted a large piece of pork. Its crackling was so crisp that Kate sent some of hers flying across the table, to much merriment. Stephen had not tasted such delicious food for eleven years. He was seated with his back to the wall, next to Mrs Henshaw, and he was so numbed by the strangeness of all this that he became almost incapable of speech. He, as the guest, was served directly after Mrs Henshaw. The vegetables were set on the table in thick Denby dishes: carrots and cauliflower. Roast potatoes surrounded the joint and were added to the plates by Dick, who carved.

'Will you have two potatoes, Helen?' he asked Mrs Henshaw, who said one would be enough and then changed her mind and asked for two small ones.

'Gran always says that,' remarked Kate, sitting opposite Stephen, next to her sister.

'I saw you riding when I arrived,' said Stephen, making an enormous effort to speak naturally to this nice little girl with her plaits and her turned-up freckled nose.

'Oh yes,' said Penelope. 'We were giving the ponies a good school. They're still not very fit after spending months out at grass in the summer, and hunting starts soon.'

'What about your own school?' asked Stephen.

Kate thought this remark the height of humour. She told him about their school. In prison he had heard plenty of talk about blood sports and had read about protests. These girls enjoyed hunting because they liked riding their ponies over the fields and jumping the fences they met; that was exciting, and a challenge. He asked about the ponies, to be rewarded with their full life histories.

'Have you come far, Mr Baxter?' inquired Mrs Henshaw, interrupting this flow as Stephen held the carrots so that she might easily help herself to more.

'Only from Oxford,' said Stephen.

'You live there?'

'I'm staying there for a while,' said Stephen. He set down the dish on the mat and carefully picked up his own knife and fork once more. He was eating very slowly, afraid that his table manners had deteriorated in prison.

'And what do you do?'

I'm an ex-con.

'I'm a management consultant,' Stephen said firmly. 'But I'm thinking of going into computers.'

'Oh, are you? Selling them, do you mean?' asked Mrs Henshaw.

'Yes. For the small business or private individual,' said Stephen. 'Or maybe offering a service.'

'You've missed the boat, haven't you?' said Penelope bluntly. 'The time to get into all that was a couple of years ago. Now they're everywhere.'

'They'll get cheaper and simpler,' prophesied Stephen.

'I tell Dad he ought to get one,' said Penelope. 'It would help on the farm. Tell him when to shear the sheep and pay the bills and all that.'

'I don't need a computer to tell me there are bills on my desk,' said her father wryly. 'And I've been shearing sheep for more years than your age.' He was smiling at his daughter as he spoke, proud of her shrewdness, Stephen saw; proud, too, no doubt, of her youthful good looks and confidence.

Rose wondered who would want to look up recipes on floppy disks, whatever they were, as she'd heard advised, when there were so many excellent cookery books about. Mrs Henshaw thought people spent enough time, as it was, gazing at television screens, ruining their eyesight, without harming it further by peering at flickering green writing.

60

As the talk round the table became more general, Stephen was able to remain silent. He listened to the lively chatter, but his main attention was concentrated on the food. To his jaded palate, it tasted ambrosial. The pork melted like butter; the vegetables, lightly cooked, had a crunchy bite to them; the stuffing was aromatic, and the apple sauce smooth and tart. He did not notice that Mrs Henshaw was casting speculative glances towards him as he scarcely raised his eyes from his plate.

The girls had second helpings. Stephen longed to do the same, but felt too inhibited; besides, if he did, he might not be able to manage the pudding which, if it matched the first course, would be worth tackling.

It was. It was blackberry and apple crumble, with thick cream. Afterwards, there was Stilton.

Mrs Henshaw toyed with a crumb of cheese as Stephen brought himself, with an effort, back to the reason for his visit.

'Mrs Henshaw, do you know where the Carters went?' he asked.

'Well, the daughter got married, didn't she?' said Mrs Henshaw.

'Married! Lois! Did she?' Stephen was truly astonished.

'Yes. That seems to surprise you,' said Mrs Henshaw. Was she an old flame of his, with whom he wanted to take up again?

'Yes, it does,' Stephen admitted. He thought of the times she had been invited to partner Frank, and how the pair had never advanced beyond very superficial friendliness. Frank had once said that Lois had built up some sort of invisible barrier around herself. She'd take quite a bit of storming, he'd joked, and had said that, though she was not unattractive, he was not tempted to assail her virtue.

'She came into some money, I remember,' said Mrs Henshaw. 'The old lady seemed rather worried about it, but of course she didn't want to move. It meant such an unheaval.'

'I suppose so,' said Stephen. 'She wasn't very fit.'

'She went into a home,' said Mrs Henshaw. 'I remember that. We thought it a pity. She seemed rather vague, but not

61

ready for that – but then, who is? Maybe I will be, one day, and they'll get rid of me from here.' She looked round at her family. 'I'm lucky,' she said, and told Stephen that she had her own flat above the garage but she always had Sunday lunch with the family, unless she was invited out or had asked a friend to join her. Apart from this, she was independent, and she had met a number of nice old ladies and a few couples since she came to live at the farm. She played bridge several times a week, she said.

'Do you know where Lois and her husband live?' Stephen asked. 'Or her married name?'

'No. We never got any letters for them. I suppose the post office sent on their mail.'

'Oh dear.' Stephen looked so cast down that Mrs Henshaw feared she had been correct in supposing he carried a torch for Lois.

'I wonder if I could remember about the old lady,' she said. 'My memory's not what it was, but I did have a talk with Mrs Carter once. Let me see – we walked round the garden together and she said she didn't want to leave because she had so many friends in the village. But she'd given up her bridge. Lily Knapp might know where she went – she was angry with Lois for uprooting Mrs Carter. As she'd come into all that money and was getting married, she could have left her in the cottage with a housekeeper, people felt.' She glanced warily at Stephen; perhaps she should not have pronounced Lois heartless. 'Of course, no one knew quite how much money it was that Lois inherited, but I think her mother was afraid she was marrying because of it.'

'It's possible, I suppose,' said Stephen.

'There was something unusual about where it came from – some unexpected source – but I can't at the moment think what it was,' said Mrs Henshaw. 'I'll remember as soon as you've gone.'

Please don't, Stephen silently besought her. Please forget it for ever.

'If it's important, I could ring Lily Knapp up – such a lovely name, don't you think? And she's a lovely person,' said Mrs Henshaw. 'I got to know her through bridge. She might have Mrs Carter's address.'

62

Stephen had known Lily Knapp. He must not admit it.

'Would you do that?' Lily Knapp would remind Mrs Henshaw of the source of Lois's wealth if she did, but he must let that pass.

'Of course I will,' said Mrs Henshaw. For all she knew, Lois's marriage had not lasted; marriage was not, nowadays, very durable.

Lunch over, everyone helped to clear away except Mrs Henshaw, who went to her flat to telephone. Stephen was allowed to wash up the glasses, which were not put into the machine; the two girls had their own jobs, putting things away and setting aside scraps for the Labrador, which had lain in front of the Aga throughout the meal. When it was done, Rose made real coffee in a jug, which she brought into the sitting-room. Her mother soon joined them, carrying a scrap of paper. She sat on the sofa and patted the space beside her, indicating that Stephen should sit there.

'Lily Knapp says that Mrs Carter went to a home near Bath,' she told him. 'Lily went to see her there several times. She wasn't too unhappy – it was the sort of place where you could have your own furniture and so on. But she was much more forgetful, and she didn't recognize Lily the last time she went. Mrs Carter was moved soon afterwards. I've got the address of the second place. Here it is.' She handed Stephen a scrap of paper covered in firm, black handwriting.

Mrs Henshaw did not report that, in Lily's opinion, Mrs Carter would not have deteriorated so rapidly if she had been at home for, after all, that was only her view and it reflected against Lois. You could not blame the girl for seizing her chance of marriage, and an old lady around the place, particularly a dotty one, was not going to be any help to the newly-weds.

'The nursing home is bound to have Lois's address,' said Mrs Henshaw. 'That's if Mrs Carter is still alive. Lily hasn't had any news of her for years, I think she feels badly about not keeping in touch, but there wasn't much point when the poor old thing couldn't recognize her.'

Stephen asked if Lily Knapp had mentioned Lois's married name. She'd been unable to remember it, said Mrs Henshaw.

At this point, Dick Wainwright laid down the newspaper and said he was going to give the lawn a last mow before winter, thus foiling Stephen who had been silently rehearsing a speech in which he offered to do this very thing. He had thought it would be a real way to repay part of the hospitality he had received. Now he had no choice but to utter more words of thanks, and to go.

'Odd man, that,' said Rose, when he had driven away. 'Very shy. Kind of old-fashioned.'

'Yes,' said Mrs Henshaw. She did not mention that Lily Knapp had told her on the telephone how Lois Carter had come into her fortune. She had been left the estate of her friend Marcia Dawes, who had been murdered by her husband because he wanted to marry another woman and Marcia would not let him go.

'He was sentenced to life,' Lily Knapp had said. 'But you know what that means. Out in a few years to do it again.'

The case was still being discussed when Mrs Henshaw and husband had moved into Primrose Cottage, but because they had not known any of the participants, except fleetingly the Carters, they had not taken much interest in it. Badger's End had new occupants and Stephen Dawes had been in gaol for some time, at first on remand and later beginning his sentence. Gossip had mentioned that Marcia and Lois were very great friends, the bequest endorsed that. Lois's marriage had astonished everyone. Her spinster state and her devotion to Marcia – she was always at Badger's End, it seemed – had supplied an obvious, if facile, excuse for Stephen's straying.

Their luncheon visitor had said his name was John Baxter. He was clearly under some strain, keeping himself strictly in check. He looked extremely respectable but ever so slightly *passé* – it was the only apt word she could think of to describe what, in a woman, could have been defined as faded gentility.

Mrs Henshaw had no real reason, beyond a hunch, to think that they had just entertained Stephen Dawes; she would keep the possibility to herself.

Whoever he was, the man had clearly suffered.

That evening, Stephen sat in his small, austere hotel room with the loose-woven sand-coloured curtains drawn over the windows to shut out the darkness. He had a lot to record in his notebook as he thought about the day. His present surroundings had seemed, until now, the height of sybaritic luxury, but his treatment by the Wainwrights had been a miraculous experience. Recollecting it, savouring every second in retrospect, he could smell again the ashy tang of the wood fire; he could hear the silence. He could taste, in memory, that amazing meal.

If they had known who he was, the Wainwrights would not have let him enter the house.

But I'm not a murderer, he reminded himself, unless to drive one's wife to suicide was murder. Many a man was an adulterer without provoking such a consequence.

The tenants were leaving Ivy Lodge tomorrow. He would make it his home and also – he faced the fact that he needed one – his refuge. He would ride out any storms from the neighbours as he had endured the years in prison. He could do without other people if he had to; he had proved that. From Ivy Lodge, he would hunt down Lois, who should have prevented Marcia from killing herself.

She might have driven her to Sussex, stood by while she jumped, even pushed her.

No!

Hardened though it was now, Stephen's mind would not accept that idea. Such things happened, and stranger things than that, but Stephen could not see Lois in such a role. She was truly fond of Marcia – even loved her. Nothing was ever too much trouble for Lois to do for her friend.

Would she help her to die, if that was Marcia's wish? Could Lois have convinced herself that to do so would be an act of love?

She might, if she had known about Marcia's will.

Someone must have helped Marcia find the solicitor who had drawn it up. Stephen knew that she would have been reluctant to make such an effort herself.

Money had opened the door to a new life for Lois; she had unloaded the burden of caring for her mother on to professionals and had found a husband, all, it seemed, as the result of her new prosperity.

Cupidity could be a very strong motive – in this case, not to kill, but to connive at another's self-destruction. And that was a crime.

8

Stephen woke with his usual suddenness at six o'clock the next morning. Some habits died hard, and he still expected to hear a warder's tread.

He packed his small bag, and after breakfast he paid his bill, leaving the hotel without making an impact on anyone there. No waiter or waitress, or maid, or even the receptionist, remembered him other than vaguely when he had gone. They were used to guests who came and went almost anonymously.

Possession of Ivy Lodge would not be his until midday, so Stephen went there by way of Anderton. He found a pay-and-display parking lot this time; there was plenty of space on a Monday morning. After leaving the car, he walked slowly through the town, past the bank where Ruth's husband, Mr E. F. Mansfield, must, at this very moment, be countenancing loans and refusing overdrafts. He went into W. H. Smith's and bought a paper; then, passing a florist's, he stopped. There was an Interflora sign in the window.

Seconds later he was inside the shop, ordering two azaleas, one to be sent to Mrs Wainwright, the other to Mrs Henshaw. He could not think of an appropriate message, and asked the girl to say, simply, that they came from John Baxter.

'What – no best wishes? Nothing like that?' asked the girl.

'No.'

He knew that if he had not walked past the florist's, he would not have thought of this, whereas once the idea would have sprung automatically into his mind. Stephen had been the sort of man who gave women flowers on their birthdays and other special days.

From the florist's, he went to Pam's Pantry, where he ordered some coffee, unfurled his paper, and began looking at the crossword. He could stay here indefinitely, ordering occasional cups of coffee, he thought. No one was going to chivvy him on to the next part of the daily routine and once he had paid his bill he could leave the place and go wherever he liked. Stephen found the newsprint blurring beneath his gaze as he read the clue: *Foreign sea song played Venetian*. He blinked rapidly, swallowed, and wrote in *Merchant*. Most of the other answers followed, and then, when he got stuck, Stephen folded the paper up, paid, and left.

He would need some stores for Ivy Lodge, he thought, and turned into a supermarket. How bright and well stacked its shelves seemed! He wandered round in a daze, wondering what to buy. As he picked up a packet of butter, he realized that he should be carrying a wire basket. It would be too much to be accused of shop-lifting. He put the butter down again and hurried towards the entrance, his gaze darting to right and left. He had done very little household shopping during the years of his marriage and was unfamiliar with the procedure. However, there was a pile of stacked baskets by the checkout, and he took one, then went back to the butter area. He'd need bread, too. Was that sold here? He prowled around the aisles, afraid that he looked conspicuous among the brisk women shoppers who seemed to know exactly what they wanted and where to find it as they pushed their trolleys round. He was glad to see that there were a few other men in the store; the staff were quite accustomed to older widowers no more self-assured in this area than Stephen, the bachelors who popped in during the lunch hour, and the divorced fathers who came mostly at the weekends, stocking up for their children's access visits and sometimes accompanied by serious small girls who supervised their purchasing, or eager little boys who swung on the trolleys and loudly suggested what to buy.

Stephen put half a dozen eggs in his basket, and a packet of bacon. Then he saw the bread. It was all wrapped in plastic and there was no warm baking aroma, but he saw croissants in a sealed bag. He had forgotten that there were such things.

When he reached the checkout, the girl suggested that he

needed a carrier, and off he went with his packages, a happy advertisement for the supermarket chain. He was back in W. H. Smith's, killing time by browsing among the magazines, when, like a burst of excited starlings, a dozen or so schoolchildren entered the shop. They descended on the showcases where Biros, crayons and rubbers were arranged. Some went to the magazine section and began riffling through the pages of various journals.

Stephen turned around and saw her. At least, if it was not Susannah, the girl was just like the one he had seen in Melton St Lucy. She was with another girl who had long blonde hair in a plait. They were selecting pencils. He went nearer and heard them discussing what they needed for an art lesson.

The fair girl was short of cash.

'I'll lend you some till Friday,' said the one Stephen was certain was his daughter. Her voice was high and sweet.

'Oh Sue, you angel! I'll pay you back then, I promise,' said her friend.

Sue!

Stephen felt dizzy.

'I'll write it in my book,' said Sue, taking out a small notebook and making an entry.

'Anyone would know your dad worked in a bank,' said the fair girl, but without rancour.

'Interest if you don't pay by Friday afternoon,' said Susannah, smiling but firm.

Stephen, carrying the gardening magazine he had been looking at, followed them to the till and was the next in line. He stood watching them when they left the shop, and saw them cross the road to go into a snack bar.

Didn't they eat their midday meal at school?

It seemed that he had a lot to learn about teenage freedom – not that Susannah was yet a teenager. Perhaps she came shopping every Monday.

He drove fast to Fairbridge, so buoyed up by his morning that he did not feel remotely ill at ease when he went into the estate agent's office and asked for the keys of his house.

There were one or two points about the inventory, said the very young man in a pale grey suit who gave them to him, but their Mr Brand would be in touch. He was out with a client just now.

Stephen thanked the young man, who must have been in short trousers when he went to prison and might not know his history.

Five minutes later he was opening his own front door.

Stephen was out on the lawn, putting into an upturned flower pot, when someone called his name. He lifted his head and missed the putt.

'I thought you'd be counting the spoons,' said Frank Jeffries, coming towards him, hands in his pockets, smiling.

Stephen's heart had automatically begun to pump hard at the sound of a voice when he had thought himself quite alone, and he breathed deeply to mask his brief agitation as he turned.

'Messrs Grigg and Whittaker seem to have done that very conscientiously,' he said lightly, and leaned on his putter, waiting for Frank to reach him.

'Congratulations,' said Frank, and gave him a hearty thump on the shoulder. 'It's great to see you here. You're looking well.'

'Whatever are you doing in Fairbridge?' Stephen asked. 'Got another criminal down here, have you? It's rather off your beat.' He spoke jestingly, his expression broadening slowly into a smile. To Frank, it was painful to watch the other man's features develop a sort of rictus until the eyes warmed and the conditioned, artificial response suddenly became real.

'Apologizing for failing you last week and taking so long to see you,' said Frank.

'That wasn't your fault,' said Stephen. 'You've thought of everything. I'm grateful, Frank.'

'I'm sorry it wasn't more,' said Frank.

Between the two men hung awareness of Val's refusal to let him enter her house.

'Come along in – how long can you stay?' Stephen asked. 'Half an hour? Five minutes?' He was used to rationing time.

'I told Val I'd be late – that I was seeing an important client in another county,' said Frank. 'It's the truth.'

'Oh!'

'I'm taking you out to dinner, to celebrate,' Frank added.

'She'll think you're with another woman,' said Stephen.

Frank shrugged, as if to say, who cares?

'You'd better watch it,' said Stephen. 'Adultery can get you a life sentence.' As he led the way back to the house, Stephen realized that he had made a joke – not a very good one, perhaps, but nevertheless a joke.

Frank had determined to see Stephen that day, wherever he was. He might lose his nerve about the house at the last minute and still be at the hotel in Oxford; Frank had telephoned there and found that he had checked out. That afternoon, he had rung Grigg and Whittaker and, learning that the keys had been collected, had driven straight over, a distance of fifty-two miles. He did not know what to expect. Stephen might be depressed, hit by nostalgia; experiencing grief for his mother; or he might be angry at the deterioration, over the years, of the house, and be busily listing damage done by the tenants. Though dusk was falling when he arrived, there were no lights on and the bell went unanswered. He had tried the front door, found it unlocked, and walked through until he could see the tall figure bent over his putter beyond the overgrown rosebeds that bordered the lawn.

Stephen looked fitter than the last time Frank had seen him, which was a month earlier when they made final plans for the days after his release. As they returned to the house, Stephen strode out. On Frank's first visit to the open prison, he had been horrified by Stephen's shambling walk, which he had not had a chance to notice in the restricted conditions of the other prisons, but it had soon improved with his changed circumstances. Stephen had worked on the land and had played cricket; he was fit.

As they went indoors, Stephen was switching on lights. Bulbs were missing here and there, removed by the tenants, but the place was lit after a fashion.

'What's the time? What does one do now – have tea?' Stephen asked. 'How do I entertain you, Frank? I did some shopping but I forgot about tea and coffee. I'm used to having these things done for me, you know.' Again the light jesting tone; it hit Frank hard.

'Tea would be just right,' he said. 'I brought a few bits and pieces for you. There's a box in the car – I'll get it.'

He went out to his BMW and returned with a large carton which he set down on the kitchen table. Meanwhile, Stephen had found two pottery mugs in the dresser but, as Frank came back, he replaced them and took out two delicate china cups and saucers, the last survivors of Mrs Dawes's Royal Doulton tea service. Frank understood his action at once, and rootled about among the shopping for the Earl Grey that was there, as well as the Typhoo tea bags. He'd remembered a lemon. Marcia had always served China tea.

'I wasn't sure what you'd need,' Frank said. He had feared that Stephen would have been unequal to the challenge of stocking his larder, and he was sure the departing tenants, who were moving into a new house, would have taken every last thing with them – as they had, even to the rolls of lavatory paper. Frank had brought Andrex; he was sure you didn't find that in prison.

Stephen was examining the carton's contents. There were cornflakes, washing-up liquid, and marmalade. Lost for words, he looked at Frank as he unpacked some fresh-roasted coffee.

'There are one or two other things,' said Frank, going out of the room. He returned with a carrier bag. 'Just a few little oddments you may have been missing.' He took a bottle of whisky out of the bag. There was also some Crabtree and Evelyn soap and a bottle of Paco Rabane aftershave. 'I thought this would be nice – even with that beard of yours, I see you still shave your cheeks,' Frank added. 'And maybe the beard will go. Some girl may complain.'

'Girls!' said Stephen, as if Frank had said he might meet a Martian.

'One day,' said Frank firmly.

He had tried to think of things he took for granted but would miss if deprived of them for any length of time. It was so sad that Stephen had no family to support him now. Frank would never get over feeling that he had let his friend down

unforgivably by not winning an acquittal for him, but intel-
lectually he had to accept the strength of the prosecution
case. It was gut instinct which had convinced him that even
if Stephen had wanted to kill Marcia, which was unthink-
able, this was not how he would have done it. For one thing,
he would have covered his tracks more skilfully. He could
believe, though, that Marcia was vicious and devious
enough to take Stephen with her as she died. Frank had
never really liked her, though there was little about her to
dislike actively. But she could hate, and she was jealous.
When her father had died of a sudden heart attack, she had
not gone to the funeral because she still resented his young
second wife.

'What have you been doing?' Frank asked, interrupting
Stephen's attempts to thank him.

'Driving around large chunks of England most of the
time,' said Stephen.

The kettle had boiled, and he made the tea, assembling
pot, cups and saucers on a tray.

Frank, following the thought that had prompted Stephen
to reject mugs in favour of bone china, and now led him to
suggest that they had tea in the sitting-room and not at the
kitchen table, realized with relief that Stephen's sensitivity
had not been destroyed.

The two men went into a room at the front of the house.
The carpet was threadbare and the curtains were faded. To
Frank it looked very shabby, but within months, he was sure,
Stephen would be selling the house and seeking a modern
flat somewhere – maybe in London: it was easier to be
anonymous there than in a small country town.

Three packing cases full of books stood open in front of the
hearth.

'I went straight up to the attic and got them out,' Stephen
said. 'It won't seem right till I've unpacked them. I'd forgotten what there was.'

After his arrest, his mother and Frank had rescued his
personal possessions from Badger's End and brought them
here.

'I'll need more shelves, I expect,' said Stephen. 'I got
sidetracked when I found my golf clubs.'

'We'll have a round soon,' promised Frank. 'A golfing weekend somewhere nice. How about that?' He'd force Val to accept it. Inwardly, at the thought of his wife, Frank sighed.

As if reading his mind, Stephen asked how Val was.

'And the children?' he added.

'Oh – they're fine. Fiona wants a pony for Christmas,' said Frank. This meant that Val intended her to have one. 'Stephen, I feel so badly – '

Stephen cut him off.

'I quite understand,' he said. 'Why should Val accept your judgement when twelve good men and true disagreed?'

'Oh – my country, right or wrong, you know,' said Frank. 'My friend, too.'

'You don't have to apologize for Val's very natural suspicion,' said Stephen.

'The kids are great,' Frank rushed on, and related a remark of Jamie's about some space exploit. 'They're all into space these days, boys,' he explained. 'Ponies for girls, but rockets for boys.'

'Talking of children,' said Stephen. 'I've seen my daughter.'

'What?' Frank sat up and gaped at him.

Stephen had not really meant to tell Frank as much as that, but he was feeling an urge to unburden himself, to pour forth thoughts that had been suppressed for years. During his incarceration, his meetings with Frank had been his most rewarding moments, and he knew that he owed an immeasurable debt to their friendship, forged in boyhood. Frank had gone far beyond the bounds of professional duty in looking after his interests all this time.

'That letter you sent on from Mother's solicitor,' he said. 'She'd had Ruth traced. The letter was in case anything happened to her before I got out – as it did.' He told Frank about it, and what he had done. 'Married to a bank manager – Ruth's all right,' he ended. 'To think I'd worried myself silly in case they were starving.'

'Social security stops you from starving these days,' said Frank.

'Did you know Lois Carter was married?' asked Stephen.

'No! God, Stephen, you're full of news,' said Frank.

Stephen described his weekend travels.

'It's been marvellous, really. The freedom – driving about. It's been like a holiday, in a way. Then the kindness of those people yesterday – Mrs Henshaw and the Wainwrights. Of course, it was all won under false pretences . . .' He let his sentence trail away.

'Not really,' said Frank. 'You didn't do it, remember? What are you going to do next?'

'Find Lois. Ask her to explain why Marcia fitted me up like that.'

'Wouldn't it be better to put it all behind you now?' Frank suggested. Nothing could be done about the past; Stephen must make what he could of the future.

'I'd like to understand,' said Stephen.

'Lois won't be able to tell you anything you don't already know,' said Frank.

'She might let slip something that could have shown what Marcia was planning – something she forgot, or didn't mention at the time,' said Stephen. 'She won't be on her guard, now. And she'll probably be surprised to see me.'

'She'd have stopped Marcia, if she'd had any idea of what was really in her mind,' said Frank.

'She did all right out of it, though, didn't she?' said Stephen.

'Well, they were devoted – or rather, Lois was devoted to Marcia,' said Frank. 'I did wonder a bit about that friendship.'

'It wasn't like that,' said Stephen. 'Or not on Marcia's side. She just accepted Lois's – well, homage, if you like. As she accepted mine. She was used to being adored by everyone – her father, but that went sour when he remarried – me, and Lois. Then I let her down. She couldn't stand another betrayal, as it seemed to her.'

'Hm. Not everyone would see it quite like that,' said Frank. 'Women change, don't they? You fall for them – probably because of good old sex, one of them turning you on more than another, and you convince yourself – often against reason – that she's the girl for you. Then you find you're living with a person you hardly know and don't much like, you've got kids and a mortgage, a position to maintain and heavy work pressures – lots of balls in the air, like a juggler. Drop one and they all go. Even the kids go in the end – turn into punks or something. It's all a giant con.' He stood up. 'Let's get you a bit more sorted out. Then we're going to the Nag's Head.' Unuttered was Frank's plan to dine early in order that he might get home soon enough to limit the inevitable recriminations.

Their talk had edged riskily near to soul-searching.

'The books, then,' said Stephen. 'Let's get them put away.'

They spent the next hour unpacking and shelving Stephen's books, which had been carefully packed in the order in which they had previously been arranged. His mother's books were still in boxes in the attic. Then they sorted through some of Stephen's clothes.

'They don't look right. I don't look right,' said Stephen, casting a downward glance at his slightly baggy grey flannels. He thought of the men in the George and Dragon the day before, in jeans and sweaters, and loose lumber jackets.

'You and I are not the type for jeans,' said Frank. 'Grey flannels are still all right, but treat yourself to some new ones. Take a trip round Marks and Spencer's – that'll clue you up. People wear sweaters a lot; a collar and tie at the weekend does seem rather formal. Remember, I've come from the office.'

'I bought some new pyjamas the other day,' said Stephen. 'Not that anyone seems to wear them these days, if television is any guide.'

'I do,' said Frank.

'I shall paint the house,' Stephen announced. 'I don't think I'm going to be able to plan sensibly for quite some time, Frank. I feel very – ' he did not want to say that he felt lost. 'Rather adrift,' he amended. 'A bit like Rip van Winkle, you know. And I'm terrified of committing some small offence and getting into trouble.'

'You won't. I mean, even if you get a parking fine, that's not going to be any sort of problem,' said Frank. 'Just a financial loss.'

75

Before they left for the restaurant, Stephen's bed had been made up in what had once been his room, and the old record player had been plugged in and found to work.

'A bed, food, books, music and drink,' said Stephen during dinner. 'What more can a man want?'

'A television set,' said Frank promptly. 'It's a thing one frequently curses because of the awful programmes, but there are some things well worth watching, and it's company.'

'That's true,' said Stephen. 'It's a soporific, too, and one I'm used to. You watch it a lot, in the nick.'

'You can hire them,' said Frank.

'I'll see to it,' said Stephen, aware that he was lucky. Other people would have been released from prison when he was. It was unlikely that any of them were innocent of the offence for which they were sentenced, but it was also unlikely that many were as well set up.

'You're not going to try to talk to Ruth, are you?' asked Frank over their brandy. Stephen's pale face was now flushed; he had eaten with appetite, and had enjoyed the wine. Frank had expected him to betray nervousness in the restaurant, but if Stephen had felt any unease, he did not display it.

'No,' said Stephen. 'It's Lois I'm going after.'

9

Stephen spent the next weeks working in the house and garden. While the weather held, he cut the grass with the old motor mower. Careless use by successive tenants had damaged its blades and it left a serrated pattern on the lawn, but, by going over his tracks again crosswise, he achieved a fair barbering to take it through the winter. He cut down the withered growth in the flowerbeds and uprooted weeds. Indoors, he cleaned off the walls and painted them and the ceilings. At Badger's End, Marcia had chosen pretty papers, but after years of austerity, Stephen had no confidence about making any such choice. He opted for white all through; that could be touched up at will or washed over with a colour later.

No one, it seemed, had discovered his identity. No anonymous letter arrived; there were no obscene telephone calls; no one painted graffiti on his gatepost or threw stones at his windows.

Most of the time, while he worked, he concentrated on the task in hand, a discipline he had learned in the last ten years, but sometimes his thoughts strayed to the schoolgirl he had seen who was probably his daughter, and he remembered the magic which had brought her into being. Now that his first anxiety about her wellbeing had been stilled, his mental unrest over Marcia's last hours grew. In spite of Ruth, Stephen had never lost the habit of loving Marcia. She had no longer stirred his blood, but he had hated making her unhappy, and felt real guilt. It was dreadful to ask your wife to give you up because you had found someone else you liked better. Wouldn't he have been deeply hurt if, in such a manner, Marcia had rejected him?

While he was working on the house, Stephen made his required reports to his probation officer, overestimating the amount of work still to be done. He must win time for finding Lois before there was pressure to think constructively about his future. There was a job the officer thought might suit him, but Stephen still insisted that he wanted to work for himself.

At length the day came when he set out for the nursing home whose address Lily Knapp had supplied. He took some flowers and a large bunch of grapes.

To his surprise, the place was not an institution, but a brick house in a small country town. There was a well-kept garden at the front.

He rang the bell and waited; then, when there was no answer, rang again. After a while he tried the handle, found the door unlocked, and went inside. There was a strong smell of boiled cabbage and urine, all too familiar. A very old lady, wearing a curious shapeless dress – or perhaps she was shapeless – made of some woolly fabric, stood at the rear of the hall clinging to a walking frame. Her sparse white hair spikily haloed her small, trembling head.

'I was looking for Mrs Carter,' said Stephen. 'Could you tell me where to find her?'

The old woman stared at him blankly and began mumbling.

Discouraged, Stephen advanced towards a passage that led into the recesses of the building. He went along it and came to a kitchen where two women in overalls, whom he took to be nurses, were drinking tea and chatting. They looked up as Stephen appeared.

'Could you help me – is it possible to see Mrs Carter?' he asked.

'Mrs Carter?' The women looked at each other questioningly. 'We've no Mrs Carter here,' said the older of the two.

Had she died? It was all too possible.

'Oh – er – when – ' Stephen took a grip on himself. If Mrs Carter had died in this place there would be records. There would be a note of where bills had been sent, wouldn't there? 'How long ago did she – she was here six or seven years ago,' he said.

'Seven years is a long time at eighty,' said the nurse who had spoken. She was dark and sallow, with a spot on her chin caused by eating too many cakes in the patients' kitchen.

'She wasn't as old as that,' said Stephen. Mrs Carter, if still alive, would be eighty or thereabouts now, but not then.

The second nurse – they were both untrained – a plump girl with small brown eyes like currants in the pale dough of her face, was prepared to be slightly more helpful.

'Mrs Rowan might know. She's been here for yonks,' she said. 'Come along and I'll ask her.'

She swept out of the kitchen, and Stephen, as he followed, had to fight an almost overwhelming impulse to flee from the building.

Mrs Rowan turned out to be a patient. She sat in a privileged spot, as was her due as the longest-staying inmate, in a wing chair near a huge television set in a room where ten old ladies and one old man sat about in various stages of disintegration. Mrs Rowan herself was not totally fragmented; she turned a white, withered face towards Stephen

78

when she saw him behind the nurse. Only one other head turned to look at him, and it wasn't because the television was offering a riveting spectacle; few of the old people were looking at it. It was on very loud.

The pasty nurse turned down the volume and spoke to Mrs Rowan.

'There's a gentleman asking for Mrs Carter,' she said. 'I don't remember her. Do you?'

'Oh yes,' said Mrs Rowan straight away. 'Batty old thing, she was, like most of us here, but for a bit she could still play cards. No bridge – we couldn't muster a four – but we played rummy. Does that sound like her?'

'It could be,' Stephen said, and hesitated, but he had to ask the question. 'Is she dead?'

'I don't know. Got too poorly for them here – kept wandering off and forgetting where she was,' said Mrs Rowan. 'She was physically not too bad, you see, and she kept escaping. You'd think they'd lock us in, wouldn't you? But most of us are past all that. She went on somewhere else – now let me see, where was it?' She cogitated, but could not come up with the answer.

Stephen turned to the nurse.

'Wouldn't there be some sort of record? A discharge address?' he said. 'I'm most anxious to find her.'

'A relative, are you?' said the doughy nurse.

'Er – yes,' said Stephen firmly. 'I've been out of the country and lost touch.'

'Well, I don't know,' said the nurse. 'Matron's out and the secretary's gone off. It would be a bother to look.'

Stephen understood people much better now than he had done ten years before. He knew at once that this was no question of ethics. He thanked Mrs Rowan and began moving towards the door, taking his wallet out of his pocket as he went. The nurse followed, and when they had moved out of sight, he set down his burden of flowers and grapes and extracted a ten-pound note, which he showed her.

'I'm sure one of your charities could use this,' he said smoothly. 'If you would be kind enough.'

The note had disappeared into the woman's overall pocket before he could blink. Without a word, she opened

the door of a small room across the passage. This was
furnished as an office with a desk by the window and a row of
filing cabinets along one wall. The nurse opened a drawer in
one of the cabinets and looked through various files, then
pushed it back with a clang and went through another.

Wouldn't medical notes follow a patient from one home to
the next? Stephen was beginning to feel discouraged when
the woman crossed to the desk. In one of the drawers she
found a large address book, and, under Carter, an entry,
scored out, to show it was no longer valid.

Discharged to Aston House, Stephen read, and a date over
four years ago.

'Where is Aston House?' asked Stephen.

'I think it's in Salisbury,' said the woman. 'I don't know
exactly where.'

Her burst of cash-induced energy had gone.

'Well, thank you,' said Stephen.

What an appalling place! Those patients were prisoners
just as much as he had been; how long must poor Mrs Rowan
wait there, with no parole except death?

Aston House might be worse.

He found it without too much difficulty. It was listed in the
Yellow Pages of the telephone directory, and the town map
of Salisbury in his road atlas showed the road. This was a
much less attractive building than the first place, a gaunt
Victorian edifice set behind a high wall. He had, again, the
sense of entering prison as he drove through the gateway and
parked.

This time, the door was opened to him. He saw a smiling
young woman who, when he asked for Mrs Carter, said that
yes, of course he could see her.

'But I doubt if she'll know you,' she said. 'She doesn't even
know her own daughter. Would you just wait a minute while
I deliver this tray and then I'll take you up.'

She turned to pick up a tray laden with six mugs of tea
from a table in the hall, and opened a door on the right.
Stephen heard her speak brightly as she entered the room
beyond.

There was the same smell of urine here, but without the
cabbage. Some landscapes, done in watercolours, hung on

80

the walls of the hall, which were painted cream. The nurse soon returned and led Stephen upstairs to a large, bright room where three ancient ladies lay in bed and three others, wearing warm dressing-gowns, sat in armchairs.

'End bed on the right,' said the nurse. 'I'll be back to see how you're getting on as soon as I've done the tea.'

Gazing round in pitying horror, Stephen thought all the old ladies looked like witches. Two of the bedridden were asleep, mouths agape. Two in chairs watched him with dulled eyes, and one of these two smiled feebly. Stephen did his best to smile back. His prison experience had not prepared him for this, and he saw that his first judgement had been hasty, or else there were good witches, for this old lady watched him with a benign expression as he approached the end bed, whose occupant was knitting and humming a tuneless dirge. The knitting was grey and hung loosely from large wooden needles.

He would not have recognized Mrs Carter but, as she looked up at him, focusing on him, he saw that it really was she – Lois's mother, the shell of a woman with, it seemed, no memory.

But with manners.

'Have you come far? Do sit down. How nice of you to drop in,' she said, and graciously accepted the flowers and the grapes.

When he mentioned Lois, he drew blank. Mrs Carter just smiled and talked about life in Malta before the war. She pulled the grey knitting off its needles and began to undo it.

Stephen remembered that Lois's father had been in the Navy. He asked about Lois several times.

'How is your dear mother?' Mrs Carter inquired, and went on to reveal what delicious custard they served in this place.

'Quite a good hotel,' she said. 'And with a sea view.'

He excused himself at last and paused beside the benign witch, who had never stopped watching him. She might be deaf, he thought. Still, there was nothing to lose by trying.

'It's Mrs Carter's daughter, Lois, I want to trace,' he said. 'She does come to see her, doesn't she?'

'Oh yes – once a month or so,' said the good witch. 'I can't be quite sure when – it's catching, you know: senility.' Her thin hands plucked at the bedclothes. 'The nurse will be able to tell you – the one who brought you up. She's a dear. Her name's Maureen.'

He met Maureen as he went downstairs, and she told him that Mrs Reynard came every second Thursday, in the afternoon.

So that was Lois's new name, and she would be here at the nursing home next week.

'She's got a business to run, that's why she doesn't come more often,' Maureen went on. 'But some of them don't get visited at all.'

'Does it do any good? Visiting, I mean, when they don't know who's there?' asked Stephen.

'Who's to say they don't know subconsciously?' said Maureen.

'One old lady up there seems quite bright,' he said.

'Oh yes. Mrs Hunter. Poor old thing, it's a pity she's here. She's very frail, you see, and they won't take her in places that don't do bed cases, but there's no one for her to talk to. We pop in when we can.' She smiled at Stephen, a nice, good woman who did her best.

Probably Lois helped her husband run whatever business he owned, Stephen thought, driving away. He was glad that Mrs Carter was in this much nicer home than the first one.

While Stephen waited for the second Thursday in the month, he built some bookshelves and went again to Anderton, where he saw Susannah at lunchtime once more, buying a birthday card. For whose birthday? Ruth's was in May. For one of the brothers? She'd cut a finger; he noticed a Bandaid stuck round it. She was with the girl with the plait again, not a boy. Some very small girls – or they looked small and young to Stephen – were with boys. It was surely much too soon? Most of the girls, of whatever age, wore earrings, he saw; Susannah's were small gold studs. He gave an extra coat of emulsion paint to the kitchen, for some of the old staining had come through what he had already applied. A series of tenants had allowed layers of grease to form on the walls, and though he had washed them several times, it had been impossible to get rid of all the splash marks and stains. Stephen recognized in himself that this drive towards cleanliness was symbolic, reflecting his search for a new beginning.

On Thursday, he parked in a corner of the space available outside Aston House and waited. Several cars were already there, and two more soon drove up. From each, a middle-aged woman got out and went into the home. Was either of them Lois? Would she be easily recognizable after so long? He planned to speak to her when she came out, and told himself that it would not matter if he spoke to the wrong person – he could simply apologize for his mistake; that wasn't an offence – merely an error. He tried to recall Lois's appearance. She was short and sturdy, with dark curls and a fresh complexion. He remembered that she had been physically strong. No task in the garden had been too challenging for her, and he had known her to hire a circular saw to fell trees in the spinney at Primrose Cottage. It was ten years, not twenty, since he had seen her; she was unlikely to have changed a great deal.

A large, dark-green van turned in at the gate. Stephen thought it must be making a delivery, but its driver parked in line with the last arrival. A woman got out, slid the door to and walked up to the front door. She wore a brown tweed skirt and a quilted khaki anorak jacket of a type he had noticed so many women wearing that it seemed to be almost a uniform. She had wiry grey curls.

Stephen got out of his car and walked round to look at the van. On it was painted *Reynard's Garden Centre* and an address in Somerset.

He had found her, and her address, and he need not speak to her today: he could call on her at her place of work any time he chose.

He wondered if, while she was in the home, his visit would be mentioned. He had left no name. Well, if it was, let her wonder who the caller could have been. She'd soon find out.

Maureen, however, was off duty and Mrs Hunter was asleep; the grapes had all been eaten, and the flowers were on a central table so that Lois never knew that anyone had been to see her mother.

10

Stephen drove westwards on a day which began fine and clear, but the weather clouded over before he had gone far. Soon, rain was spitting down, splashing up at him from the road and spattering his windscreen as passing traffic sent up waves of water. Then his windscreen wipers stopped working and he had to stop to get them mended. This delayed him, since he had to leave the main road and find a garage which could help him. He had expected the journey to take about three hours, but now he would not reach Witterton until the afternoon.

The clouds broke up later in the day, and it was fine, though already getting dark, when he reached the garden centre. It was on a by-road leading into the village from the main Exeter road, a long building with a large parking area outside, part of it covered so that cars could load while protected from bad weather. A range of garden furniture was displayed beneath this cover, and among the chairs and tables, some of wood, some of white plastic and some wrought iron, stood groups of gnomes.

This was the right place. Stephen's pulse quickened. Here was where he would find some of the answers.

He walked through the shop entrance and saw racks of seeds on view, together with rows of garden implements, wheelbarrows, trugs, hoses and watering equipment. Beyond, there was a paved yard, approached by swing doors. Here, there were plants in pots and tubs, and a few customers in raincoats and waterproof headgear. A grey-haired man in a green overall in the showroom was attending to someone buying peat. Another assistant manned the till. It seemed that you helped yourself to the plants or the goods you required, loading them on to one of the large, wooden-floored trolleys ranged against a wall. As well as all this, there were pots of jam for sale, and tablemats, trays, tea towels, and other items he would not have connected with gardens. There was a book section, whose contents were concerned not only with horticulture but also with cooking and wild life. Stephen remembered nothing like it from the days of his freedom; he had simply visited various nurseries when buying plants; there had not been all these sidelines, nor could you get, as here, it seemed, everything from one place.

He did not see Lois, but then the business must be her husband's; she was, perhaps, at home, wherever that was. There was no house attached to the centre.

He went up to the till, which was tended by an alert-looking youth.

'Mrs Reynard about?' Stephen asked.

'Not just now,' said the youth. 'Can I help you, sir?'

Stephen did not realize how rare was this respectful form of address nowadays.

'Is Mr Reynard about, then?' he pursued.

'Mr Reynard? No way!' The youth almost laughed. 'There's no Mr Reynard,' he added.

'Since when?'

'Since always,' said the youth. 'Mr Harris, over there – he can tell you,' he added, indicating the older man Stephen had already noticed.

Stephen walked over to Fred Harris, who had now finished with peat and was advising an elderly couple about their lawn. Stephen waited patiently while he attended to them, and when at last they had gone, Fred turned to him.

'Now, sir,' he said. 'Sorry to keep you waiting. What can I do for you?'

'I don't know,' said Stephen. 'I was asking about Mr Reynard and your colleague over there said he's not here now.'

'No, sir, I'm sorry to say,' said Fred. 'Mrs Reynard's a widow lady. Came here when he died, nine years ago that would be. Bought the place with what he'd left her, seemingly. She's built it up well – it was nothing special then, but now we attract trade from all over the county, and even beyond.'

Stephen could almost feel his brain cells clicking as he absorbed this information.

'Nine years ago?' he said.

'That's right – just before my Sandra was born, it was, and she's coming up for ten after Christmas,' said Fred.

'You worked here then?'

'Oh yes. Mrs Reynard took me on with the place,' said Fred. 'She's out just now.'

'Where does she live? Mrs Reynard?' Stephen asked.

'Two miles up the road, just before you get to Witterton,' said Fred. 'Fir Tree House, it's called – you can't miss it. It's on the left – there's no other house nearby. It's got a long drive and stands in two acres of land. She grows a lot of stuff there.'

'Thank you very much, Mr Harris,' said Stephen. 'You've been very helpful.'

He went away without having given any reason for his interest in the deceased Mr Reynard, and Fred gave it no further thought.

Stephen drove along the road as directed. Daylight was fading fast, and he went carefully; he did not want to miss Fir Tree House but, as Fred had said, he could not fail to see it. There was a white fence and the name was clearly painted on the gatepost. He turned in at the entrance and drove up the drive. At the end was a small Georgian house of perfect proportions. There was a gravelled sweep around a lawn before the front door, and the garden sloped away to the left. As Stephen swung the car round, the lights picked up a spreading cedar tree with, beneath it, a monster gnome dressed in orange and scarlet.

Marcia had said that Lois had kept her gnomes for company. They were like the life-sized figures, dummy-boards, used in the seventeenth century to make large rooms seem peopled and ward off intruders. Figures were sometimes used as firescreens in the eighteenth century, and to startle guests, Marcia had said. She often came up with interesting pieces of information of that sort.

There were no lights showing in the house, not even one in the porch. Stephen took a torch from the shelf under the dashboard and walked up to the front door. He rang the bell.

It echoed back at him. There was not a sound – not the yap of a dog – nothing to break the silence. He rang again. Still nothing. Then he tried the door, which was locked. He went round to the back of the house, where there was another door, also locked; then, for all the world like one of his recent companions, he played his torch over the windows. They were of the sash variety, and Stephen had learned in prison how easy it was, with a knife, to force the catch and open such windows.

Before he entered the house, Stephen moved his car round to the yard behind the garage, where Lois would not see it when she came back. If he was waiting in the house for her, sitting in the dark, ready to surprise her, she'd be very shocked. She would say much more, like that, than if she had time to collect herself.

The house was neat. The kitchen was swept, the sink wiped down, not even a mug left on the drainer. A small gaudy gnome smoked a pipe on the shelf by the drainer. In the dining-room there was an inlaid mahogany table, quite small, to suit the size of the room. It gleamed with attention. Stephen was vague about period, but he thought it must be valuable – Sheraton, maybe: Marcia would have known. The chairs placed round it looked to be of the same period, and there was an elegant inlaid sideboard with graceful legs. Beyond the small, square hall was a room quite unlike the Carters' sitting-room at Primrose Cottage. Marcia had said that Lois's mother had lived in rented houses for most of her married life and had picked things up here and there as they caught her fancy, without any overall scheme.

There was certainly one here. The covers were peach, with a pale lime flowered design, and the curtains were of soft lime colour; the carpet was off-white, with one good rug in front of the hearth. Two silk pictures hung on one wall beside the mantelpiece – Marcia's work, he recognized them instantly, but of course they belonged to Lois now. In a display cabinet, the one they had had at Badger's End, a number of china pieces were set out. Stephen approached and inspected them. There were figures exactly like those in Marcia's collection. There was the Meissen figure of Mars she had bought at a sale in Guildford.

Stephen felt his spine prickle. It was right that Lois should have the cabinet from Badger's End, but how had she matched the collection it had contained? That had vanished the day Marcia disappeared. He looked round the room again, this time identifying familiar furniture. The sofa was smaller than the one he remembered, but surely the chairs were identical? Stephen went back to the dining-room and looked at the chairs there. Yes, they had been at Badger's End, he was sure.

Seeing these pieces again was disturbing, yet he should have expected to see them. They were all much better than anything Lois and her mother had owned; she would have kept them and sold the rest. But it didn't explain the china figures.

Stephen turned the lights out in the downstairs rooms and went upstairs.

There were three bedrooms, all quite a good size. The first one he went into contained a single bed covered with a deep rose candlewick spread, slightly faded. There were rose curtains, whose colour did not quite match, with sprigs of small flowers all over them, and a heavy mahogany dressing-table on which there was a Maison Pearson hairbrush, a powder pot with a silver lid, and a pink plastic comb. A red wool dressing-gown hung on the door. It was like a jolly-hockey-sticks type of schoolgirl's bedroom of several decades ago, Stephen thought, and rather pathetic. On the bedside table was a green anglepoise lamp and a book about ferns.

Depressed, Stephen moved across the landing. The next bedroom was clearly not in use, and he recognized the spreads from the spare room at Badger's End. The beds were divans, however; those at Badger's End had had walnut headboards. The dressing-table was too large for the room and probably Edwardian or later: a relic from Primrose Cottage, perhaps.

He opened the third door, turned on the light and looked round the room. The lighting was soft, sending a diffused glow over the furnishings. There were pale cream curtains, printed with delicate flowers, and the wide bed was covered in a quilted spread of the same material. The carpet was ivory, and the dressing-table was Marcia's from Badger's End. On it were her silver hairbrushes, bearing her monogram and given to her by her father.

Stephen thought he was going to choke as his heart thumped and seemed to rise up into his throat.

Of course Lois would have Marcia's furniture – her dressing-table – but not her brushes: those had been stolen.

If the police had traced them, wouldn't he have heard?

Maybe not. Maybe Marcia had left Lois a message telling her where they were, a message which, if it had been revealed, would have proved him innocent of murder.

Stephen turned out the light and left the room. There were two unopened doors on this landing and behind one was a large airing cupboard full of neatly folded sheets, towels and pillow cases. The other led to the bathroom. Stephen saw a forest of plants along a shelf, turning it into a jungle. He looked for signs of use. There were sponges and flannels – two of each – and a long-handled back brush. There were two toothglasses, each in chrome racks fixed to the wall, each with its brush suspended. Two bathcaps hung on the door, one yellow, one pink.

He went downstairs as fast as he could and let himself out of the house by the front door, banging it behind him. For minutes he stood there, gasping, inhaling the fresh, damp country air in which there was the tang of the sea, not ten miles distant.

He had to get away, compose himself, work out what it meant.

As he walked past the garage to collect his car, he hesitated. Should he have a look in there before he left? It wouldn't take much time. He had seen a row of keys hanging on a rack in the kitchen. Stephen entered again by the window he had already used, and took one which had a large tag on it labelled *Garage*.

One space inside the garage was empty; the other was occupied by a blue Mini. Stephen shone his torch round. A hose was coiled on a hook on one wall, and a large tin of Castrol XL stood on a shelf, with a plastic bucket and a brush attachment for the hose. He went over and looked at the shelf on which stood also some tins of touch-up paint, car polish, a large sponge and a roll of stockinette cloth. It was all very neat.

Something made him glance down and sideways at the front of the Mini. It had been driven up close to the wall, and between its wheels and the brickwork was a dark bundle. Stephen shone his torch on it and saw black plastic. Plants, he thought: a tree or shrub. He felt a weird compulsion to touch it, and bent down, reaching out to the end nearest him.

It was not a tree or a shrub. Stephen gripped the end in his two hands, then moved them upwards along what was strangely firm and yet soft. His heart began to drum, accepting horror before his mind was able to do the same. He stood up and went round the Mini to the other side, where the far end of the bundle lay, and there he felt the head. For what he had felt at first was a pair of feet, and as his hands moved he had touched human limbs beneath the wrapping of plastic.

Hardly knowing what he was doing, Stephen pulled at the plastic wrappings. The sheeting had been turned in and tucked round the neck, but it was not tied. He folded it back and saw dark hair, pale at the roots. Then, sick with dismay and shock, he shone his torch on to the face.

She had always been pale, but now she was a weird, purplish colour. He noticed a few tiny red specks in the eyes, which were open. She was fatter, and her skin, even in death, was lined, but he knew at once that this was Marcia.

Part Two

1

'How could he? How could he?' Marcia had stormed to
Lois, whom she had summoned to Badger's End by telephone.

Only a week before, at a dinner party, Marcia had told her
guests what a perfect marriage theirs was, and now Stephen
had destroyed her world.

'You can't trust any of them,' said Lois, meaning men. She
felt Marcia's distress as acutely as if it were her own, watching the stiff, elegant figure in the big armchair, a handkerchief to her eyes but not a hair out of place, nor, as far as Lois
could see, a tear being shed.

Marcia and Lois had first met some time after Marcia's
father, a widower, had remarried. He had been in the RAF
during the war, and afterwards had started a synthetics
business which had prospered to such an extent that ten
years later he sold it for more than two million pounds.
Marcia was much indulged. Her only brother had died
during the poliomyelitis epidemic in 1947, and she, escaping
the disease, had become the recipient of all the attention that
would have been shared by the two children. Her mother
became anxious and overprotective, flying to the thermome-
ter at the least sign of the mildest ailment, and her father was
constantly afraid she would overtire herself. This was
unlikely, for Marcia had a natural indolence. She was sent to
a small boarding-school where she spent four years learning
very little, obtaining O-Levels only in English, Art and
Needlework. She sewed exquisitely, branching out into fine
embroidery when other girls, more practically, took up
dressmaking. Later, she went to Switzerland to be 'finished',
but here even her skiing – for which she had no innate talent
– was circumscribed by her parents' insistence that she must
not overtax her strength. At this stage in her life there was
some justification for their attitude because, in her middle

teens, she had suddenly grown extremely fast and genuinely did tire easily.

During her last term at the Swiss school, her mother, whose own increasing pallor and lethargy had gone unremarked, fell gravely ill and died. A year later her father launched Marcia into a London season, chaperoned by an impoverished lady of impeccable social standing who made an annual income by this means.

Marcia enjoyed that year, but it ended without the engagement her father had hoped for as a solution to her future. She had neither the need nor the urge to embark on a positive career, and frittered time away in brief spells spent helping friends in boutiques, soon growing bored. Occasionally she went to lectures at the Victoria and Albert Museum and mildly studied the decorative arts. Meanwhile, her father had started up another business and was preoccupied.

Then, with no warning, he remarried. His new wife was only a few years older than Marcia, who bitterly resented the interloper. Till then, she and her father had shared the large house in Kensington, looked after by a housekeeper and a daily woman. Now, Isobel moved in, and soon she had a son.

This was an unhappy time for Marcia, and not easy for her stepmother, who tried in vain to overcome the girl's jealous hostility. Marcia would scarcely speak to her, and took no interest in her small half-brother.

Her father sought advice from the woman who had earlier introduced Marcia to the social scene, and made contact, as a result, with a troubled widow whose daughter had just had an abortion. This was before termination became legal.

Lois Carter had acquired her mistrust of the male sex – and of sex – when she had had too much to drink one evening at a May Ball. She had gone in a punt with a young man whose name she never knew, thinking it rather a lark and expecting merely an aquatic experience with, perhaps, a deep kiss or two. Other girls had, with giggles, discussed such things, and more, in her hearing, but Lois had never felt even the lightest touch of male lips on hers. Her escort had tied up to a willow, helped her on to the bank beneath the tree's concealing branches and there assaulted her. Lois had been only irritated at first. His misdirected kisses were so slobbery that he seemed simply ridiculous. He kept moaning and tugging at her clothes, which was silly and annoying but, at this point, not alarming. Of course, she had expected all this to happen one day, amid romantic surroundings and after marriage. Lois knew you were meant to be carried away on a tide of rapture. Girls talked about how far you should let a man go, but now she found she had no chance to decide as a great, bulky weight pinned her to the ground. A hand tore at her knickers and strong knees forced her legs apart. Then something huge, hard and painful was thrust violently inside her, piercing her with a shaft of pure agony that made her scream, but the sound she made was muffled by the pressure of a heavy shoulder against her face.

It was over in seconds. He lay gasping like a stranded fish, still lying on her, his head turned away. After a while, he rolled off her and adjusted his clothes, and Lois, sniffling, did the same. Then he took her back in the punt.

The next day her mother noticed her low spirits, and, as time passed without any change in mood, became anxious. It did not take long to get the sad tale out of the girl. Mrs Carter was appalled, but thought Lois had lost her self-control on a tide of alcoholic passion. With luck there would be no lasting damage, and the episode would be a useful warning. But as a result of this single encounter, Lois became pregnant.

Friends helped Mrs Carter arrange the abortion. When Marcia's father appeared, with his proposal that she should take his daughter and her own around the world at his expense, Mrs Carter was so grateful that she would have done almost anything to help Marcia, towards whom she soon became protective, as did most people. It was thus that Marcia and Lois met at a time of crisis in both their lives.

Soon after their return, when her stepmother was pregnant again, Marcia met Stephen. She was spending a weekend in the country with a debutante acquaintance, who was still unmarried, and whose mother gave weekend houseparties for a variety of reasons, not least the dullness of her husband. Stephen, staying nearby with a schoolfriend, Frank Jeffries, came to play tennis on the Saturday. He partnered Marcia, who made little effort but, because of her height and reach and a naturally good eye, was a useful doubles partner. At the end of their victorious first set she, as was her habit, flopped into a deckchair exuding fatigue and expecting to be brought a glass of lemonade. Stephen was intrigued by the contrast between her robust appearance and apparent fragility. She was pretty, and she seemed shy. Later, he realized that what he took for shyness was a reluctance to exert herself even into making conversation. At the time, he yearned to shield this golden girl from life's buffetings.

Why shouldn't he, thought Marcia: someone must offer her an escape. She told Lois that he was like a knight of old, with his courtly ways, and responded gently to his passion.

They had been married for twelve years when Stephen asked for a divorce.

Marcia's reaction startled him. She wept and yelled, like a child denied a treat, tearing at her own hair and then beating at Stephen's chest with her fists in what was, in fact, a tantrum. Until now, she had always been very controlled – too much so, he had often felt, in their intimate moments, though she welcomed his attentions with languid pleasure. In this area, as with the rest of her life, Marcia was lazy and disinclined to think of anyone but herself. She had not seemed to mind the fact that they had had no children. Latterly, Stephen had begun to wonder whether a family would have changed things: her dormant emotions, which he had been unable to stir to any great extent, might have been aroused by an infant. For she had emotions, as was now made plain.

To Marcia, what was threatened was impossible to tolerate. She would not let it happen.

At the first attempt, she succeeded. Their furious quarrel ended in a sexual reconciliation, with Stephen aroused to passion by remorse, but some weeks later, when he brought the subject up again, she raged afresh, and, horrifying Stephen, threatened to kill herself.

'How would you like that?' she stormed. 'It would be your fault.' She knew her man, and added, 'That would spoil your fine affair, wouldn't it? It would haunt you.'

This time, there was no passionate resolution. Stephen

became quiet and withdrawn, but was always kind and considerate at home. Occasionally, they made gentle love. A year passed before, once again, he asked to be released, and now he told her that there was a baby on the way.

That night, Marcia slit her wrists with her nail scissors. She did not do herself much damage but there was quite a lot of blood in the bathroom.

White with shock, and feeling very sheepish, Stephen told Dr Watkins the reason for her action when Marcia was safely sleeping, wrists neatly dressed. His hand shook as he poured whisky for himself and the doctor.

Dr Watkins counselled care. He would see Marcia regularly, for she clearly needed help.

Stephen had to play along with Marcia now. He and Ruth could not build a life on the ruin of Marcia's.

A week after this event, Stephen had come home to find that his things had been moved from the main bedroom, not into his dressing-room next door, but into one of the guest rooms at the far end of the house. Marcia made no reference to these new arrangements, and so he did not comment. Apart from this, life went on as before. Stephen told Ruth, who had thought that Marcia's earlier threat of suicide was simply made to frighten Stephen, that he would bring the subject up again when things had settled down. But he had lacked the nerve to do so until his euphoria after Susannah's birth gave him courage, and then the world went mad.

The real separation between Stephen and Marcia had begun with their move to Badger's End – welcomed by Mrs Carter, who thought their coming would improve her daughter's social life and thus her marriage chances. But the only unattached man Lois seemed to have met through them was Frank Jeffries, and nothing came of that.

Before the move, Marcia and Stephen had lived in a small house near Reigate but, when she was twenty-five, Marcia gained control of money settled on her by her father when he remarried. Until now, Stephen had refused to use interest from this fund to pay their mortgage or for any of their day-to-day expenses, but he had seen that she was discontented. She had always lived in a large house, in a certain style, and to deny her this because he was too proud to let her pay for it seemed to him, upon reflection, to be merely stubborn. He gave in, and was rewarded by the transformation in his wife.

Her days were now happily filled supervising renovations to the house, as she set in train a much more extensive programme than Stephen had anticipated or thought necessary. While Marcia attended to the house and its furnishing, buying furniture at auctions and bringing swatches of various fabrics home to choose from, Lois undertook the restoration of the garden. Things grew for her; she took slips from other people's gardens and they always struck. Under the impression that he was planning his own surroundings, Stephen agreed to Lois's suggestions for a revised layout, hiring machinery and doing a lot of the work, to her design, at weekends and on summer evenings. The result was excellent as shrubs and roses replaced a thicket of scrub, and near the house a series of bedding plants ensured colour throughout the year. Lois found a jobbing gardener for them, but was often to be seen herself, in corduroy trousers, trowel in hand, attending to bulbs or planting out asters. She designed the water garden, a streamlet cascading down several levels to a small pool, and she was cast down when Marcia would not permit gnomes to be stationed among the plants.

Meanwhile, Stephen's expanding work absorbed him. He took for granted the apparent pleasure with which Marcia greeted him when he came home; she always asked about his day and he replied with the answer she required: that it had been quite good; he never brought his problems home. They were unfailingly polite to one another. Marcia seemed content with her round of exhibitions in London, to which she dragged Lois, and her shopping trips. Lois often went on those, too, but Marcia soon gave up trying to educate her dress sense.

Marcia did not mind the absence of children. They would mess up the house, want to keep rabbits or, worse, pet mice; cost money. At first she mildly expected to find herself pregnant but then she grew used to her undemanding life; and she saw, too, how tiring small children were, and what a tie, preventing one from doing things one enjoyed. Her days were a great deal calmer than those of the wives in Hagbourne Green who spent their time, when not coping with measles and mumps, ferrying children to and from school or swimming, or music lessons, and even, as time went on, boxing ponies to gymkhanas and spending hours plaiting manes and tails. Marcia took up embroidery again, and began to design and execute pictures in silk, which she gave to various friends, finding ideas in art galleries and making the transfers herself from prints or photographs. She was so skilful that people began to ask her to carry out commissions, and, laughing about it, she earned a little money which she did not need.

When Stephen told her that he wanted to leave her, Marcia's world was shattered. Here was a fresh betrayal: as when her father married Isobel, she had been supplanted. Jealous rage made her hysterical, but the sexual reconciliation which followed left her weak and trembling, mortified by her own abandon. She would never let it recur.

She did not tell Lois that part of it, though she told her the rest. She told her, too, that she had threatened suicide when, after an interval, Stephen brought the subject up again.

'That'd stop him,' Marcia said, with satisfaction. 'He'd never be able to look at that woman again, knowing it was all her fault.'

Lois recognized that this was just a threat, but when Marcia cut her wrists after she heard about the coming baby, Lois was frightened. What if such another gesture went too far? Suppose she swallowed too many pills one night, and wasn't found in time to be saved? Her bluff might, by accident, become reality.

It was Lois who thought of faking a suicide, one so successful that it would have the same punishing effect as if it were genuine. Then she had to sell the idea to Marcia, with some suggestions about how it could be done. It would have to be convincing enough to satisfy the police that she was really dead, so that Stephen should experience the ultimate in suffering.

'You'd have to leave him a note, then disappear,' Lois said.

At first the suggestion was simply a diversion to Marcia, who did not take it seriously, but they talked about it frequently.

'How would I live, if I disappeared?' Marcia asked in one of these discussions. 'I'd need money. If I cashed cheques, the bank would know I wasn't dead.'

'I'd help you,' Lois said. 'I'd fund you.'

'What with? You know you and your mother haven't anything to spare,' said Marcia brutally. She often stood treat to Lois on their outings, but the cost was worth it for company, and help when carrying parcels.

'You could put some money aside in advance,' said Lois, who had a small nest egg of her own.

'But if I died, or pretended to be dead and was believed, Stephen would get my money,' Marcia said. 'There's quite a lot of it. Why should he and that woman have a present of it? Besides, I'd need it.'

Lois waited for Marcia to think of the solution herself, but she didn't and had to be prompted.

'You could make a new will,' she said.

'But who would I leave it to?' said Marcia, and repeated, 'I'd want it myself.'

Lois waited again, willing Marcia to tune in to her thought waves. This time it – or something – worked, for Marcia suddenly smiled. The answer was before her.

'Why didn't I think of it before?' she cried. 'You're the one, of course! I trust you completely. You'd give it back!'

'And find somewhere for you to live temporarily,' said Lois. 'And look after you and help you. You'd have to disguise yourself a bit,' she added, veering away from the emotional. 'Dye your hair – adopt another name.'

'My things,' said Marcia, looking round the room. 'My china figures! All my clothes!' She did not mention any friends she might be sad to leave.

'If you were to leave everything to me, you'd get it all back as soon as the formalities were over,' Lois said. It was amazing how the plan began to grow as they discussed it, each suggestion setting off another.

Later, Lois thought of the refinements. When she suggested that Marcia should tell her solicitor that she was afraid Stephen might kill her, and that this was the reason for changing her will, Marcia, at first, protested.

'Adultery's enough reason for changing it,' she said.

'It will give the impression that you're disturbed,' Lois said. 'Disturbed in your mind, I mean. I think you should see Dr Watkins, too, and tell him. It will help to make it all more convincing. He'll probably give you tranquillizers, but you needn't take them.'

Marcia was not persuaded at once. There were long, intense sessions of talk when she speculated about life at Badger's End without Stephen.

'You wouldn't be able to afford to stay on,' said Lois. 'Not in the same style.'

'He'd have to give me alimony,' said Marcia.

'Not a lot, probably, as you've got money yourself,' said Lois. 'You might marry again, of course.'

The idea was wearisome to Marcia. How would she find another Stephen, to whom, by now, she was so accustomed?

'No,' she said, wondering only for an instant about sex and deciding that she could live without it; she would not let herself remember that one violent coupling which had shown her how the body could betray.

'How much would you mind leaving Hagbourne Green? Not seeing again people you've known for years?' Lois asked.

Marcia shrugged. There was no one important.

'I'd make new friends, I suppose,' she said. 'There'd be you, after all. I'd miss you, if it meant that – but it wouldn't, would it?'

'Only for a while – just while it's all being sorted out,' said Lois. 'And of course I'd keep in touch – come and see you, often, wherever you were, and make sure you were all right. Then I'd sell up here and we'd settle somewhere new.'

'Together, do you mean?' Would she like that, Marcia wondered. Well, she wouldn't want to be quite alone, that was certain, and Lois almost lived here as it was. The idea, at this point, was still just something to play with. 'But what about your mother?'

'I'd make arrangements for her,' said Lois. 'She's getting awfully vague, you know. She'd really be happier some- where where they can cope with these things.'

'In a home, do you mean?' Lois seemed to have got it all worked out.

'Mm. Before long, I won't be able to leave her alone,' said Lois. 'I often lock her into the house, as it is, on bad days. She goes wandering round the roads and forgets who she is.'

Marcia had not realized that Mrs Carter's absence of mind was more than just that.

'And the money?' she said. 'You'd simply hand it back, would you, afterwards?'

'Pay it over, as it came in,' said Lois. 'We'd have to look into what it would mean in tax terms.'

'There'd be death duties,' said Marcia.

'Well – yes – ' There would be no way round that.

'How would we spend our time?' Marcia asked.

'As we do now,' said Lois. 'Or we might start a small business. Antiques, say. You know such a lot about them. You could be the adviser and I'd do the day-to-day stuff.'

That idea had its attractions, but the whole thing was still just a fantasy to Marcia.

'Where would we live?'

'Wherever you like. Not near here, of course. By the coast, perhaps? Devon or Cornwall?' Lois had always liked the sea.

'Why not?' It was all the same to Marcia.

She did not believe in the plan until she began to find it had started to come into effect. Lois had made an appointment for her with a London solicitor. It had to be a stranger – not Frank, who had looked after their affairs so far, nor anyone local.

Marcia found it quite easy and even rather fun to carry out the interview with the solicitor. She dressed in black for the part, and whilst the solicitor suggested she was imagining things and might be wise to consult her doctor – or, if her husband had made actual threats against her, the police – he agreed that she was entitled to ensure that the errant Stephen did not stand to gain in any way by her death. After all, accidents happened.

The will was sent by post to be signed. Mrs Bishop, Marcia's cleaning woman, and the jobbing gardener were the witnesses, both told that it was just a legal document. Marcia sent it back to the solicitor, and a photostat was returned to be put in her desk, where later, as Lois knew they would, the police found it.

A new purpose had entered Lois's life, and she was amazed at her own invention. To further her aims, she carried out some research for, without the presence of a body, it would be difficult to fake a suicide convincingly. People who disappeared often turned up later; there must be, this time, strong evidence of death. She read some old detective stories that were in the house; her mother had once enjoyed them. Then she went to the library and consulted volumes on forensic medicine and the memoirs of pathologists.

'If I was really going to do it, I'd take sleeping pills,' said Marcia, who had slept soundly almost every night of her life.

'Some might be useful,' Lois said, ignoring this proof that Marcia's effort with her wrists had not been serious.

'I expect Dr Watkins would give me some,' said Marcia, and he did, though with some reluctance, when she complained to him of insomnia. She waited until her next visit to tell him that she was afraid Stephen planned to kill her.

The doctor suggested that holding on to a faithless husband was not necessarily the best plan for the rest of her life, particularly as there were no children to be thought of. Why not, he asked, get a job? Or pursue some outside interest? Marcia's general health was good and she had seldom consulted him; he judged her to be a pampered woman with too much time and money, perhaps frigid, and thought that Stephen had probably said, 'I could wring your neck,' in frustrated anger, not meaning it literally.

Lois took their plans a step forward when she found a furnished flat. It was in Bath, and Marcia was to go there as soon as her disappearance had been contrived. Lois had chosen Bath because Marcia would have no car at first, and must live somewhere pleasant with plenty of interesting things to see and do while they waited for all the legal angles to be dealt with. She took Marcia to see the flat, Marcia wearing a curly brown wig which Lois had bought. It changed her appearance amazingly, and her personality. She became quite giggly as she put it on in the washroom of the pub where they had stopped for lunch on the way to

Bath. Lois, too, donned a disguise, but she had already worn her smooth blonde wig, not unlike Marcia's own hair, on her flat-hunting expeditions, and she added plain-lensed spectacles with winged frames which she had bought at a theatrical outfitter's. She had taken immense trouble over finding a flat to suit Marcia; it had to be elegant and spacious, for you could not uproot a camellia and plant it in alien soil, expecting it to thrive.

Lois had told the man from the estate agency that her friend Mrs Morse (she chose the name of a favourite rose) was recently widowed. His manner was suitably subdued as he showed them round.

Marcia thought the flat was enchanting. Its owners had gone abroad for a year and were anxious to find a careful tenant who would cherish their precious belongings. The pale decor was the sort of thing Marcia herself would have chosen. She could not really believe they were going ahead with the plan as 'Mrs Morse' agreed to lease it; it was like being small girls playing at 'house', she thought, admiring the well-arranged kitchen which, though small, was more modern than hers at Badger's End.

Lois dipped into her savings to pay the first month's rent in advance, telling the agent that Mrs Morse's affairs were still not settled and until they were she would attend to things. There was so much to think of, for Marcia must not cash cheques after she disappeared and ready money would be the most immediate problem. Lois was nagged by the worry that the law might not presume Marcia dead for seven years, thus delaying, all that time, the settling of her estate and depriving them of income.

'You'll have to jump over a cliff into the sea,' she told Marcia.

'What? I couldn't possibly,' said Marcia. 'It would kill me.'

'Exactly,' said Lois. 'That's what everyone will think has happened. You won't really do it, of course. It will just seem as if you did.'

'How will anyone know?'

'Something you own could be found nearby. Maybe a scarf,' said Lois. Would that be enough? It would have to be at a place where the high tide washed the beach and could be presumed to have swept the body away. Cornwall, with its granite rocks and wild, leaping waves, would be ideal but was too far.

'Beachy Head,' said Marcia. 'That's the spot, isn't it? People are always jumping off there.'

That was a good idea, Lois thought. She remembered the white, high cliffs and the angry sea below. She had been there several times, and it was always windy, so windy that any scarf would blow away. Something weightier would have to be left as evidence – Marcia's handbag, possibly. Would it be washed up if it was thrown into the sea?

Marcia wouldn't want to part with it, or the precious personal contents, but she might have to be persuaded. Then chance would play its part. A murderer might, to get rid of it, hurl it after his victim, and in the dark, a missing shoe could be overlooked.

She went on planning, while Marcia allowed the idea to divert her from the reason for all this scheming, and the baby grew within the body of Stephen's mistress.

.

2

Lois chose her moment, after she and Marcia had been to an art exhibition in London. It had bored Lois, but she had trotted round in Marcia's wake and stared dutifully at various paintings by young artists of whom Marcia said they should be aware. Lois had taken them both to the station in her Morris Minor, and now they were having a drink together at Badger's End before she went home to face whatever her mother had been up to while she was out. Last week, Mrs Carter had caught the bus to Guildford and then, after buying a blouse and a pair of gloves, had forgotten where she lived. She had paid by cheque, and the shopkeeper had sensibly rung up her bank to find out her address. Mrs Carter had returned safely, remembering about the bus herself, but Lois feared that shop-lifting would be the next step in her mother's decay. Still, any such excess would justify sending Mrs Carter to a home. Lois had already chosen one and put her name down. This was an intermediate sort of home, which accepted people who were physically well enough to dress themselves and manage the day. As soon as they failed to do this, the home turned them out, but it had connections with others who cared for the more frail. Mrs Carter must take her turn on the waiting list, but it was time to prod Marcia. Lois's tactic had been to let the idea, now firmly planted, lie undisturbed in Marcia's subconscious for days, then nourish it towards fruition with some aptly applied remarks.

'That baby won't vanish, you know,' Lois said when they had each finished their first glass of sherry and were well into the second. 'It must be due soon, and once it's born that woman's going to have much more hold over Stephen.'

'He'll support it, I suppose,' said Marcia.

'It won't end there. You know how soft he is – he may like the child,' said Lois. 'Go all gooey over it – he's just the sort to do that.'

What she said was true.

In the early years of their marriage, Stephen had expressed regret that there were no children and once he had suggested that they should consult Dr Watkins about it, both of them going together, but Marcia had burst into tears and asked if he really wanted her to go through a lot of embarrassing tests. He never referred to the subject again.

'He might just walk out, without a word,' warned Lois. 'If he did, he'd beat us to it. That woman would win.'

When Marcia did not answer, Lois got up and refilled their glasses. She automatically did this sort of thing at Badger's End, as if she were part of the family.

'Are you going to let him humiliate you?' she asked. 'I wouldn't, in your place. Think of the gossip.'

'There'll be talk, won't there, anyway? If I kill myself?' said Marcia.

'You're not going to kill yourself,' Lois reminded her. 'And when people think that you have, the talk will all be sympathetic towards you. He'll be condemned. Isn't it better to make sure that's the sort of talk there is – kind to you and against him? It will all come out, you see, and the woman, whoever she is, will be disgraced too.'

Lois was curious about the woman's identity. She had suggested that Marcia have Stephen watched so that they could discover who she was, but Marcia didn't want to know anything about her rival. It seemed odd, to Lois, that she did not want to rush round and tear the woman's eyes out, but then Marcia never lost her dignity. Lois's own manner towards Stephen had been distinctly cool in the last months.

Marcia was remembering how nauseatingly proud her father had been about the arrival of his own second family. Men had this thing about sons, and the baby might be a boy. It would be some consolation to destroy in advance any chance of pleasure Stephen might have.

'If we're going to do it, perhaps we should get on with it before the wretched little thing arrives,' she said.

Lois had had a motive in trying to force a decision now.

'The tides are high at night next week,' she said. 'It would be an ideal time.' High tide was necessary to account for the body, entering the sea in darkness, being washed away. 'If we miss the tide, we may have to wait a month.' Or find some other method of laying the false trail, and she'd worked this one out so well. 'The flat's there, ready for you,' she reminded Marcia. 'There's a bright new life waiting.'

'I'll be on my own,' Marcia said.

'I know, but you're often on your own here. You'll be able to sew some pictures, just as you do here.' Lois could not see that Marcia's life would be so different; she just wouldn't have Stephen there any more, which should be a relief to her, Lois considered, after the way he'd been behaving. 'There's plenty to do in Bath. You'll make friends. Just be careful – you've been widowed – you and your husband lived in Rhodesia and, with the future there so uncertain, you decided to come home after he died. If people ask you about it out there, you must say it's all too painful – you're still so upset about your husband, you don't want to talk about it. No one will press you, if you say that. And I'll come over as often as I can.'

Lois must put spunk into Marcia now, fan the flame of her

anger. She would have to keep Marcia strong during the weeks after her supposed disappearance, especially when she discovered how Lois had elaborated upon the original plan. For Lois had devised a far more severe revenge than they had discussed.

Lois never physically touched Marcia. She was unaware, even in her own mind, of the true nature of her emotions, but she recognized that anything that hurt Marcia also hurt her. Marcia was not tough, as others were, and she needed protection which Stephen was no longer providing. Lois would soon supply all that was lacking, and at the same time gain the perfect companion and a source of income for life. She would be able to lavish on her friend all the energy which at present was dissipated by the demands of her mother. Marcia must finally, when legal hurdles were overcome, be installed in a beautiful place surrounded once again by her own lovely possessions, with opportunities to pursue her artistic bent. Their life would be full and rich, and Marcia would never be able to escape for she, Lois, would know her secret and she would hold the purse strings.

In the end, Stephen precipitated events when, the next Tuesday evening, he told Marcia that the baby girl had been born. Again he asked her to let him go, and again she refused.

'I'll be leaving anyway, then,' he said, grimly. 'Not at once, but soon. I'll make proper arrangements for you and, as soon as that's done, I'm going. I'll telephone Frank tomorrow.'

He looked defiant, and something else, too: it was almost as if he had been drinking, yet Stephen was always abstemious. Marcia, a stranger to it herself, did not recognize elation. His demeanour, however, was enough to spark off another suicide threat.

This time he reacted coldly.

'You're being hysterical,' he told her. 'You'll have a perfectly good life without me. It's just marriage you'll miss – being married – not me.'

Marcia went off to her bedroom in tears. When Lois came round early the next morning she was still red-eyed, and when Mrs Bishop arrived to clean, Lois led her aside to whisper that Mrs Dawes was rather upset this morning.

108

Things hadn't been right for some time, she said, and Mr and Mrs Dawes had had a dreadful row last night in which Mr Dawes had threatened to do his wife an injury.

'Oh, he never!' exclaimed Mrs Bishop. 'Oh, poor thing!' Feminine loyalty was thus easily won and Mrs Bishop, at Stephen's trial, repeated that Mr Dawes had threatened his wife. Defence counsel established that it was hearsay evidence and not admissible, but the words took effect, one more brick in the case against Stephen.

'We'll do it tomorrow,' Lois said. 'Agreed?'

Marcia, who was genuinely exhausted, nodded. There had been a new determination about Stephen the previous evening; she was going to lose out, either way, but their plan gave her a chance to hit back.

'Right. Then tomorrow morning, as soon as Stephen's gone to the office and before Mrs Bishop comes, you go over the garden and through the woods to Horseshoe Lane. I'll be there, waiting, with the car. Make sure no one's coming along before you get into it – I'll signal all clear with the lights, but you look too. You'll have to crouch down out of sight till we're away from here. After that, you're Mrs Morse. I'll take you to the flat, but I'll have to hurry back to take your car to Sussex and leave it near the cliff.'

Marcia did not ask how Lois planned to return to Hagbourne Green from Sussex.

'My clothes,' she said. 'I'll have nothing to wear.'

'You will,' said Lois. 'Don't forget the stuff I've already taken over to the flat. You can't take anything else – no case – but when Stephen clears things up at Badger's End, I'll offer to deal with your clothes. I'll say I'll give them to charity. He'll agree – he won't want to bother. You'll have everything else back in time.' And so, in fact, it developed, although Marcia had to wait until Lois had officially inherited the clothes. Several weeks earlier, Lois had persuaded Marcia to go through both her and Stephen's wardrobe, ostensibly for the Scouts' jumble sale, but in her case putting out clothes she still enjoyed wearing. These had all gone to Bath, together with spare underclothing. 'You can buy some more,' Lois added, to console her. 'There are good shops in Bath. You'll enjoy doing that.'

For the last few months, Marcia, at Lois's suggestion, had been cashing larger weekly cheques than usual, both on the household and her own account. By this time she had accumulated a considerable sum in cash, and now, choosing her words carefully, Lois suggested that Marcia should write her a cheque for as much as a thousand pounds, if there was money enough in the bank to meet it.

'I can say you lent it to me to buy a new car,' she said. 'Knowing the Morris is on its last legs. It's just the sort of generous thing you'd do, and it will look like a last gesture.' And so it did, when the police questioned Lois about it. She'd paid the cheque into her account at once; large cheques shouldn't be left lying about, Lois had said.

Marcia enjoyed the sense of bestowing patronage. She had willingly written the cheque.

Stephen was late home that night. He had telephoned to say he would not be back for dinner and, when he came in, he told Marcia that he had an appointment to see Frank the next day about a settlement for her. He hoped, in time, when she felt less bitter, that she would decide to divorce him.

'I told you what I would do if you went on with this,' Marcia said, and went up to her room.

Before going to bed himself, Stephen paused outside her door. There was no sound. Gently, he tried the handle. The door was unlocked and he opened it a fraction. She was sleeping peacefully, just as she always did. He pushed the door wider, so that the light from the landing would show him any suspect bottles of pills by her bedside, or a note on the dressing-table. He saw neither.

Stephen's own mind was at last made up, and he slept soundly that night. Marcia did not come down to breakfast the next morning, so he went along to her room before leaving the house. He never left for the office without speaking to her.

He knocked on the door, and when she did not answer, went in.

Marcia, in her dressing-gown, was sitting at her dressing-table brushing her hair. Their eyes met in the mirror. Her face was pale, but the eyes were clear.

'I won't be late tonight,' he promised, the last words he spoke to her.

As soon as he had gone, Marcia moved with what was, for her, considerable speed. Under her dressing-gown, she was already dressed in a blue wool suit that Lois had told her to wear. Lois had left an old raincoat of her own for Marcia to put on over this. She was to wear a strong pair of comfortable shoes such as she might choose to drive in. Lois had taken her handbag away the previous evening, saying that she was going to leave it in Marcia's own car at the clifftop. She had got Marcia another, almost its twin, and had bought a duplicate make-up kit and a purse. She had thought of so many details that would never have occurred to Marcia, who was reassured by this thorough preparation.

But it still seemed a game as she went across the garden and over the fence into the woods. Lois won't be in the lane, she thought. I'll come back and we'll forget it all.

'What if I meet someone?' she'd asked.

So early in the day, it was improbable.

'Ignore them,' said Lois. 'Then they'll remember that you weren't yourself.' Marcia was the least likely resident of Hagbourne Green to be taking a walk at such an hour. 'Just watch out when you get to the road. If I see anyone, I'll open the bonnet of the car and be looking inside as if something's wrong. But time it for half past eight exactly.'

Marcia met no one as she hurried through the fallen leaves along the bridle path where she and Stephen, in earlier years, had sometimes walked at weekends. She reached the outlet into Horseshoe Lane and peered cautiously beyond the concealing bushes and trees. Lois's car was there. The lights flashed once, and in seconds Marcia was crouching on the floor in the back, inhaling dust and fumes and complaining loudly.

Six miles on, Lois allowed her to get into the front passenger seat and put on her wig. Unknown to Marcia, she had already carried out the most difficult part of the plan. Through her reading, she had developed a healthy respect for the work of forensic scientists and knew that an actual journey to the spot with Stephen's car would be the safest way to arrange the evidence she wanted to prepare. During the previous night, Lois had taken the Rover. It was risky; Stephen might hear the garage doors, might hear tyres on the gravel; but Marcia's room and the spare bedroom where he had slept for so long both overlooked the garden, and the garage was set a little apart from the house. If neighbours heard the car pass, so much the better: they would think it was Stephen, when they later thought about what must have happened.

Lois knew where everything was kept at Badger's End. It had been easy, in advance, to take the spare keys of the Rover and a pair of Stephen's shoes without Marcia's knowledge. On Wednesday night she had ridden up on her bicycle, wearing a man's cap, rubber boots and a plastic raincoat, and gloves, so that she would leave no traces of her own in the car. She had Stephen's shoes in a carrier bag.

She was anxious about starting the Rover, lest she was heard, but it fired at once and the engine ran sweetly as she backed it out of the garage.

If anyone saw the car that night, so much the better. At the wheel, in her cap, her hair tucked up, she could be mistaken for a man.

By dawn, the Rover was back in the garage, and Lois had cycled home to Primrose Cottage. Pressed into the rug which Stephen kept in the car's boot were some tiny fibres from the blue wool suit which Marcia was now wearing, carefully collected earlier by Lois and retained in an envelope. There were also some strands of her hair, drawn from her hairbrush – only two – too many would overdo it. Beneath the driver's pedals she had rested her feet, wearing Stephen's shoes, in which she had clumped over some yards of Sussex soil with plastic bags over her own socks. His shoes, in a plastic carrier, were now in the boot of the Morris.

Luckily, Marcia had not asked why they did not use her car for the journey to Bath, instead of the Morris, so that Lois could drive it straight down to Sussex. For Lois wasn't going to Sussex. She had already done everything she could there. One of Marcia's black patent pumps lay near a gorse bush on the headland. Lois had walked to the edge of the cliff, the wind tearing at her so strongly that she feared it might blow her over. She had cast Marcia's handbag from her, flinging it into the gale. It might never be seen again, and if it was found, because there was money in it, the finder might say

112

nothing, but it could be the most convincing piece of evidence that Marcia had died.

No one had seen her in the dark. There had been no moon and no stars, just herself and the night.

The second of Marcia's shoes was in the boot of the Rover, under the rug, where it might have fallen if she had been bundled up and carried there.

Before locking the garage, Lois took Stephen's large adjustable spanner from his toolbox and walked quietly over the lawn to the garden pool she had helped to make. She slid the spanner silently into the water.

She wouldn't have been able to do that if a gnome had been there, guarding the pool and watching her with his vigilant eye.

3

'What about my letter?' Marcia had asked. 'He won't know what I'm supposed to have done unless I leave one.'

'That's true.' Lois's plan would be wrecked if such a note were found, but she could not risk disclosing a hint of it to Marcia until it was too late for her to back off. Mrs Bishop, arriving soon after Marcia's departure, would see any envelope left addressed to Stephen. 'Where will you put it?' she asked.

'On the drawing-room mantelpiece,' said Marcia. 'Or in my bedroom.'

Lois decided that a head-on tackle was the best way.

'You don't usually leave notes like that for Stephen, do you?' she asked. If such communication was necessary, Marcia left messages on a wipe-clean plastic memo pad in the kitchen. 'Won't Mrs Bishop think it strange? She knows you were upset the other day – suppose she puts two and two together and raises the alarm? She might, you know.'

'What – open the note?' asked Marcia. 'Surely not?'

'If she was worried, she might just be curious enough to

steam it open,' Lois said. 'She'd be justified by the result, in this case. There'd be a hue and cry before we'd had time to get away.'

'What do you suggest, then?' asked Marcia.

'Well, you want to make sure that Stephen finds it himself,' said Lois. 'Does Mrs Bishop go into his room every day?'

'He makes his own bed, but usually she dusts around.'

'So it's no good leaving it in there,' said Lois.

'I could tuck it into his pyjamas under his pillow,' said Marcia. 'Then he won't find it till he's given up looking for me and gone to bed.'

'That's a good idea,' said Lois.

'Yes. He'll spend the evening wondering where I've gone,' said Marcia with satisfaction.

As they drove off together, Lois asked her if she had put the note in position.

'Yes,' said Marcia. 'He'll be shattered when he finds it.'

'Won't he, just?' said Lois, smiling as she looked at the road ahead.

It took them almost three hours to reach Bath, and Lois was anxious to start back for she had a lot to do at Badger's End before Stephen's return. He was never home before six o'clock and latterly had often been really late, so that when Marcia said he had promised not to be late this evening, Lois felt alarm.

'When will he be back, then?' she asked.

'Oh, he didn't say.' Marcia laughed, a harsh, bitter sound. 'Who cares?'

Lois must say nothing to make Marcia suspicious. Once the police had begun to treat her disappearance as a murder investigation, she would see what a far better plan it was than a mere suicide. The gravity of the situation then would reduce any risk there might be of Marcia confessing to the hoax, for she would have laid herself open to a serious charge of some sort. Lois was not sure what exact offence they were committing, but that it was one, she had no doubt. Even if they were to plead that it had been done to teach Stephen a lesson, they would scarcely escape scot-free. At the least, there would be a great deal of unpleasant publicity which

Marcia would never endure. The threat of that would keep her staunch, Lois was sure: and the successful revenge.

She had brought their lunch – cold salmon, a salad, and a bottle of champagne as it was a celebration. They ate early because Lois must leave without delay.

She had also brought some dark hair rinse.

'Do it right away and put your hair in rollers,' she said. 'Then you needn't bother about the wig.' Lois knew that Marcia already rinsed her once-blonde hair; by now it had faded naturally. 'You mustn't wear it straight,' she warned. 'Tomorrow you should make an appointment to have a perm and a proper dye. Then there's a lecture in the afternoon on Watteau – you'd enjoy that.' Lois handed her a leaflet advertising the lecture, and a sheaf of notices about other forthcoming attractions.

'But you'll be coming over, won't you?' said Marcia.

'No – not right away. I'll phone you, but I'll have to be at home tomorrow. The police are sure to want to talk to me,' said Lois. 'After all, I'm your closest friend. They'll be looking for you, you see. They'll interview lots of people, asking if anyone's seen you.'

'I suppose that's right,' said Marcia. 'I suppose you really wouldn't go off for the day if you thought I'd killed myself. You'd be rather upset.'

'I should think I would,' said Lois emphatically. 'And I'll have to look it. Now, you'll be all right, Marcia – oh, you did remember the money didn't you? The envelope you had?'

'Yes.' It was in her new handbag.

'Good. Then you've nothing to worry about. Remember, pay cash for everything, even clothes. You can explain that you've moved here from Rhodesia and your bank arrangements aren't straightened out yet.' She hesitated. 'You'll have to be tough, you know, Marcia, when you read about yourself in the papers.'

'Will it be in the papers?' Marcia showed surprise.

'Probably, because you'll have vanished, you see,' said Lois briskly. 'Now, I must get back. I'm picking some plants up at a nursery on the way home, to explain where I've been today, if anyone asks. Specialist-grown ones. And I'd better be there when Stephen rings to ask if I've seen you. He's sure to do that.'

And there was her mother. There was always her mother. Last night, Mrs Carter's Ovaltine nightcap had contained four of Marcia's sleeping pills, so conveniently prescribed by Dr Watkins and taken from Badger's End without Marcia noticing. Mrs Carter had complained that the drink was too sweet but had meekly swallowed it down: Lois had added extra sugar to mask the taste of the sedative. She had left the house this morning before her mother woke up, leaving her breakfast tray beside her. The coffee was in a thermos, and more tablets were dissolved in that. Mrs Carter was not used to drugs and would, Lois hoped, be drowsy all day. With luck, there would be no callers at the cottage; some chances had to be taken.

'You'll be all right, Marcia,' Lois told her firmly.

'Yes. Yes, I will. It will be quite fun,' Marcia decided. The champagne had taken effect. 'I'll like to think of him worried to death.'

'There's drink in the kitchen cupboard,' said Lois. 'Sherry and gin, and some wine. And you've got the television for company.'

'I wish you'd let me bring away that work I was doing,' Marcia grumbled. She had wanted to take her current needlework picture, but had to admit that a suicide wouldn't do that, and Mrs Bishop, if not Stephen, would remember what she had been working at.

'Go out and buy the bits to start some more,' said Lois. 'There's sure to be the right sort of shops here. And you can read – I've got you a few novels.' She pointed to some paperbacks. 'The books that were here looked a bit dry.' Marcia was not a great reader but it would be a way to pass the time. 'If you feel a bit down, just remember what Stephen's done to you, Marcia,' Lois advised. 'He deserves whatever comes to him.'

'You're right,' Marcia nodded. 'I'll do some shopping this afternoon. I might start a bedspread.' She had long planned to design one.

'Good idea.' A big project would keep her occupied. 'There's enough food for a bit, but don't run low,' Lois added. 'And remember you're Mary Morse.' Marcia had refused to be Florence, the rose in full, and perhaps that was wise; it wouldn't have come to her naturally. 'I must go now,' she said.

Lois's eyes misted with tears as she left Marcia alone, for the very first time in her life forced to fend for herself.

Marcia, however, hummed under her breath as she tidied up the lunch things. There was some salmon left. The flat was quite sweet and she wouldn't be in it for long. For a little while longer, to Marcia, it was still a game as she thought about dropping the identity she had had for so long and adopting another. What an odd thing to do! But what had it really amounted to, after all? She was a rich man's daughter, a rising man's wife – her name had been theirs. She might as well be Mary Morse, and herself.

She carried out all Lois's instructions, washing her hair and winding her newly dark locks up in rollers before using the drier which Lois had shown her. There were heated rollers, too, for the hasty revival of collapsed curls. Marcia thought the flat was extremely well equipped, not realizing that Lois had supplied everything she thought her friend could possibly need. When her hair was dry, she went out and bought the rudiments of a new set of embroidery equipment, pretending to the shop assistant that she was a novice needlewoman. Playing such a role was quite amusing.

The rest of the day dragged. She had tea and a biscuit, then watched television, much as she would have done at home. There was a piece of fillet steak to cook for her supper, and frozen peas.

Marcia poured herself some sherry and sat sewing in the quiet, elegant room. Stephen would be at Badger's End now, looking everywhere for her. He wouldn't find her note until he gave up the hunt and went to bed.

She supposed he would do that – not run off to that other woman? He wouldn't just do nothing about her disappearance, would he?

Lois drove back to Hagbourne Green, pausing at the shrub specialist's nursery on the way to pick up her bundle of

117

plants, already ordered and paid for, and, she was thankful
to see, waiting for her. This was her alibi for the day, for
which she needed her own car. She put her foot down,
pressing the old Morris Minor to maximum effort. Suppose
Stephen were already home? How would she save her plan?
But he wasn't.

It would not matter if her car was seen at the house. She
could say she was worried because Marcia hadn't answered
when she telephoned that morning, and had said nothing
about going out early.

Lois had a key to the house; she always kept an eye on
things when Marcia and Stephen were away.

First, she returned Stephen's shoes to his cupboard. Next,
she retrieved the suicide note from under his pillow and put
it in her pocket. Later, at home, she burned it. Then she
bundled up every easily portable possession of Marcia's that
had any value and put them in a holdall she had brought for
the purpose. She wrapped the porcelain in towels from the
airing cupboard and put the jewellery into some socks. She
stuffed Marcia's silver hairbrushes, the peppers and salts,
some coasters and a rose bowl into a pillow slip. She took
Stephen's dress studs and cufflinks. Then she laid waste to
the place, tipping over drawers, turning lamps over. With
her gloved hand, she broke the french window, then
unlocked it and left it open. Gritting her teeth, she used a
sliver of glass to cut her own finger and let some drops of
blood fall on the carpet. She knew her own blood group and
Marcia's were the same. They had both been donors; Lois
still attended but Marcia had fallen away. With her glove on
again, she rubbed at the spots on the carpet with her handkerchief, damped at the tap – just a bit – not too much. She
put the sliver of glass she had used in her pocket to get rid of
later and, as she did so, her hand met the spare keys of
Stephen's Rover. She had almost forgotten them! She put
them back in the bowl in the kitchen where they were
kept.

Later, when questioned, she told the police she had called
at the house and found everything orderly, but Marcia
absent. It was the truth.

When she reached home, Mrs Carter was still in bed. That

morning she had not woken until nearly ten. After calling vaguely for Lois, she had eaten her breakfast, supposing that Lois had told her she was going out and that she'd simply forgotten, as so much escaped her memory now. Then she'd gone to turn on her bath. While it was running, she had felt sleepy again and had gone back to bed.

The bathwater ran slowly at Primrose Cottage, so the overflow outlet just managed to keep pace with the intake and no flood greeted Lois. She heard the water running away as she came round the side of the house past the drain. At first, she was afraid her mother had had an accident and that was not part of the plan. Apart from the complications of inquiries, she was fond of her mother, who in rational moments could still be a pleasant companion, though she harked back too much, for Lois's taste, to bygone days when her father, a naval officer, was still alive and before times were hard. They had never referred, after it was over, to Lois's misadventure, but the bond between them remained strong.

Lois hurried upstairs and turned off the bath taps. Her mother was snoring lightly, the breakfast tray still beside her, the thermos empty. She had had no lunch, obviously.

She'd be none the worse for her lost day. She would have no recollection of it, and that would be all to the good, thought Lois as she wound a plaster round her finger, which had bled freely into her glove. She put the holdall containing Stephen and Marcia's possessions into the cupboard under the eaves in her room. Then she took her mother's tray downstairs.

All the hot water had run away and there was none to wash up the used crockery.

Lois was thirsty. Champagne had that effect. She made herself some tea while she waited for the water to heat up again in the boiler. She would have liked to telephone Marcia while she had the chance with her mother asleep, but Marcia thought she was driving down to Sussex.

It was lucky she had taken all Marcia's sleeping pills, Lois thought; she might need more. She made sandwiches for supper, using up some rather nice pâté she'd got in the fridge. Then she settled down for the telephone call Stephen

would surely make to her, as soon as he came home to find
the house turned over and Marcia missing.

He did. He described, briefly, the state of the house and then
asked if Marcia was with her.

'I haven't seen her all day,' said Lois. 'I've been out
myself, buying plants, but I rang up before leaving and got
no answer.'

'She'd said nothing to me about going anywhere,' said
Stephen. 'Did you know her plans?' Lois always did.

'No – I didn't think she was doing anything special,' said
Lois.

'What time did you ring?' asked Stephen.

'About nine,' said Lois. Mrs Bishop would know that she
hadn't rung later than that. 'I was a bit worried, actually –
she'd been so upset lately – I popped in on my way back and
she was still out. But everything was quite all right then. In
the house, I mean.'

'Did you come in?'

'Yes. I was worried, you see,' Lois repeated.

'Everything was locked up? There was no sign of a
break-in?'

'None at all – oh, Stephen, what can have happened?
If only she'd come with me! I did ask her to, but she said
poking about at a nursery looking at plants would bore
her.'

'I'm sure she's perfectly all right,' said Stephen. 'She's
probably rung the police and gone round next door. Her
car's here, so she can't be far away. I'd better get on and ring
them – the police, I mean.'

'I'll come up,' said Lois. 'I'll just settle mother.'

Lois knew that Stephen would have been pleased to see
her if Marcia had merely gone next door after discovering a
break-in, for she would calm Marcia more successfully than
he could, and now she must act as if things were as they
seemed. She was curious to see what the police were making
of the situation, and she was at Badger's End when Detective
Inspector Simpson noticed that the french window had been
broken open from inside. She saw their attitude harden

towards Stephen. She had already said that she had been to the house that afternoon, so that there was an explanation for any traces she might have left.

She was well pleased with what she found and the way the police were talking to Stephen. She had not expected that to happen so soon.

Mrs Carter woke up when Lois returned. She was shocked and upset to learn that Badger's End had been burgled and Marcia seemed to have disappeared.

4

Marcia lay in her unfamiliar bed in Bath, with her hair strangely brown. She wore one of her own nightdresses, and had used her usual brands of cleanser and nightcream, thoughtfully supplied by Lois. What was Stephen doing now, she wondered.

Her pleasure in his certain ultimate dismay made up for her own apprehension. She had never before, in her life, been quite alone like this, in a place among strangers.

He might not have found her note yet. He'd be wanting to tell her what he'd arranged with Frank. When he discovered she was not in the house, if he didn't run off at once to that woman, he'd probably telephone Lois. Would she be back yet from Sussex? He might try ringing other friends and it could take him ages to give up and go to bed. When he saw that her car had gone, he might ring up the police before he found her letter.

How seriously would they take the report of a missing wife? Not very, until the note was found, she thought.

It had been a long day, and she fell into her usual sound sleep before she had done a great deal of speculating.

In the morning, she woke later than her normal time, and at first wondered where she was. The bed was comfortable; she stretched out in it as she remembered and thought of how Stephen would be feeling. She pictured the hang-dog look he would wear on his face. The police would search for her car today; how soon would they find it?

She'd been quite surprised when her suicide threats had not been enough to bring Stephen to heel. The discovery had toughened her and she wanted him to suffer. Now she felt calm, and not in the least suicidal; that had never been genuine, but her own anger had surprised and alarmed her; she did not like extreme emotion.

'I'm Mary Morse,' she told herself, getting out of bed and drawing on a long-since-discarded dressing-gown which she had kept for unscheduled guests – though such people almost never came to Badger's End. 'I'm newly widowed, and as I bravely adapt to my new life, I'm going out today for a hair-do, and then to attend an improving lecture.' She giggled. It was like acting in a play.

It would be nice to talk to Lois, but she had been instructed not to ring up except in the direst emergency, and then to say she was Hawking's Plants, about the order, in a disguised voice. Lois had enjoyed all their planning. She was a good friend. Some people might find such devotion cloying, Marcia thought, but she understood how circumscribed Lois's existence was, with her mother, and what an outlet she, and Badger's End, had provided. There was a gap in Lois's life, and she filled it. Marcia, eating Weetabix, reflected that that upset when she was young had put her off men for life, but perhaps she had never liked them much.

How would it be when they settled down together? Perhaps it wouldn't come to that. Lois could make the money over to her again, or to Mary Morse, after it was all sorted out, and they could part if it didn't work out. But it probably would: Lois could be trusted to undertake all the boring aspects of life which would irritate Marcia. She would fetch coal, pay bills, peel potatoes. Meanwhile, Marcia could buy beautiful pieces of furniture and sell them again at a profit. She would enjoy that. They might have a shop with an expensive and a cheaper area: Lois could strip pine and cater for less advantaged customers while she dealt with the élite. Marcia felt a slight pang about Mrs Carter being bundled off to a home, but no doubt she'd be, in the end, better and happier where there were plenty of people to look after her.

122

She was getting on; she wasn't young when Lois was born. Talking to her was no longer amusing, and on bad days, when she was very forgetful, required so much patience; she was like a demanding child. Soon it would be too much for Lois to manage, so, all in all, everything would work out for the best in the end.

She had her hair done, amazed at the difference dark curls, instead of her own smooth fair hair, made to her appearance. She had darkened her eyebrows to match this new scheme. There would be time for a nice lunch in rather a pleasant café she'd spotted on the way to the hairdresser's, before she must find the lecture hall.

Stephen would be pretty desperate by now, she thought, and wondered if the police had found her car yet.

Lois rang up late that night, after her mother had gone to bed. She said that the police had been combing the woods all day and going round the village making inquiries. It had really been quite exciting, said Lois, since she knew that Marcia was, in fact, safe and sound. Stephen was very upset, she added, and he'd spent all day with the police. She'd ring again soon.

Marcia did not learn the details of what had happened at Badger's End for several days, for there had been no notorious discovery of a murdered body to alert the press. A small paragraph in some papers told readers that Mrs Marcia Dawes, 35, was missing from her home. One paper said that an intense police search had been mounted and that her husband had been helping police with their inquiries, but after some time he had been allowed to leave. Marcia thought it was natural that Stephen would be helping the police; she did not understand the significance of the newspaper report until Lois came down late on Sunday night.

It was almost midnight when she arrived. She knew it would have been wiser to stay away, but she was anxious to see how Marcia's nerve was holding out, and felt she must prepare her for what she would soon discover about the extra vengeance being wreaked upon Stephen.

Lois had seen Frank, who had confided to her that the police were taking a very grave view of things and he was extremely worried for Stephen.

'What do you mean? You can't mean they think – oh!' It was easy for Lois to show distress.

'They think she's dead and that Stephen killed her,' said Frank bluntly. 'They're doing tests on his car. I don't know what that's going to tell them. Perhaps they think he took her away somewhere in it and dumped her. She's been in the car enough times, God knows – it won't be hard to prove that, I don't doubt. But as for the rest – well – you know Stephen. Chivalrous to a degree.'

'They hadn't been getting on,' Lois said. 'There was this woman.'

'Yes, but that doesn't mean he'd kill Marcia, for God's sake. You know that, Lois.'

Lois hesitated, seemed about to speak, and then stopped herself.

'What is it, Lois? What were you going to say?' Frank asked.

'It's too awful,' Lois mumbled. 'Best forgotten.'

'What is? Come on, Lois, out with it,' Frank urged. 'Anything you know might be useful.'

Lois looked at him with her large blue eyes.

'He threatened her,' she muttered. 'She didn't want a divorce, and he threatened to kill her. She told me.'

'What?' Frank stared at her, his ruddy face suddenly pale. 'You can't be serious, Lois! When was this?'

'Oh, months ago now, the first time. But they had an awful row the other night – let me see – when was it? Oh, Tuesday, that's it. That woman's had her baby, you see, and Stephen brought it all up again. About leaving, I mean.'

Frank, consulted about a settlement for Marcia, knew about the quarrel, but Lois's disclosure stunned him.

'I told her he didn't mean it, of course,' Lois had said, in a quiet little voice. 'Oh Frank, do you think he did?'

'No, I don't,' said Frank robustly. 'Marcia made it up.'

Now Lois had to tell Marcia that the police thought she had gone from the house during Wednesday night, for no one but Stephen could attest to having seen her on Thursday. She did not, at this point, mention her own alleged telephone call on Thursday morning. Marcia must be made to see why this new plan, which Lois would say she had worked out in case anything went wrong with what they had decided upon together, was so much better than the earlier idea, and why it had had to be put into operation without Marcia's knowledge.

She said that Marcia's car would not start when she got to the house on Thursday afternoon. There was not much time: Stephen would soon be home, so she had staged the robbery – and look! Here were many of Marcia's most precious possessions – her brushes, her collection of porcelain. Lois had brought the holdall with her, retaining Stephen's property which could, later on, be sold.

Marcia was thrilled, as Lois knew she would be, by the restoration to her of her belongings.

'I took them away when the car wouldn't start,' said Lois. 'That was when I put plan B into action.'

'I can't think why it wouldn't,' said Marcia, pinning on a diamond brooch that had been her mother's. 'It's always been most reliable.'

'No – well, these things happen,' said Lois.

'What do they think happened to me, if burglars were supposed to have broken in?' Marcia asked.

Lois shrugged.

'You may have been kidnapped, or perhaps even killed,' she said. How much should she tell Marcia now? It would be better if she learned from her that Stephen was under suspicion rather than from the press or television when she was alone. 'They've taken Stephen's car away,' she said.

'Whatever for?'

'To their lab. To examine it,' Lois told her.

'But why?'

'In case he took you off somewhere and dumped you.'

'What – killed me, you mean? Stephen? Oh no!' Marcia was half appalled and half laughing.

'Would it be so strange? A couple of years ago you'd never have said he'd be unfaithful, would you?' Lois asked her. 'And don't forget, you told Dr Watkins and the solicitor that he'd threatened you.'

'But that was to show that I was upset enough to kill myself,' said Marcia. 'And to explain the will.'

'The will would be explained by his infidelity,' said Lois.

Suddenly Marcia saw where all this was leading.

'You planned it like this!' she said. 'You meant them to think Stephen had killed me! But what about the note? Wasn't that found?'

'I destroyed it,' said Lois, and waited for the outburst of protest she expected.

But it did not come. Instead, Marcia was regarding her with amazed respect. What an audacious plan!

'Why didn't you tell me you'd got all this up your sleeve?' she asked.

'You mightn't have agreed,' answered Lois.

Would she have, in advance? Marcia wasn't sure. She weighed it up in her mind.

'I think it's marvellous,' she said. 'He will have a bad time, won't he? But as no one will find me, he won't be arrested.'

Lois would let her go on thinking that for a while. Time enough later to point out precedents for murder charges where bodies had not been found. Lois had checked and found a case not so long before where a woman's body seemed to have been fed to some pigs; those responsible had been charged and convicted. In another case a woman had disappeared from a liner and a man had been convicted of pushing her overboard. No, a body wasn't essential if the evidence was there.

In fact, it was not until Stephen's trial that Marcia became aware of the full ingenuity of Lois's preparations.

Lois did not tell her, either, that her precious possessions were a form of insurance in case it took years to settle her estate. They could be sold off, bit by bit, if that became necessary. Later, some furniture had had to go.

'I looked at the points on your car,' Lois said now. 'But that wasn't the trouble.'

'Points? What are they?' Marcia asked.

'They stick sometimes,' Lois said.

'I think you've been rather clever,' said Marcia.

5

Marcia's first fascination with being totally alone soon faded as the winter dragged on.

Lois tried to structure her days for her, drawing up schedules of things she could do each week. There were lectures and exhibitions, and even the cinema, as a means of passing the time. When Marcia still seemed restless and discontented, Lois suggested voluntary work of some kind. Marcia must not take a paid job because she could produce no cards for an employer.

'What sort of work?' asked Marcia.

'Help in a hospital?' Lois knew as she spoke that this idea would fall flat. 'Or with old people?' She racked her brains for a better plan. Marcia had always avoided the dark side of life. 'Further education?' she tried.

So Marcia enrolled for a daytime class devoted to English literature, as the art-appreciation class which attracted her was full. The lessons were not demanding; the teacher was a pleasant elderly woman; the students were amiable, and most of them widowed, so that Mary Morse's plight was only different because she was so much younger than the average. Wonder was expressed that she had no job to fill her days, and as soon as essays had to be written, Marcia dropped out.

Lois came every four to five days. She would rush eagerly up the stairs, bursting into the flat full of healthy energy, and her visits restored Marcia. Often she had to restore the flat as well, for Marcia, accustomed to Mrs Bishop, did very little cleaning, although she was so neat that only removing the accumulation of dust and the need to polish the furniture ever struck Lois as being necessary. Both grew depressed as the weeks passed and nothing happened to Stephen. He was taken off for questioning a number of times but not arrested, and Marcia's estate was frozen.

Lois found acting her new role towards Stephen a relief. She was now the horrified friend who believed that he had killed his wife, so she never went up to Badger's End.

At last, however, the police, having failed to persuade Stephen to confess, decided they had built up a case and the papers went to the Director of Public Prosecutions.

Meanwhile, Lois and Marcia's funds were dwindling. Bored, Marcia had been on a number of spending sprees; she was unused to practising any sort of economy and Lois dreaded asking her to begin.

It was time to take things on a stage. Lois made further plans and was ready when Marcia's resolution faltered.

'I can't keep it up,' Marcia had told her. She was sitting wanly in her chair, clearly having wept before Lois's arrival. 'I just want to go back to Badger's End and have things as they were, with Mrs Bishop coming in, and the house so nice, and my life going on like it used to.'

'Marcia, you can't go back,' said Lois. 'It's too late. Everything's changed – it could never be like that again. If you did, you'd be in dreadful trouble for deceiving the police.'

'I could say I'd lost my memory,' said Marcia sulkily.

'Well, I haven't lost mine, and they'd soon find out where you'd been all this time,' said Lois grimly.

'It was your idea,' said Marcia.

'That's quite true,' said Lois. 'But it was all done for you, Marcia. You wanted to punish Stephen and spoil things for him with that woman. We've done that – he's not seeing her. Frank told me. She hasn't stuck to him, and he's keeping away from her because he doesn't want all the publicity to affect her. The papers would soon be on to her, you can bet, if they knew who she was.'

'Is that so? That she hasn't stuck by him?' asked Marcia. 'Yes.'

'He'd be glad to have me back, then. He wouldn't want to leave after all,' said Marcia.

'Do you really think so? After all this? He's had a rough time, you know, in and out of the police station being questioned for hours – locked up, probably. Not that I'm breaking my heart for him,' said Lois. 'Marcia, I could survive a trial and going to prison. I don't think you could, and it might come to that, if we back down now.'

'Prison!'

Lois wasn't sure if that would be their fate, but it seemed likely; hours and hours of police time had been taken up with the case, and no doubt thousands of pounds of taxpayers' money had been spent on it. They would hardly escape with a fine. To her, the fact of defying authority was a stimulus: she was hugging herself with secret glee at what she had set in train, and meant to see it through. Marcia must be braced up and persuaded to persevere.

'Every time you feel low, you must think about going to prison and how dreadful that would be,' Lois instructed. 'Things will get better soon. Something will happen. Even if Stephen isn't arrested, you won't be here much longer.'

'Why not? What can change?'

'I've been preparing the ground for myself – for mother and me,' said Lois.

When she went off like this for the evening, coming home late, Mrs Carter now thought she was meeting a friend – a man. She had invented his name, Mike Reynard. He was a farmer. At the appropriate moment, she would tell her mother that they were going to marry and so Primrose Cottage must be sold.

During a recent fit of bewilderment by her mother, Lois had talked to the solicitor who looked after their affairs – not that there was much for him to do, but he had made her mother's will. As a result of this, and a conference with Dr Watkins, she now had her mother's Power of Attorney and could sell the cottage, with or without Mrs Carter's consent.

Mrs Carter was overjoyed at learning of this man in her daughter's life. Forgetting how she had welcomed the arrival of the Daweses in Hagbourne Green, she now thought that Marcia's disappearance had its benefits, freeing Lois from a demanding friendship. Mrs Carter still maintained the view that marriage was the wisest goal for any woman and, if Lois found a husband, she would also gain security.

Lois told Marcia her plan.

'I've got to vanish, too, you see,' she said. 'Everyone's going to think I've got married.'

'Married! You?' Marcia's unkind mirth at this prospect was enough to divert her from her own self-pity. 'You can't bear men,' she said, and tittered.

'That's not true. I got on all right with Stephen and Frank,' said Lois. 'They weren't silly.' She went on to ask Marcia where she would like to live, once they'd made their real break. Property was much cheaper in the West Country than around Hagbourne Green; Lois thought that, even without Marcia's money, with the sale of Primrose Cottage she should be able to buy a small house and a stake in a business. She'd begun looking around; something that they could build up would be the best sort of investment because they could buy in low.

She left Marcia resigned to hold on longer. Ten days later Stephen was arrested and charged.

There were flurries of excitement on television and in the press – shots of Stephen being hurried away between burly police officers and driven off in a large car, interviews with people who lived in Hagbourne Green and who all said what a nice man he had seemed to be. No one said much about Marcia.

He was not allowed bail, and interest waned in the months before the trial, but both Marcia and Lois were keyed up now. Marcia laid the blame for her unhappy winter upon Stephen, and used it to fuel her anger against him in the rare moments when she wondered if they had gone too far.

He'd be acquitted. Without a body, the jury would decide in his favour and he would have been punished adequately. He'd have no happy future without a wife, and with no mistress either.

Marcia had made two silk pictures in the long winter evenings while she listened to radio plays or, with half an eye, watched television. The needlework required close attention, so that while working she often lost track of what was happening on the screen. She had no ear for music and gained no pleasure from hearing it in any form, although Lois liked jazz and even some pop – something that added to the discord between them later. When the pictures were done and she had had them framed, Marcia took them to a shop where she had seen old lace, quilted cushions and patchwork, which was just coming back into vogue, for sale.

The shopkeeper enthused over the pictures, bought them both and said she would take any more Marcia produced.

It was in this shop, some weeks later, that Marcia met Hugh Vaughan.

He had come in to potter about. He pottered a lot, and was attracted by some snuff boxes lined up in the window. He saw Marcia talking to the proprietor; she was delivering a third picture which portrayed St George standing triumphantly over the dragon. Marcia had found the original illustration in an old book in the flat.

Hugh Vaughan was entranced, and bought it at once.

He was a retired tea planter, a bachelor. With the birth of Sri Lanka, he had been forced into early retirement without the full pension he had expected. Whilst in Ceylon, he had read publications such as *The Connoisseur* and built up a fine collection of classical music on records. He had always intended to marry but had never quite got round to it, meeting no Miss Right either on leave or in Ceylon. He had had one turgid affair with the wife of another planter; the resultant gossip and scandal had killed the romance, and afterwards he had been both more cautious and more discreet in his entanglements.

Now, resettled, he was lonely. After buying Marcia's picture, he bore her off for coffee which extended to lunch. By this time he had learned of her sad situation, and, as he had friends in Rhodesia, had sought to find a mutual acquaintance, but Marcia, alarmed, remembered Lois's advice, allowed herself to look weepy, and clammed up at once, saying to talk about the country brought back memories which made her sad.

Both had time on their hands. Hugh took her to a concert, which she hated and could barely sit through with any pretence of pleasure; Marcia was not accustomed to dissembling for the benefit of others. Later, they went to a stately home in his car; this was a more successful expedition, and with a sigh Hugh realized that Marcia had no music in her soul.

131

She bloomed in the warmth of his attentions. They made further outings to beautiful houses; both were knowledgeable, in differing ways, and both enjoyed these excursions. When he kissed her one day, she was mildly stirred. He was no longer young; he had thin, greying hair and the yellowish complexion of a man who has spent most of his life in the tropics, but he was male, and he was treating her with tender respect, as Stephen had done. Her body, if not her will, responded, encouraging Hugh, who nevertheless drew back. He must not rush things; he could not afford to marry now, so he must be certain that she did not misunderstand.

They had not got as far as sleeping together when Lois found out. She saw Hugh leaving the flat when she arrived without warning one evening in May. She had been to make final arrangements for her mother at the home for which she had put down Mrs Carter's name, and which now had a vacancy.

At first she did not connect the tall, apparently oldish, man she met in the hall with Marcia, but when she reached the flat, she found Marcia flushed, her brown curls not as neat as usual, and two used sherry glasses on the coffee table.

'Oh Lois! I didn't expect you till Friday,' said Marcia, as guilty as any deceiving wife.

'That man was in here. The one I met downstairs,' snapped Lois. 'Two glasses.' She pointed.

Marcia actually blushed.

'That was only Hugh. He bought one of my pictures,' she said.

Hugh had, in fact, left earlier than usual after bringing her back from one of their expeditions. He was going to a concert that evening.

Lois had realized that Marcia was happier these last few weeks, and had thought she was settling down to her new way of life. She had never foreseen this: she could lose Marcia to a man, if she wasn't careful, although in fact she could also bring her down, if that threatened. She could say Marcia had made the car journey to Sussex the night before she disappeared; she could deny all knowledge of the false trail of clues and maintain that Marcia had carried out the whole plan herself.

But the incident frightened Lois. She decided to close a deal for a nursery garden at Witterton which she had seen; it wasn't quite what she had hoped for; it was running at a serious loss, and the house available nearby wasn't as big or as attractive as what she had planned for Marcia, but both had potential, and there was plenty of land with the house where she could bring on plants. Lois, in her researches during the winter, had concluded that this sort of venture would suit her much better than dabbling with antiques. Popular gardening was an expanding industry; it was work she already understood and was interested in, and it had a future. Fir Tree House, too, offered scope for renovation and that was Marcia's line. The alterations would have to be carefully budgeted for, and carried out when the money could be spared. That would take care of Marcia's time for several years. They could use the furniture from Primrose Cottage until Badger's End had been sold, then keep whatever Marcia most wanted from her former home and sell the rest. However Stephen's trial went, her death would be presumed when it was over, and her estate would be resolved.

Lois did not refer to Hugh again, but she moved fast.

As for Marcia herself, she did not really want all the bother of a consummated affair. She had had no other lover than Stephen, and the strangeness of someone new would be rather alarming; besides, although Hugh caused her to feel minor urges, minor they were, and minor they remained. She enjoyed his company, not so much for itself as for the mere fact of being escorted about by a man. While she was with him, she forgot about the forthcoming trial, which she dreaded. Once it was over, she would forget Stephen utterly, but first there would be the press reports and media fuss, with references to her; Marcia had been aloof, austere, according to some journalists; lonely to others. She did not recognize herself in these descriptions.

She was pleased when Lois told her they were moving, and decided not to tell Hugh until the last moment, for she liked things to be pleasant and wanted no emotional scenes. In the end she wrote him a note, posting it the day she left Bath and saying she hated goodbyes. She was going to live with her sister in Scotland, she explained; Scotland was far enough away to dissuade him from pursuit.

Hugh was sad for a time, and he missed her. He had found no one among his Rhodesian acquaintance who had ever met her, but he did not attach importance to that, limited though the white society was out there; after all, he had not lived there himself. He soon met a charming, though older, widow, who was enamoured of Bach, and afterwards remembered Marcia merely with mild nostalgia.

He kept her needlework picture.

6

As she read the reports of Stephen's trial in the newspapers, Marcia found it hard to believe that this was happening to the man to whom she had been married for so long. It was unreal, like a dream. There were photographs of Stephen taken before his arrest, and of the van transporting him back and forth to court. There were shots of Lois, in a new oatmeal suit bought specially for her appearance as a witness, and of Stephen's mother, looking thin and drawn. Marcia had never felt really at ease with Mrs Dawes. Though nothing remotely critical was ever said, Marcia had felt that the older woman thought her idle. When she came to stay at Badger's End, which was rarely, Marcia had fussed dutifully round her and urged her to make the most of the rest she could enjoy under their roof before resuming the treadmill of her work.

'It's a treat for Stephen's mother to come to us,' she would say to people. 'I love to pamper her.' She had always taken trouble as a hostess.

As the trial went on, Marcia continued to believe that Stephen would be acquitted. Gossip in Hagbourne Green was optimistic about his chances, though, Lois reported, most people were sure he was guilty, for what other explanation was there?

'I'd never have thought it of him,' was the general opinion.

'The jury was convinced that Marcia Dawes was well and truly dead,' said Lois after the verdict. 'And Stephen was the only person with the motive and opportunity to kill her.' She smiled at Marcia, a smug, complacent smile which Marcia was too disturbed to notice.

Prison for life! What a sentence!

Marcia took a grip of herself. He deserved it – he had destroyed her life, after all. She found that she could still work herself up into a rage about what he had done, and feel hatred for both Stephen and the woman who had schemed to part them.

Well, that relationship had perished. She had never come forward, both the press and Lois declared. There were no hidden whispers about who she was and whether she would stand by Stephen – indeed, some of the more lurid comments had referred to the killer's 'worthless romance'.

Life didn't mean life. He would not be hanged, and he would be let out again after perhaps fifteen years, thought Marcia. Lois thought that it might be less, but kept that to herself.

A month after the trial ended, they moved into Fir Tree House and Marcia resumed her maiden name, although she went on calling herself Mary and posed as a widow. Now she could use her birth certificate to establish her new identity, simply suppressing the fact of her marriage. She applied for a driving licence, giving the true details about when she had passed her test, and obtained one. Lois made a new will leaving everything to Mary King; she had done well from the sale of Primrose Cottage. Although Marcia's estate would take some time to settle, a more positive life began for both women.

Marcia was able to put both her own sense of grievance and Stephen, its cause, from her mind as she concentrated on the work to be done at Fir Tree House. In a way, it was a rerun of the early years at Badger's End, except that the house was much smaller and Lois was penny-pinching about the budget so that the work was done in stages, as it could be paid for. And there was no Stephen.

It wasn't Stephen himself so much that Marcia missed: it

was more the absence of an admiring man about the place, but soon, in the shape of the workmen, she had several who appreciated her plans for the house. Their demeanour was always respectful, and Marcia's own manner towards them did not encourage familiarity. While she supervised their labours, Lois was busy turning the nursery along the road into a garden centre; she was aided by Fred Harris, whom she took on with the place, and as they got their new format organized, Marcia helped design the showroom. Fred had put Lois on to the builder who was doing the work at Fir Tree House. The builder knew a draughtsman who drew the plans for the reorganization and presented them for planning approval, which was granted. For more than three years, Marcia was perfectly content and fully occupied with these activities. She made the curtains for Fir Tree House, and when they were done she started her bedspread at last. This was not patchwork in a conventional sense; it involved using the patched pieces, some of them large, of fabric that matched the curtains in a redesigned manner so that the delicate floral sprays of which it was composed were differently displayed. It was mounted on fine net, and backed with cotton sateen so that it did not slip when placed, at last, on the bed. It took her over a year to make. After that she resumed her pictures, and time began to hang heavy again.

Lois now had two men helping with the garden work at Fir Tree House, raising plants for the centre; she built a greenhouse for her seedlings. She was too busy to wait upon Marcia's whims as she had done in the past. The garden centre was expanding fast; profits and spare cash were ploughed straight back into it and there were few treats at Fir Tree House. Tax had bitten into Marcia's estate in a way Marcia had not foreseen, although Lois had, but she had not known the extent of the estate itself. What Lois ultimately received, however, was more even than she had expected; it enabled her to salve her conscience over her mother, when her condition deteriorated, by moving her to a more expensive home, and it guaranteed the success of the centre.

Things which for years had mildly irritated Marcia about Lois's want of taste now became really annoying. The gnomes which she placed here and there in the garden were only a small aspect of this; Marcia frowned at some of the items sold at the centre – the imitation wrought-iron plastic furniture which she thought vulgar, the vivid awnings – even some of the larger begonias and the giant dahlias.

'People want them,' said Lois. 'More people have my sort of taste than yours, Marcia. And plastic furniture's cheaper than redwood.'

'You said we'd have an antique shop,' Marcia grumbled.

'Get yourself a job in one, if you want to,' said Lois, who had early cherished a dream of Marcia, in a chic overall, taking over the pay-out or perhaps some of the office work at the centre; she had seen the impossibility of this fantasy before she had tested it out on Marcia. 'Get yourself paid cash – then you won't have to pay extra insurance or tax.'

This idea was very attractive. Marcia did not at all like being handed her allowance, like a child its pocket money, by Lois each week, nor having Lois tell her that she did not need a new suit or a dress when she had a wardrobe full of clothes she had owned for years.

'Just because all you ever wear is a filthy old pair of trousers,' Marcia complained.

'I always change in the evening,' Lois protested, and it was true: she often came home smelling of fertilizer or, if she had been working outside, of sweat, and always had a bath before dinner, which nowadays they took turns to cook. Lois had given up wearing skirts; tights laddered too easily; she wore trousers at home as well as for work.

They had no social life at Witterton. When they first arrived, the vicar had called, and one or two older ladies from the village; they had been invited to drinks, and had gone once or twice, but because they never invited anyone back – at first the excuse was that the house was still upside down because of the work being done there, and later Lois had said, when Marcia wanted to entertain, that she was too tired when she got back from work to bother with being polite – and as they took no part in village life, such contacts died.

Lois, at first, did most of the household cleaning but, as the business grew, she had less energy for that; she would not let Marcia employ a woman to do it for them, however; she was afraid to let someone else into the house.

Marcia found a job in an antique shop in Shawton. She went round them all, asking if any of them needed help, and her elegant appearance – although she had put on some weight – and evident knowledgeability when she picked out objects on view, brought her two offers. She took the position at the more selective of the two places, her waning confidence restored.

Lois was uneasy, at first, about Marcia going off on her own and having a life apart from her, but things were different, now, she reasoned, from the Bath days. Marcia was no longer lonely, Lois told herself, quite wrongly; she was older and had seen the merits of a tranquil life. An interest would be good for her, become a hobby.

Marcia soon became friendly with Jack and Barbara Payne, who owned the shop, but she quickly saw that she must keep them and Lois apart. She told them that when her husband died, her old friend Lois Reynard had taken her in, since she was almost penniless and very distressed as the result of her bereavement. Lois, however, was rather antisocial: she didn't like entertaining, and since Fir Tree House was hers, and Marcia there by her kindness, she could not invite her own friends in, much as she would like to do so.

The Paynes accepted this, and sometimes they asked Marcia to stay on for a meal after work.

It was through the Paynes that eventually she met Andrew West, who went to them after his wife's death when he moved from a large house to a cottage and had some good furniture to sell. Marcia helped him with the interior decoration of the cottage, advising on fabrics and colours.

Lieutenant-Colonel Andrew West, after his retirement, had had a job in the accounts department of a local plastics company; not a lofty position in their hierarchy, and undemanding, but it kept him, as he said, out of mischief. He had had to give it up when his wife became ill; now he had time on his hands, though he was busy enough at the cottage. He was a very neat worker, spilling almost no paint and, though overalled, always looked clean while papering or painting. His fastidiousness appealed to Marcia.

Lois knew she was advising someone on decor; she saw Marcia making curtains; but the name of the customer was never disclosed and Lois thought it was for a couple. Marcia, too, had learned to lie, both deliberately and by evasion. After her professional assignment was over, she continued to visit Rushmere Cottage as a guest.

One day, over a year after their first meeting, Andrew leaned towards her as they said goodbye at his cottage. He put a hand each side of her face and his touch was soft and cool. Even before he gently kissed her lips, Marcia had felt her own response.

'Goodbye, my dear,' he murmured.

Marcia, who by now had taken over the small car she and Lois ran as well as the centre's van, drove off with her heart thumping rather fast. She thought she had forgotten such sensations, living as she had in comfortable chastity for so long. It seemed, however, that they had merely lain dormant, like seeds beneath the soil, she thought fancifully, waiting to spring into life when the sun shone.

Like Hugh, Andrew was a lot older than Marcia.

'I must like older men,' she thought, amused at herself. Earlier generations had such good manners, of course, like her father – although, to be fair, Stephen had had perfect manners, too.

She would manage this friendship as she had managed Hugh, she thought; and imagined she could contain her own emotion.

But Andrew, unlike Hugh, had been married. He was lonely, and wanted a wife. He went slowly, because these things must be taken a step at a time. He already had Marcia's friendship and a lot of her company; he was not in need of a housekeeper as he was a capable man who could cook for himself, and he had an excellent cleaning woman, so he was far from helpless, as many men are when suddenly bereft.

Marcia liked his company. He was interested in old churches and she enjoyed the trips they made together, rather as Hugh had taken her to stately homes. Each widened horizons for the other.

He proposed to her six months after that first light kiss,

which he had followed with some warmer, though still restrained, salutes.

Marcia turned him down, but gently. She did not want to lose his friendship but – even forgetting the complications which would make marriage very difficult – she wanted to avoid commitment. Marriage meant taking on the rough side of life as well as the smooth, and she was not willing to do that.

'I've rushed you,' he chided himself. 'You haven't got over Harry yet, have you?' Harry was the late Mr King. He went on to say that he hadn't got over Betty yet either, and never would, but he had learned to accept it. You went on, as you did if you lost a limb, making the best of what was left.

'I can't leave Lois,' Marcia said. 'We pooled our resources when we moved down here. I had just a little money; it made all the difference to being able to buy the house and get the business going.'

'I see,' said Andrew. 'But we wouldn't need your capital, my dear. Not unless you would find the cottage too small.' If they married, perhaps Lois could repay Marcia gradually. He must guard her future for, as his widow, she would receive no army pension, marrying him after his retirement.

Marcia knew that, indeed, the cottage would be too small, but although she did not intend to put it to the test, she had been offered an alternative life, and the knowledge that it was there made her still less tolerant of Lois, who had grown coarser over the years. She was now careless of her appearance, and often strode in muddy boots through the kitchen. She played Radio One very loudly when she was at home, and watched comedy programmes on television. She kept a bottle of whisky in her office and often came home smelling of it, only to pour another stiff tot which she took upstairs to her bath. Pop music would sound through the house as she soaked the stiffness from her joints in very hot water, often inadequately cleaning off the rim of grime she left.

Willy-nilly, Marcia, these days, often had to clean and polish; she did not mind polishing her own pieces of furniture, but she did not enjoy cleaning, or cooking, though, when it was her turn in the kitchen, she always produced an elegant and tasty dinner. Lois, however, had given up trying, and simply tossed various ingredients into an electric slow cooker, so that on many evenings the meal was an undistinguished stew.

Three months after his proposal, Andrew skilfully seduced Marcia. Once she dropped her guard, her senses took over and she readily entered into their new relationship. Every Wednesday afternoon, when the shop was closed, and after lunching together at the Three Horseshoes in Shawton, they now went back to Rushmere Cottage and made love in Andrew's comfortable double bed, with the curtains drawn against prying eyes, though the cottage was well screened from the village street by a tall yew hedge, and little traffic went that way. Once a week, it turned out, was enough for both of them – pleasant for her, delightful for him, though less ecstatic than that side of his life had been with poor Betty. But that was to be expected, he thought philosophically, although he had hoped, due to Marcia's comparative youth, for a rather more active response than he seemed able to arouse.

During this time Marcia and Lois began to quarrel seriously. Their rows usually started over trifles, such as what to have for supper – Marcia disliked Lois's perpetual stews, and Lois wanted something more substantial than the braised sweetbreads or poached fish which Marcia would prepare, having bought the food while in Shawton. Lois retaliated by making her stews even stodgier, and Marcia sought out recipes for lighter dishes. They clashed over television – Lois could not abide the arts programmes which Marcia always wanted to watch, and would stump noisily upstairs to her room, where she would turn the volume of her radio up very loud so that the sound of pop music penetrated through to the room below.

Then one day she brought a new giant gnome home. He was nearly two feet tall, with a gaudy face, a bright red hat and orange breeches, and she put him in the middle of the small circular lawn in front of the house.

'You're not planning on leaving that thing there, are you?' demanded Marcia as soon as she saw him.

'He's the guardian of the house,' said Lois, who was already well primed with whisky to face the trouble she knew

141

she would have with Marcia over the gnome. He was the prototype for a new line, and she'd ordered two dozen for the centre. It was time to show Marcia who was boss, Lois had decided. It was she who paid the bills, so she should call the tune. Lois liked gnomes and wanted them around the place; Marcia must put up with them.

They quarrelled violently that night, Marcia telling Lois she had no taste and Lois wanting to know where Marcia would be without her – alone and moping in some hovel, while Stephen lorded it about with his new wife and a string of kids, for sure, she declared. In the end, Lois had become maudlin and began to cry, a spectacle that nauseated Marcia.

'I get no thanks. I work and slave for you – and very gladly – but you take it all for granted,' Lois snivelled. 'You could never manage alone, and you know it.'

'You're revolting,' said Marcia.

The following morning, Marcia loaded the large gnome into the wheelbarrow and took him down to the bottom of the garden near the compost heap, where she tipped him unceremoniously on to his face on the ground.

It was dark when Lois came home, but she saw that he was missing and tracked him down by torchlight. Marcia had not even put the barrow away.

Lois placed the gnome under the big cedar tree near the house, and there he remained in a position of truce, though they did not speak to each other for three days.

The quarrel was on a Tuesday, and the next afternoon Marcia spent with Andrew, to whom she displayed new ardour. He was encouraged to propose again, and though she declined once more, he detected a change in her tone. His heart lightened. He would win her yet.

7

The next time they met, Andrew suggested they should take a holiday together.

Marcia had not been abroad for years.

At first, when Marcia said she was longing for some sun, Lois had said that foreign travel was impossible, even if they could afford it, a thing of the past to be put out of her mind. But when Stephen had been in prison for nearly five years and the business showed a profit, she relented, and began to think about their passport problems.

Her own was easy: she had changed her name to Reynard by deed poll to facilitate the transfer of Marcia's estate and avoid business complications. Marcia's own passport had not survived the sale of Badger's End. Lois did not know what had happened to it and Marcia's papers; perhaps they were in some lawyer's office. She had fetched Marcia's clothes herself, when Stephen's mother was packing up his personal things after the trial.

'They were left to you,' said a grim-faced Mrs Dawes. 'They're all very good. You're not as tall as she was, but no doubt you could have them taken up, that is, if it wouldn't upset you to wear Marcia's things.'

'Why should it?' asked Lois calmly. 'Not if she wanted me to have them.'

'Will you take them all, then, please?' Mrs Dawes requested. 'Go through them at your leisure and dispose of anything that's of no use.'

Thus had Marcia been reunited with her wardrobe nearly a year after she had abandoned it.

Marcia applied for a passport in her maiden name, sending a copy of her birth certificate. The vicar of Witterton testified that the photograph supplied was her true likeness, and Marcia had to endure travelling as a spinster.

Since then, they had taken the car to France several times. Lois, however, was increasingly reluctant to leave the business. She did not enjoy their foreign trips and fretted while Marcia lay in the sun or chatted with other holiday-makers. She still drew admiring looks, though she had put on weight. Lois was always afraid they might run into someone from Hagbourne Green who would recognize them, hence her insistence on independent travel in their own car. Anxiety made her ill at ease, and she would sit silently drinking while Marcia sparkled in company.

143

Marcia hesitated only for an instant before agreeing to Andrew's suggestion. She would handle her own passport throughout: people did not scrutinize it too closely as to married status or otherwise. If anyone addressed her as Miss she would laugh it off. Mary would pass as a diminutive for Marcia.

She might even alter her passport.

'Lois hates going away,' said Marcia. 'She gets liverish with too little to do, and I feel quite guilty at taking her from her pots and plants.'

'Where shall we go?' smiled Andrew. 'You choose.'

'Oh – the West Indies, please,' said Marcia at once.

Andrew suppressed his own desire to tour France in the spring, taking in castles and cathedrals. To soak up the sun with Marcia would be bliss indeed, and what was more, could take place sooner. They might even go to France later on, he thought, if he could afford it. The idea that Marcia should pay for herself crossed the mind of neither.

Andrew said he would get some brochures. They could look at them next week. Or, since that was so far off, why did he not bring them round to Fir Tree House?

'Why not?' said Marcia.

Lois was going to have to learn about Andrew. That last row had been the final straw. They could not go on like this for the rest of their lives, locked in a prison of conspiracy.

'I can't think why you haven't asked me round before,' said Andrew. He had heard from the Paynes about Lois. 'Some old dragon of a lady gardener,' they had called her. They had once been to the centre, more from curiosity than anything else, since there was a good market-garden shop in Shawton where they bought plants for their tiny patio behind the shop, over which they had a flat. Lois had been visible in the office, small and tough-looking; very butch, they told one another anxiously, wondering if Andrew was on a hiding to nothing with Marcia. Andrew had told them that he thought Marcia was not unlike the Sleeping Beauty, caught in a web from which she needed rescuing. 'I've been quite hurt,' he added lightly.

'Well – I have explained about Lois,' said Marcia. 'She

144

helped me when I needed it. I have an obligation to her – or I had. I can't go on feeling like that for ever'. She sighed. 'I used to give lots of dinner parties, once,' she said, and thought how long ago they seemed: those dinners at Badger's End, very often with Lois preparing much of the food. Even her cooking had fallen away since then.

'Perhaps you'll soon start them again,' said Andrew with meaning. 'I'll come in on Sunday.'

'Come to tea,' said Marcia. Lois was always at the centre on Sunday, one of her busiest days.

Andrew was still at Fir Tree House when she came home, and to Lois it was a repeat of the time she had run into Hugh, in Bath, but much worse, for this time she met Andrew face to face and had to be introduced.

Andrew saw a stocky woman with wiry grey curls, wearing corduroy breeches and long dark green socks, with no shoes on, for she had left her boots in the back porch and walked through the house into the drawing-room, thinking the car outside belonged to some customer wanting to see her. Though she did no business at the house, beyond growing on stock, on rare occasions people had called there when the centre was closed. Andrew looked at Lois's hard blue eyes and florid complexion; she was so exactly like his worst imaginings that he turned at once to Marcia for the reassurance of her warm regard.

She'd got herself into this trap in all innocence, Andrew saw, and he became all the more determined to pluck her from it. In many ways he was not unlike Stephen, seeing his role as that of a protector.

Lois, in turn, saw a tall, lean man with iron-grey hair and a small clipped moustache. He had shrewd grey eyes.

'You're home early, Lois,' said Marcia calmly. She and Andrew had lost count of time as they weighed the merits of various islands, discussed dates and reminisced about where they had been in the past. They decided on single rooms, in spite of the exorbitant cost. Andrew thought one could not ignore convention; Marcia wanted privacy. She was filled with restless longing. Andrew was her way of escape from Lois; he could restore her to the sort of life she had had before Stephen's defection.

145

'This is Andrew West,' she told Lois. 'Colonel West. Andrew – Lois Ca–Reynard.' She had nearly said Carter. Lois glared as she nodded curtly at Andrew.

''D'ye do,' she grunted. 'I'm going upstairs to change.'

'Stay to supper, Andrew,' said Marcia, as Lois left the room. Her eyes were shining. She was suddenly determined to bring matters to a head. She and Lois had not spoken since the affair of the gnome – she had told Andrew about it, for he noticed the creature as he parked his car, and Marcia had felt obliged to disown it.

Andrew was no coward. He was more determined than ever, now, to wrest Mary, as she was to him, from her prison. Lois would soon find another friend, one who shared her tastes, he thought, ambiguously, and everyone would be happier as a result. He might as well begin at once to assert himself. He accepted.

Lois reappeared in about ten minutes, her hair still damp from the shower she had taken; she wanted to lose no time in returning to chaperone Marcia. She wore dark purple corduroy trousers and a bright orange Shetland wool sweater with a patterned yoke. She poured herself out a very strong whisky as Marcia announced that Andrew was staying to supper.

'I see,' she said, and went out of the room.

Marcia giggled like a schoolgirl. She felt totally reckless. 'She's upset,' she said. 'Never mind. There's sure to be enough – it's her week as cook and she always makes stews.'

'I expect she's tired,' said Andrew tolerantly. 'After all, she's been working all day, hasn't she? Can I do anything to help?' He saw no point in alienating Lois even further: the women must part as friends.

'We could lay the table,' said Marcia. Lately, they had eaten all their meals in the kitchen, a slide from the standards that Marcia thought they should maintain.

As they set out Marcia's best silver, she planned how she would remove it when she married Andrew. She would make Lois pay her a regular allowance; it would be a way of returning to her only what was rightfully hers, after all. The future looked suddenly bright, as they sat round the table eating casseroled pork, followed by blackcurrant ice-cream made with their own fruit. Andrew kept the conversation going, trying to draw Lois into it by asking her about the business and discussing what plants thrived in the area. Then he turned to foreign travel, and the holiday he and Marcia were planning to take in January. His gaze met Marcia's: she sent him a smouldering glance that quickened his pulse. When he got her away to tropical climes, he would sweep away that last reserve, he vowed.

Lois had produced a bottle of claret, saying they usually had some wine on Sundays. She drank most of it herself, and then opened another. In response to Andrew's questions, she had told him a certain amount about market demand and status gardening. He could see that building the business up from its small start, as she had done, had required not only hard work but a shrewd commercial sense, and a knowledge of horticulture that had by now become extensive. To succeed, she had had to be tough. He saw, too, that Mary needed support. She would not do well alone, his pale, lovely girl, he thought fondly. What more natural than to lean for support, in all innocence, on this sturdy girlhood friend?

Over the Stilton, he reflected that his own married son and daughter would approve of his choice when at last they met Mary. His son, who had followed him into the army, was in Northern Ireland at present, and his daughter, who had married an American, lived near Boston. She worried about her father. He might take Mary to see her after they'd been to whatever island they chose.

He kissed her on leaving, lightly but firmly and possessively on her soft mouth, and pressed her arm warmly.

'See you on Wednesday,' he said, and, watching them, Lois heard.

'You can't go away with that man,' Lois said, clattering plates together in the kitchen after Andrew had gone.

'Why not?' said Marcia. 'What I do is my business.'

'It's not. We depend on each other.' Lois stumped out of the room and poured herself half a tumbler of whisky, which she brought back with her into the kitchen, taking a large swallow from it on the way.

'You've had quite enough to drink,' said Marcia in a prim voice.

'Don't you tell me what to do,' said Lois.

'The same goes for you.' Marcia set her lips together. Another shouting match such as they had had a few nights ago was not to be endured. Quarrels and loss of temper were so undignified.

'Men are only after one thing,' said Lois. 'I saw how he looked at you.'

'Oh – and what are you after?' said Marcia. She did not mean it in the way Lois interpreted it, but it provoked an outburst of such venom that Marcia quailed as Lois launched into a recital of her own dedication to Marcia's interests.

Marcia flung down her drying-up cloth and walked out of the kitchen, leaving Lois sobbing drunkenly into the washing-up water. She stayed in her room the next morning until Lois had left for the garden centre; in the evening, neither spoke, and Tuesday followed the same pattern. Lois was frightened. If Marcia could plan to go away on holiday with a man, she was capable also of leaving Lois, to live with him permanently. Such an idea was terrifying. Lois could not live without Marcia; everything she did was for the ultimate good of her friend. Besides, it would be dangerous to see too much of any outsider, male or female. They had so much to hide. Their quarrel must be mended, but she could not find any words with which to try to effect a reconciliation. In the evenings, Marcia was glacial, sitting silently sewing. Lois, as a gesture, even forbore to turn on her favourite television show, sitting gritting her teeth in silence, thumbing through a gardening magazine while Marcia sewed placidly on.

They would have to talk on Thursday, Lois thought, leaving for the third morning without seeing Marcia. One Thursday a month, in the late afternoon, they went to Sainsbury's for a big household shop. Marcia liked Sainsbury's and would potter about picking up oddments not on the list, while Lois sternly pushed the trolley round collecting the regular items. Another Thursday was Lois's day for visiting her mother; on a different one she made up the books at the centre, and on the fourth Thursday she sent out her bills. If there was a fifth Thursday in any month, it came as a bonus and was used for odd jobs that had accumulated.

But today was Wednesday, when Marcia had said she would see that man again. Marcia did not work on Wednesdays, early-closing day in Shawton, but went into town to have her hair done and change her library book. She had taken to reading fiction since her time in Bath, and borrowed historical novels. She always had lunch out on Wednesdays, but Lois did not know where she went.

That morning, Lois told Fred that she had toothache. The pain was so bad that she must have it seen to at once, which meant postponing an appointment with a customer who wanted some advice. She had put this off until the next day and secured an emergency appointment with the dentist. Would Fred lend her his car to go to Shawton, and would he, meanwhile, deliver some plants, which had been promised for the following day – a simple swop of plans? Fred agreed to lend Lois his Ford Escort; this had happened before; she was an excellent driver and he never minded.

In Shawton, Lois lingered outside Jonquil's Coiffures on a double yellow line, uncertain of the time of Marcia's appointment. It used to be half past eleven, but so much had changed. More than once, she circled the streets, returning to her post, not wanting to incur the wrath of a traffic warden. The third time round, she saw Marcia emerge and walk off down the street. Marcia would have recognized the van, but Fred's car was anonymous. Lois slid into gear; luckily she was facing in the right direction.

She saw Marcia turn in at the Three Horseshoes, a two-star hotel which was the best that Shawton could offer. Lois drove under the archway and into the yard, where she saw the Mini already parked. Nearby was a maroon Maestro. Andrew West had been driving a maroon Maestro on Sunday.

Lois parked the Ford and went into the hotel by the saloon-bar entrance. The Three Horseshoes was popular at lunch-time; its bar food had been commended in several guides and it attracted shoppers, business people and, in season, tourists. There was also a restaurant which served *à la carte* and

149

table d'hôte meals. Where would they be, Marcia and that man? Lois peered through the smoke of the saloon bar across to the lounge bar, which was set at right angles so that much of each was visible from the other. There they were, at a corner table, drinks before them which he must have ordered in advance as there hadn't been time since Marcia arrived.

Lois waited in the car park in Fred's car, not troubling to hide beyond pulling her tweed hat down over her face as they came out together nearly an hour later – at least they were not arm-in-arm – and got into Andrew's Maestro. They were so engrossed in their conversation that they noticed nobody else, Andrew gazing down at Marcia as he opened the passenger door for her, Marcia smiling back at him in what Lois found a nauseating manner.

She followed them out of the yard, through the town and across to the Exeter road. Three miles on, the Maestro turned down a lane, and five minutes later it reached a small village where it entered a gateway between two stretches of high yew hedging. Lois drove past.

She turned at the end of the road outside a small church, and drove slowly back, parking short of the cottage which she had seen beyond the hedge. She waited there for two hours. Then she gave up, for the centre needed her, even if Marcia did not, and Fred would want his car.

Why had Marcia not taken her own car to this place, which presumably was where the man lived? If it was all above board, she would have done so, Lois reasoned – perfectly correctly: Andrew was old-fashioned enough to be seeking to protect her reputation. Yet they planned to go away together.

He meant to marry her. Lois saw it clearly, and just as clearly, knew that Marcia would do it, if only out of spite.

Marcia, in fact, had made up her mind. She told Andrew so that afternoon, wrapping the towelling robe she kept at the cottage around her.

'If we both still feel the same after our holiday,' she said, as a safeguard. It was her only way of escaping from Lois;

150

without money, she could not otherwise leave, and Lois would not give her any if she simply packed and left, Marcia knew. She'd come round in time, she thought; she'd accept the inevitable and make a financial adjustment.

She had her birth certificate. Would she need a death certificate for her alleged husband? Would there be any way Andrew could discover that she was not Mrs King? Surely not. She'd have to make discreet inquiries: there would be a way round it; there always was if you looked hard enough for it.

Andrew was ecstatic.

8

Lois worked late at the garden centre that night. There was always plenty to do if she did not want to go home, and lately she had spent more and more time there.

They had been happy. In those first years, with Marcia totally dependent on her, Lois had rushed eagerly back to Fir Tree House every day, anxious to see how the work in the house had progressed. Marcia had wanted to hear about her day, too. It had been a good partnership. Marcia had put on weight straight away, and lost the pinched look she had acquired during those months in Bath; it was only then that Lois fully understood what a strain that time had been for her, while Lois herself was busy playing her role as dead woman's grieving friend and arranging their future.

Now this man posed a real threat. Lois would have to fight him for Marcia, and subtly. So much was at stake; it was a conflict she dared not lose, for if Marcia became too involved with him, their safety would be imperilled.

She would apologize for last night's scene, Lois decided. She would even take away the large gnome which had sparked off last week's row, if it would please Marcia.

She drove home in the van, put it in the garage and went into the house.

Marcia was in the kitchen preparing the dinner. She had

not pulled the blind, and Lois could see her through the window as she approached the house. She was singing: Lois heard the tuneless hum as she opened the door.

Marcia never sang.

Lois wavered in the passage by the back door. She took off her boots and set them against the wall, then started towards the kitchen, but her courage failed her, and instead she headed off towards the dining-room where the whisky was kept. Fortified by a large slug – she had already had one in the office – she set off to apologize.

Marcia, too, had meant to be nice. She had planned to soften Lois up in the next week or two, get her into a good enough humour to be able to tell her that she was leaving and wanted the return of her money. She would not put the garden centre in any sort of jeopardy: an arrangement whereby Lois kept the capital but paid Marcia the income would do. The centre was thriving now; Lois could manage easily. When she no longer had to pay high nursing-home fees for her mother, things would be easier still. They must part on good terms; Lois had proved herself a loyal friend all those years ago; she had helped her achieve a great revenge upon Stephen, but she had gone too far. If they had kept to the plan for merely a fake suicide, at any time Marcia could have relented – reappeared pleading loss of memory when she judged Stephen had been sufficiently punished. No one could have proved otherwise if she stuck to her story. Marcia successfully thrust from her mind now the knowledge that she had soon accepted the excessive penalty Stephen had been made to pay. Anyway, life didn't mean life. He'd get out one day.

The thought that she was planning to commit bigamy did not enter her head and, if it had, she would have quashed it: Stephen's wife was dead.

'Hallo,' she said brightly to Lois, magnanimous now with the future so bright.

'I'm sorry about Sunday,' said Lois gruffly, not meeting her eye. 'I've got rather unsocial lately. Your friend was quite nice.'

Marcia knew that this speech represented an immense effort by Lois.

'Yes, he is,' she said.

'Have you known him long?'

'Nearly three years,' said Marcia.

Lois had not expected such an answer Blood pounded in her head as she realized that Marcia had been meeting Andrew West secretly for a long time, hiding the truth about their relationship all those months. She breathed deeply, trying to control her jealousy and terror. If she kept calm, the threat would pass. Marcia would tire of him and his nasty demands. She must know in her heart that no man could offer her such loyal friendship as she, Lois, had done all this time.

Marcia thought it would be wise to change the subject.

'I'm making that chicken thing you like,' she said. 'With the grapes.' It was a dish that had featured at dinner parties at Badger's End. 'Go and have your bath. It won't be long.' She thought that Lois looked tired. She was swaying slightly, standing there in her breeches and socks like a middle-aged child, and beneath her ruddy complexion there was a bluish tinge.

'Yes – all right,' said Lois. She turned away and left the room but there was a delay before Marcia heard her plodding heavily up the stairs. She'd paused to refill her glass.

Soon, from the bathroom, came the throbbing beat of Radio One. Stirring her sauce, Marcia strove to ignore it. She laid the dining-room table, setting out the good silver again. It was a pity to spoil a delicious meal by eating from pottery plates and using the kitchen cutlery.

'What's this, then?' said Lois, when she came down again in her orange sweater and purple trousers. She'd bought both the garments by mail order, and the first time she wore them, Marcia had ostentatiously fetched her sunglasses and put them on. 'It's not a birthday,' Lois stated.

'We've been getting slack,' said Marcia. 'It's because we don't entertain. I think I'll have a dinner party.'

'Will you? And who will you ask?' said Lois. 'Your fine friend from Sunday, I suppose, and how many more like that have you got tucked away?'

'Don't be silly, Lois,' said Marcia. 'I've got plenty of friends – Jack and Barbara from the shop, for a start – and

153

it's only because of you that I haven't asked them here before. They all know you're difficult and that's why I don't invite them.'

'Difficult! Well – ' Lois's face reddened.

Before she could go on, Marcia made an effort to retrieve the situation.

'I know you don't like entertaining after a long day at work,' she said. 'Though you liked parties when we were younger.'

'I didn't,' said Lois. 'I only went to them because mother wanted me to catch a husband. That wretched business loused it all up for me. I hated them after that.'

'You hated men, you mean,' said Marcia. She looked across the table at Lois, now pushing chicken, carrots and rice around her plate. 'You even hated Stephen.' Suddenly a great truth struck Marcia. Lois's act against Stephen had not been simple revenge for Marcia's sake; she had been exacting a price from him for what had been done to her by another man years before.

Lois did not answer. She shovelled a forkful of food into her mouth, spilling sauce down her chin. Marcia eyed her with distaste.

'Lois, for goodness' sake!' she burst out. 'You used to know how to behave! Must you eat like a peasant?'

'I am a peasant,' Lois muttered. 'I till the soil.'

'Nonsense! You're a good business woman and you work hard,' said Marcia, attempting to be air. 'But you mix with all sorts. Perhaps it affects your standards.'

'And what about your standards?' demanded Lois. 'Spending all afternoon in bed with that man. That's what you were doing, weren't you? You weren't just looking at holiday brochures. You're just a tart – you're no better than that woman Stephen got hold of.'

As soon as the words were out, Lois wished them unsaid. She bent to her plate again and munched on, taking greater care not to overload her fork.

Marcia laid down her knife and fork. She wiped her mouth and placed her napkin on the table beside her; then she pushed back her chair.

'What have you been doing?' she asked, and her tone was

icy. 'Have you been spying?' For a wild instant she imagined Lois on a ladder outside the bedroom window at Rushmere Cottage. There could have been a chink in the curtains through which an onlooker might have seen what was going on. The idea was intolerable.

'It's all so beastly,' said Lois, looking at her now. 'They slobber so. They're awful. How could you let anyone do it to you?'

'You know nothing about it,' said Marcia. 'You had one drunken tussle and were unlucky enough to get caught. It's not like that at all, between civilized people. It's pleasant and natural, in moderation – like drink. Look at you, Lois! Do you know what you look like? You used to be quite a pretty girl.'

Lois was unable to swallow the food in her mouth. She spat it on to her plate, and Marcia shuddered.

'Please,' she said, and then, for after all she had tried hard to be nice and Lois had not met her anywhere near halfway, she lost patience. 'Lois, I'm not prepared to go on living with you like this any longer. You're possessive and selfish, and your habits are disgusting. You're turning into a drunk and you'll lose your head for business if you go on like this. I'm leaving. I'm going to marry Andrew. He's been asking me for a long time and I've always refused because of you, but I've changed my mind and I told him so today. We'll get married as soon as we can.'

Lois stared at Marcia. Panic filled her.

'You can't do that!' she shouted.

'Oh yes, I can. Who's to stop me?'

'I will. I'll tell him what you did,' said Lois.

'You won't, you know,' said Marcia. 'And if you did, he'd think you mad. He wouldn't believe you.'

'He will, when I've finished,' said Lois.

'He'll just think you a silly, jealous, drunken sot,' said Marcia scornfully. 'Besides, you did it all. I was just playing a trick on Stephen, to teach him a lesson. I'd have gone home again after a few weeks, when he was sorry and had broken off with that woman. It was you who took it all much too far.'

'If it wasn't for me, you'd be living alone somewhere with

no one to look after you,' Lois said. Her voice was low, almost a snarl.

'I wouldn't,' said Marcia. 'I'd have met someone else – as now I've met Andrew.' She did not refer to Hugh.

'You didn't want anyone else. You've forgotten – you were bitterly hurt and angry and you wouldn't forgive Stephen – you'd never have done that, if he'd begged you to. You didn't want the shame of him leaving you – all the talk – that he liked someone else better. That man Andrew thinks you're a widow – he's in for a shock when he hears the truth.'

'He's not going to hear the truth,' said Marcia. 'And you can think what you like about the past if it gives you any comfort. I realize now that you didn't want to help me at all. You were getting back at that other man, but it wasn't his fault, it was yours. You were drunk then, and you're drunk now.'

While she was speaking, Lois stood up. She came round the table towards Marcia, who was looking at her with scorn, sitting calmly while Lois, her face crimson, loomed over her. Some spittle trickled down Lois's chin.

'I won't let you go,' Lois said, and suddenly she sprang at Marcia, gripping her by the throat as she sat at the table, shaking her head from side to side.

Lois had not intended to hurt Marcia; she meant only to force her into submission, but in a very few seconds, after making some grabs at Lois's arms and a few choking sounds in her throat, Marcia went limp. She was dead when Lois released her.

She'd had a heart attack, Lois thought as she began frantically trying to revive Marcia. She patted her face, then slapped her, calling her by name. When this brought no response, Lois rushed into the kitchen and was violently sick in the sink. There she gasped and sobbed for some time, finally splashing cold water over her face. After that she returned to the dining-room to look at Marcia. Perhaps she wasn't really dead after all, but was simply unconscious and by now would be stirring.

But she wasn't.

156

Marcia was slumped against the chair, her head on one side, her legs sprawled. Lois shifted her on to the floor. She was very heavy, an inert mass of flesh and bone. Lois crooned over her, murmuring that she hadn't meant to harm her, begging her to wake up. Then she began to apply mouth-to-mouth resuscitation. She had never learned how to do it, but had read about it and seen it demonstrated on television. She did what she thought was right, pinching Marcia's nostrils and putting her mouth to Marcia's, breathing into her. She carried on for a long time, the rhythm broken only by sobs. Marcia's lips were flaccid; her body was slack.

At last Lois gave up. She went into the sitting-room where the curtains were drawn and the fire, by now, had died down in the hearth. She sat there, unmoving, for nearly an hour. Then she went out to the garden shed and brought in some black plastic sheeting of the type she used to wrap plants. She laid the long roll on the floor of the dining-room and bundled Marcia into it as if she were a tall bush. The body was very heavy; Lois could not lift it. She had to drag it out of the room and into the kitchen. Next, she fetched a garden cart, loaded the body on to it and took it out to the garage where, with difficulty, she heaved it into the van. After that she returned to the house, cleared away the meal and washed everything up.

She had lost Marcia, but so had that man. And as Marcia Dawes was already dead, and Mary King did not exist, she had nothing to fear. All she had to do was dispose of the body.

She knew she should do it at once, but she had run out of strength. Lois sat in the sitting-room, trying to brace herself for what must be done. She used whisky to try to conquer her grief and fear, and in the end she passed out. When she came to, it was too late; dawn was breaking.

She had to take the body out of the van before driving it to the centre where it would be needed for the day's work. She backed the van out of the garage, turned it, and reversed it into the garage again. Then she hauled the black bundle out. It was rigid: rigor mortis had set in. Lois dragged it across the floor of the garage and placed it in front of the Mini.

It would be quite safe there until darkness returned again.

Part Three

1

Stephen crouched in the garage with the body of Marcia, for whose killing he had served ten years of a life sentence, unable to move as he tried to absorb the fact.

She looked different – not just because of death; her hair was dark with a reddish tinge, and her face was almost plump. Even so, he had no doubt at all about her identity. To make sure, he pulled back the black sheeting and then the neck of her expensive silk shirt to expose a mole on her shoulder.

Marcia had not died all those years ago, but she had been murdered now. He knew it as he closed her poor, staring eyes.

He stayed here, bent over her body, in a weird, belated leave-taking, unable to make any sense of his discovery. Then, as the first shock abated, he wrapped her up again.

He must get away. Now it was vital that Lois did not find him here while he decided what to do. He locked up the garage, returned the key to the house, and got into his car. At the end of the drive, he turned left, away from the garden centre, towards Shawton. It was dark now. Several cars passed him. A mile or so down the road he came to a lay-by and pulled in. He turned off his lights, opened the door and got out of the car, walking round to the kerbside, away from the traffic. He stared across the field which bordered the road.

A law-abiding citizen, he thought, discovering a corpse, would summon the police. Stephen was a law-abiding citizen; when his wife was missing and his house ransacked, he had instantly called the police and had been grievously punished, afterwards, for committing a mortal offence of which he was innocent. So reporting what he had found to the police was no longer his immediate impulse.

It was quite a time before, standing there in the darkness, Stephen saw that the discovery of Marcia's recently dead body would clear him of that earlier charge. She must have been living here with Lois all these years, using some other name, and Lois had never been married. Mr Reynard had been invented to aid the deception.

Lois had killed Marcia, and meant to dispose of the body. That had to be the explanation. But why? The implications of it all began crowding in on him as he started to accept fragments of the truth. Lois had been devoted to Marcia: there was no doubt about that. She had inherited all Marcia's estate, so, unbelievably, the devotion was mutual, and strong enough for Marcia and Lois to conspire together in their fearful plan against him. And now, somehow, things had misfired and Marcia really was dead.

Had they known he was out of prison? Had that caused the rift between them? There had been nothing in the press about his release, but the women could have known it was imminent; after all, for a whole year, since parole was agreed, he had known the exact date. Lois might have anticipated that he would look for her. The man at the garden centre could have told her that someone had been there, asking for her — and Mr Reynard.

Stephen wanted to mull it all over and work out how it had been managed, but there was no time for that now. The police must be told about the body and Lois must be arrested before she could dispose of it, for surely that would be her plan.

Stephen got back into his car and drove along the road till he came to a telephone box. The instrument in it was not working, and he had to go on for several miles before he came to another. He dialled 999, asked for the police and, when he was connected, told the officer who answered that there was a woman's body in the garage of Fir Tree House, Witterton, the home of a woman known as Lois Reynard. Then he rang off, without giving his name. He must wait on events without being directly involved. Exoneration for the past would follow.

As he pushed his small car along the road, hurrying back to home and sanctuary, Stephen cursed aloud in his anger. However bitterly Marcia felt, how could they have fitted him up like that, sentencing him to such a fate for a mere act of

162

adultery? And what about the relationship between the two of them? Oddly enough, he found that harder to accept than the fact of how they had framed him.

Hours later, after he reached Ivy Lodge, Stephen's impulse was to telephone Frank at once, and he lifted the receiver to start dialling the number, but before it could begin to ring he changed his mind. It was very late, and Frank would be asleep. What could he do now? It could wait until the morning. Soon he would be pardoned. The news would be in all the papers and he would be cleared of his disgrace, a free man. He would be able to claim acquaintance with his daughter.

He should be rejoicing, he told himself. He'd intended to find out the truth, and he'd done it, far more easily than he had ever expected. But what a truth it had turned out to be! At the moment, all he felt was shock and horror. He told himself that, in time, he would accept it and be able to reap the benefit, but at the moment he had to digest the fact that his wife had lived on all these years when he had thought her dead. The puzzled grief Stephen had known so long ago was reawakened, and he mourned.

That night, he lay awake in bed imagining what would be happening now at Fir Tree House, the police vans, the flashing lights, the questioning.

It was Lois's turn to be in a cell, to undergo interrogation.

All day, Lois had wondered what to do with Marcia. Burying her in the garden seemed an obvious solution, but even the night before, she had known she could not do it. She could not dig a pit and inter Marcia there, where every day she would see the spot. Besides, if she were missed – by that man, for instance, Andrew whatever his name was, or the Paynes at the antique shop – and searched for, it was possible that the police would look for her in the garden. They had before, at Badger's End – had dug up several sections of the vegetable garden where the soil had been recently turned. Oh, she'd say Marcia had gone away, but that man might not accept such an explanation, Lois knew: not when they were on such close terms.

She still couldn't bear to think of that.

Many years ago, Marcia had officially been accepted as having died from a blow on the head, with her body being disposed of over a cliff. Lois would dispatch her now, as was most appropriate, in the same manner. There were plenty of sheer cliffs near Witterton; she needn't go far. This time she could take no account of the tides, but with death due to heart failure, there was no need to fear discovery of the body. If it were to be found, Lois would say that they had had an argument and Marcia had driven off into the night. With the Mini parked at the cliff top, this time it would be accepted as a genuine suicide.

Lois was in no hurry to return home that evening. There would be no Marcia waiting for her. For years, Lois had hurried eagerly back after her day at the centre. When had things changed? How long ago was it that she had started to feel anxious about what sort of mood Marcia would be in and how their evening would go? For how long had she needed to fortify herself with whisky before going back? It had all been so gradual that Lois could not remember when the atmosphere between them had begun to sour.

As the day wore on, it had seemed incredible that such a thing had happened – that Marcia was dead. Lois did not worry about the house; no one was due there in her absence – it was not the week for the window-cleaner, and the gardeners never went near the house or garage. But Mary King was due at the shop. Belatedly, Lois telephoned from the office and explained that she had a bad cold and had lost her voice. She would not be in for several days.

Lois had kept her postponed appointment, that afternoon, with a client who wanted advice on how to save labour in her garden. When she returned to the centre, Fred told her that a gentleman had been asking for her. Mr Reynard, he'd wanted, in fact, until Fred explained. Then he'd asked where she lived. He'd left no name.

'He'll be back, if he wants something,' Lois said, only half attending, but as she drove home, the last to leave, for there would be no routine trip to Sainsbury's today, she wondered why someone would want to speak to Mr Reynard, whom no one had ever met, and felt a small thread of extra concern weave itself into her major anxiety about what must be done tonight.

No one was waiting at the house, however. All was in order, as she went inside to fortify herself well with whisky before going out to the garage. She was going to put Marcia's body into the sea, and she would leave Mary King's car nearby.

But the body was still ramrod stiff. There was no chance of fitting it into the rear of the Mini, behind the seats, as she'd planned, intending to find her own way home by any method after abandoning the car.

She dare not delay while she thought of something else. Though visitors were rare at Fir Tree House, there were occasional charity collectors, and the man whom Fred had mentioned might still call. She heaved the body into the back of the van as if it were a bundle of trees. It was heavier than the saplings she delivered, and Lois had to struggle, but she was strong. When it was done, she covered it with sacks. Then she set off for the coast.

During the very hot summer of 1976, she and Marcia had swum from a beach twenty miles west of Witterton. It was reached by a path leading down from the cliff at Watch Point, where there was a popular coastal walk. The headland itself was approached by a gated road over farmland, along which, in the darkness, Lois now drove her van.

There was no moon, and she had turned out the lights of the van so as not to attract attention before driving it near the cliff edge. She could hear the sea soughing and sighing, and the wind ruffled her hair as she dragged the bundle out of the van and unwrapped it. Lois was glad she could not make out Marcia's features clearly in the darkness. She took off Marcia's diamond and emerald ring – Stephen's ring, which she regularly wore – reminded of it only because she felt it as she rolled Marcia over, removing the plastic sheeting. She had to use her own saliva to moisten Marcia's finger enough to allow her to slip the ring over her knuckle. Lois's own finger – even her little one – was much too thick for her to wear it during the journey home. She wrapped it in a handkerchief and put it in her breeches pocket.

When Lois returned to Fir Tree House, she found a white

police patrol car parked outside the front door, with a very bored constable sitting inside it. Lois's pulse quickened. Had she exceeded the speed limit somewhere on her way to the beach? It was highly likely. Luckily, she hadn't yielded to the temptation to stop at a pub on the way back, though her mouth was dry and her system clamoured for alcohol. But she'd had a couple of drinks before setting out. Would that send her over the top with the breathalyser?

She drew up in front of the garage, turned off the van's lights and got out as the constable approached, shining his torch.

'Mrs Reynard?' he asked.

Finding no one at home when he called to investigate an anonymous message, which had been treated with some scepticism by the officer who had taken it down, but nevertheless must be followed up, Police Constable Cuthbert had gone down to the village to see if anyone there knew where the householder might be. At the Grapes, he learned that the two women, Mrs Reynard and Mrs King, who shared the house, kept to themselves. Reporting back, he was instructed to hang about till one or other returned, or until otherwise ordered. Cuthbert had wandered round the grounds while he waited, much taken with the gnomes, especially the big fellow under the tree on the lawn. He was sure, even before he spoke to Lois, that the call was a hoax, but he had to go through the motions.

'Yes,' Lois answered. 'What can I do for you, officer?'

'Might I just take a look in your garage, Mrs Reynard?' asked Cuthbert.

'Yes – certainly you may,' said Lois. 'But why do you want to?' Her heart began to thud harder.

'We've had a report. It has to be followed up,' said Cuthbert.

'What sort of report?' No one could have seen her – only the gnomes.

'Just a report that needs investigating,' Cuthbert said.

Lois opened the garage doors and he went inside. To demonstrate that she had nothing to conceal, she switched on the light, which cast a bright glare over the stark whitewashed walls. The garage was exceedingly tidy, and walking all round it, peering down beneath the Mini, he could see no body.

'Might I look in the boot of the Mini, please?' Cuthbert requested, determined to be thorough.

Lois went off and fetched the keys of the Mini from the house. Her suicide plan had already gone wrong because the Mini was not yet at the clifftop. Never mind. She would think of something to say if Marcia were found. More worrying now was the fact that someone had been to the garage during the day and seen the body. But who? How could they have got in? The doors had been locked.

She thought again of the man who had spoken to Fred, asking for Mr Reynard, and then wanting to know where she lived, and she knew a moment of utter terror, but she kept control as the constable opened the boot of the Mini, revealing its tools, a can of de-icer and a windscreen scraper.

'What are you looking for, officer?' asked Lois, then added, with an attempt at humour, 'Cannabis?'

'There's been a report of a body, Mrs Reynard,' Cuthbert allowed her, now, to know. 'Some practical joker, obviously, but if it had been a true report, things would have been different, I'm sure you'll agree.'

'Oh really!' Lois managed to put just the right note of injured amusement into her tone. 'How ridiculous! Some child, I suppose, who sees too much television. You're satisfied, I hope?'

'Quite satisfied, Mrs Reynard,' said Cuthbert.

'Would you care to look round the house? Perhaps there are several more stacked up there?' Lois suggested, with brave sarcasm.

'That won't be necessary, thank you,' said Cuthbert. Then, as an afterthought, he added, 'The other lady – Mrs King – where would she be now?'

'She's gone away for a few days, to stay with her sister in London,' said Lois. 'I'm not sure when she'll be back.'

'This her car?'

'Yes – well – we share it. She uses it, mostly,' said Lois. 'She went to London by train. I took her to Shawton station this afternoon.'

'I see. Well, I'm sorry to have troubled you,' said
Cuthbert, and departed.

Lois watched him leave, apparently calm but starting to
shake before his rear lights had disappeared. She put the van
away and closed the garage, then rushed into the house to
pour herself almost a tumbler of whisky.

Someone had called at the house, broken into the garage –
though there were no signs of forced entry – and found the
body. Who?

Could it have been the stranger who had learned where
she lived from Fred? Had he found Marcia and called the
police? If so, why had he not waited for them to arrive? Who
was he? Why, when he found no one at home, had he entered
the garage? And how had he done it without breaking the
lock?

It was some time before Lois thought of Stephen. She had
shut her mind to the fact that one day he would be back in the
world, and she'd covered their trail so thoroughly that surely
he would never be able to find them? Could there have been a
weak link in that chain somewhere? Only her mother, who
was too feeble now and too much deranged mentally to be a
danger. But people in Hagbourne Green had known of Lois's
alleged marriage. Could Stephen have been released
already, and traced her?

He must have done. It must have been Stephen, and he
had lacked the nerve to stay with Marcia. No other explanation made sense.

Murderers shouldn't be let out of gaol, thought Lois,
pouring herself some more whisky. Life should mean life.

She dreamed of him in the night. She saw his white,
ravaged face as he stood in the dock and heard the foreman of
the jury pronounce him guilty, and as he turned away to
start his sentence, Lois woke. With the bedclothes drawn
tight round her, she lay in bed waiting for the dawn and
thinking first of Stephen, and then of her friend's body being
swept out to sea as, ostensibly, had happened all those years
ago. She thought of the cold salt water lapping at Marcia's
soft flesh, of the fish and other marine creatures who would
prey on it, and she shuddered.

2

Stephen scarcely slept that night, though he went through the motions of going to bed. In the morning, he turned on the radio for the early news. There was nothing about the discovery of a woman's body in a garage at Witterton, no reference to the earlier murder investigation.

Perhaps they had not yet established Marcia's true identity, he thought. Perhaps it was too soon for local journalists to have heard about the matter.

He got up, shaved round the edges of his beard, bathed, and brewed coffee. For more than a decade he had accepted and carried a burden of guilt because he had, as he thought, driven his wife to end her life by hurting her beyond consolation. Now, he understood that he had provoked only bitter hatred, and that Lois must have planted most of the evidence that had convicted him. He had always known in his heart that Marcia, even in anger, would never have been forceful enough to do it alone. How long had they been plotting together in those last weeks at Badger's End?

He felt physically and mentally exhausted. Proof of his innocence now existed, but he was not elated. It was tragic, for Marcia lay dead; her friend had, in the end, turned against her. Why?

Stephen forced himself to eat some toast and marmalade. He listened again to the news on the hour, but there was nothing about the body. At nine o'clock he rang Frank's office.

'Something's happened,' he said when they were connected. 'I'm not sure that I should mention it on the phone.' He was indoctrinated, now, into curbing spontaneity, fearing the worst because he knew it could happen and aware of the need to protect himself. 'I've traced Lois,' he added. 'To Witterton.'

'Well?'

'Frank – can we meet? I don't think this can wait. Are you very busy, if I come over?'

Frank looked at his diary. He had three important appointments but he knew that Stephen would not call like this on a whim, just because he had found Lois.

'All right,' he said. 'While you're on the way, I'll see if I can unscramble a few things and be free for you.'

'I'll start at once,' said Stephen.

By the time he arrived, Frank had seen one of his clients, referred a second to a partner and postponed the third till the following week. Stephen was shown straight into his office.

Frank took one look at him and then spoke into the machine on his desk, asking his secretary to bring some coffee.

'In a pot, please, Pat,' he said. 'One cup won't be enough for you, Stephen,' he went on. 'You look awful. Now, tell me what's happened.'

'Marcia wasn't dead,' Stephen burst out. 'She is now, but she wasn't then, all those years ago.'

Frank stared at Stephen, whose eyes were sunk with fatigue but very bright. The tension in him was almost tangible; he resembled a volcano about to erupt.

'Begin at the beginning,' Frank advised. He was used to hearing incoherent tales of injustice from defrauded shoppers or wronged spouses and, though it took time, in the end it was always best to hear the whole story from scratch.

Interrupted only by the arrival of Pat with the coffee, Stephen described his search for Lois and how he had gone to Fir Tree House. He related how he had seen Marcia's supposedly stolen possessions. Then he told Frank how he had entered the garage.

'I don't know what made me walk round to the front of the Mini,' he confessed. 'There it was – this bundle. Although I couldn't believe it, I recognized her at once, in spite of her hair being dyed. She was rather a ghastly colour,' he added. 'I unwrapped her enough to look for a mole she had on her shoulder. I think she was strangled.'

Frank had listened incredulously. As Stephen described finding the china pieces, and seeing the silver hairbrushes

170

with Marcia's initials on them, he had sat forward in his chair, not interrupting even with a gasp.

'So what did you do?' he said at last.

Stephen told him.

'What would you have done?' he asked. 'What would you have told me to do, if I'd rung you?'

'I'd have told you to wait at some handy pub and come down at once myself,' said Frank, and added honestly, 'I think.' But he would have made some telephone calls first.

'There's been nothing about it on the news,' said Stephen. 'Of course, I realize now, they won't know who she really was. She must have been using some other name.'

Frank picked up the telephone and asked the switchboard to connect him with the Chief Constable of that area.

'This isn't going to be straightforward, Stephen,' he warned. 'There'll be red tape, not to mention red faces, but your conviction will be quashed, I swear it.'

'Poor Marcia,' said Stephen. 'She looked awful, Frank. Older, of course, and fatter, but it wasn't only that. That dreadful hair – all curly. Hers used to be so pretty. Could Lois really have strangled her? What would make her do something like that?'

'You say there's no Mr Reynard, so it can't have been him, if he ever existed, which I agree seems highly unlikely,' said Frank. 'But there may be a third person involved – some other woman, perhaps. We'll find out. Keep your nerve, Stephen. You're going to need it.'

The Chief Constable was out, but a deputy came to the telephone when Frank explained that it was a very serious matter, connected with a previous murder conviction and the body found at Witterton the previous night.

The Assistant Chief Constable knew of no such body. He asked Frank to hold on, and shortly confirmed that none had been found.

Frank kept his voice level.

'One was reported, anonymously, at about – ' he glanced at Stephen for the time. 'About six thirty last night,' he said. 'It was seen in the garage at Fir Tree House, Witterton. Do you mean to tell me the call wasn't followed up?'

As Stephen heard this, his face went even whiter. He clenched his fists as Frank listened to the telephone.

'I see,' Frank said, and then went on, 'My information is that the dead body was one Marcia Dawes, apparently living in Witterton under an assumed name, and allegedly murdered in 1972. Her body was never found, but her husband Stephen Dawes was convicted of her murder.'

The Assistant Chief Constable remembered the case.

'I acted for the husband,' said Frank smoothly, despite worried looks from Stephen. He listened to more words from the ACC and then said crisply, 'My information, at this point, is confidential.' He listened again, said, 'Very well,' supplied his own telephone number and rang off.

'He's going to find out what happened,' Frank told Stephen. 'Then he'll ring us back. All hell will be let loose down there, I shouldn't wonder. God knows what's been going on. Nerves of steel, old soul,' he added, as he had said dozens of times during the investigation.

When the telephone shrilled on Frank's desk, Stephen jumped as if shot. Frank spoke into the receiver.

'Yes. Yes, I see.' He kept his voice level, not wanting to show Stephen how shocked he was by what he was hearing. Only for a second did the thought flash through Frank's mind that Stephen had at last cracked and was hallucinating. Stephen was as sane now as he had been eleven years ago. 'Well, hadn't you better find this Mrs Mary King, then?' he said, glancing at Stephen as he spoke. 'I can tell you that King was Mrs Marcia Dawes's maiden name. And no, I'm still not prepared, at the moment, to divulge where I got my information.'

The wires would start crackling all over the country, he thought. In minutes the fact that Stephen had been released from gaol would be known, and details of the case would be exhumed from memory, if not the files. He picked up a pen that lay on his desk and fiddled with it while he told Stephen what he had learned.

'They went to the house – a patrol car went – got there at six fifty-five,' he said. 'There was no one at home, but a constable was there when Mrs Lois Reynard, the householder, and owner of Reynard's Garden Centre, returned at a quarter to ten. She was in her van, alone. She unlocked the garage and showed the police officer that it was empty except for a blue Mini which was usually used by Mrs King, who shared the house with her. The car is registered as the property of Mrs Reynard.'

'That fits,' said Stephen grimly.

'Mrs Reynard asked the officer if he wanted to look round the house, but he declined. They're going there now. If the place is empty, they'll collect Lois from her garden centre and make her open up. She said that her friend was visiting a sister in London.'

Stephen's face was grey.

'She's dumped her,' he said. 'I ought to have stayed there, Frank. Waited at the house till the police came. Lois must have got back just after I left and moved her.'

'If you had stayed, you might have been tempted to murder Lois,' said Frank. 'She wouldn't have just stood there, you know, letting you clear yourself and wreck things for her. She might have blipped you, too. It sounds like she's turned into a very tough lady.'

'I think she was always that, only we didn't realize it,' Stephen said. He shrugged. 'What now?'

'We wait. They'll get in touch. It might take hours.'

The police would ask Lois for Marcia's alleged address in London and that would have to be laboriously checked before they started to search seriously elsewhere. Police investigations, like computer programmes, followed a strict routine, with no short cuts.

'Shall I go down there?' Stephen asked.

'No. If they want you, they know where to find you,' said Frank. 'They'll realize you were the informant. And you're not going back to Fairbridge, Stephen. You're coming home with me. We may need to act quickly.' And you need my protection, he thought. Until Marcia's body was found, there was only Stephen's word for her presence even though her fingerprints would be in the house. Had they been taken at the time of the original disappearance? Probably, though in the absence of a body, they would have been established as hers only by a process of elimination. There should still be traceable dental records.

173

'But what about Val?' Stephen said. He was too tired and wretched to make any stronger protest.

'She can't object now. You're innocent,' said Frank.

He told his secretary he was leaving the office for the rest of the day and would be at home if anything urgent arose. He was expecting a call from the police, who should be given his home number and asked to ring him there.

Pat did her best to hide her intense curiosity. She knew exactly who Stephen was.

Stephen, in his Mini, followed Frank out of the town and back to his house. It was in an area rather like Hagbourne Green, looking rural but with a lot of large, comfortable houses where professional people and senior executives lived. The original villagers had almost all moved away. The house was quite like Badger's End, but it was larger, and was painted pink. There was a paddock, occupied now by a donkey, waiting for the pony Fiona would have. Stephen parked beside Frank's BMW. The doors of the double garage were open, and it was empty.

Frank led Stephen in through the kitchen door.

'Val's out. I've forgotten where she was going today,' he said. 'Let's find something to eat.'

Stephen was recovering.

'You don't have to do this, Frank,' he said. 'I can go home. I'll be all right. It's only just a question of waiting a bit, I expect, till the police find out what's going on.'

'True, but waiting is always the hardest part of anything,' said Frank. 'And I'm not letting you do it alone. If you knew how it's bugged me all this time – knowing you were innocent but being unable to prove it!' Frank couldn't get rid of the feeling that if only he had done more, the case against Stephen could not have been proved, yet he had thought of every possible action to refute it. His biggest disappointment had been his failure, once sentence was passed and the appeal dismissed, to interest an investigative journalist or criminological expert in the case strongly enough to look into it. An interesting case, they all said, but conclusive. No one but Stephen could possibly have had any motive for murdering Marcia.

They thought he had probably hidden her jewellery and

the other valuables in some woodland spot against his release, or left them with his mistress.

It had occurred to no one that Marcia might not, in fact, be dead.

Frank sent Stephen off to the storeroom to get them both some beer while he went to his study to telephone the Home Office. The call took some time, and afterwards he found Stephen standing in the kitchen staring out of the window at the wintry garden, where the lawn swept down to the paddock. Some apple trees swayed in the wind.

'I've set a few more wheels in motion,' Frank explained, and began opening cupboards. He found a tin of Baxter's Game Soup, some cheese, and a loaf of moist home-made brown bread – Val was an excellent cook. From the diary by the telephone, he had discovered that she was doing Meals on Wheels today. Val maintained that those who were lucky in life must give something back to others.

Frank looked forward to introducing Stephen to her at last, and to watching her expression when they met.

3

When a uniformed police constable came into the garden centre at noon on Friday and, after consulting Fred, headed towards the office where Lois was trying to concentrate on the week's figures, her first thought was that Marcia's body had already been found.

She prepared herself to display shock and grief, which would not be difficult since she was still in the grip of both emotions.

The constable asked her to accompany him back to Fir Tree House as there were some points to be cleared up regarding the whereabouts of Mrs King.

'She's in London,' she said. 'And I'm busy.'

'One or two matters are not quite clear,' said the constable imperturbably. 'I must ask you to come with me.'

'Oh well – ' Alienating the young man would not help, Lois saw, and the short drive home would give her time to compose herself. It would be better, too, to be questioned there than in full view of Fred, the boy and the customers. The officer indicated that she should accompany him in his car. The drive passed in silence. Perhaps the constable did not want to break the news of Marcia's death to her until she was in her own home. When they drew up outside it, she saw that there was another car already there and, as they approached, a burly man in a Gannex coat and a stocky, younger man with curly hair, wearing a navy anorak, got out of it. Lois knew at once that they were detectives; she had forgotten nothing about the investigation after Marcia's original disappearance.

'Detective Superintendent Rodway,' the burly man introduced himself. 'And this is Detective Sergeant Burton.'

Rodway had been instructed by the Assistant Chief Constable to go himself to Fir Tree House to get to the bottom of what was going on. It could be a very serious matter. Stephen Dawes had been released from prison a few weeks previously, and his solicitor's call from Surrey must be followed up. As Mrs Reynard, formerly Lois Carter, had inherited all Marcia Dawes's considerable estate, it was highly likely that the husband felt aggrieved, since he would have expected to gain that wealth if he had got away with his crime. The call the evening before might have been made by him, with malicious intent to stir things up. Mrs King must be accounted for. Then they could all go home.

'I'm inquiring into the whereabouts of Mrs King, who I believe shares this house with you?' said Rodway. 'May we go inside, please?'

Lois did not answer. She walked ahead of the men to the front door and opened it, leading the way into the dining-room, not wanting them to desecrate Marcia's drawing-room by their presence. The uniformed officer remained outside with his car.

'An officer came to see you last night, as the result of a telephone report,' said Rodway.

'Yes – some ridiculous nonsense about a body,' said Lois. 'Someone's idea of a joke, I suppose.'

'Mrs Mary King lives here with you?' Rodway asked.

'Yes.' Say as little as possible, Lois reminded herself.

'How long have you lived here, Mrs Reynard?'

'Nine years,' Lois answered.

'And Mrs King too?'

'Yes.'

'And where is Mrs King now?'

'In London. I told the officer last night,' said Lois.

'Do you have her address?'

'No.'

'But you told the officer last night that she was visiting her sister. Surely you know her sister's address?' Rodway asked.

'I don't. It's not my business,' said Lois shortly.

'Her name, then? The sister's?'

'I don't know that either,' said Lois.

'Rather strange, isn't it, when you've shared a home all this time?'

'Not really. I've never met her.'

'I see. Well, I'd like to take a look in the garage, if you have no objection, Mrs Reynard,' said Rodway.

'Not at all,' said Lois. She took her keys out of her jacket pocket and gave them to him, first selecting the appropriate one. Rodway took it and went from the room. He left the house by the back door, noticing as he went through the kitchen the row of neatly labelled keys hanging on the wall.

Just as PC Cuthbert had done the previous evening, Rodway saw the blue Mini in the garage. He walked to the front of it and looked at the ground. There were marks in the dust. They were marks that could have a number of innocent explanations, but they could also have been made by dragging some heavy object across the floor. He noted the registration number of the Mini and went out to the uniformed officer still in his car, on whose radio he checked the details with the computer. Then he returned to the house.

Meanwhile, Lois and Burton had been talking.

'Helps you at the garden centre, does she? Mrs King?' asked Burton.

'No. She has other interests,' Lois answered.

'Nice place you've got along there. I've had plants from you,' said Burton. 'Tomatoes, mostly. They did well.'

177

'Our stock is all high quality,' said Lois.

'And what are Mrs King's interests?' Burton pursued.

'She helps in an antique shop.'

'Oh, where?'

'In Shawton.'

By the time Rodway returned, Burton knew the names of Mrs Mary King's employers, but had learned little else about her.

'You'll have no objection, I take it, Mrs Reynard, if Sergeant Burton just has a quick look round the house?' Rodway stated.

'Not at all,' said Lois. 'But what are you looking for?'

'Nothing special,' Rodway replied, with perfect truth. He nodded at Burton, who went out. 'The car in the garage – the blue Mini. Mrs King used it, you told PC Cuthbert last night, but it's registered in your name?'

'That's correct. I bought it for her to use,' said Lois.

'Very generous of you,' commented Rodway.

'Not really. She wasn't left well provided for,' said Lois. 'I was. The business is mine.'

'And the house?'

'Yes.'

'You drove Mrs King to Shawton station to catch the London train?' Rodway asked.

'Yes.'

'Which one, Mrs Reynard?'

Lois knew about the trains. She'd put plants on them to be collected at the other end. She gave the time of the afternoon fast train to Paddington.

Burton soon came back into the room and nodded briefly at Rodway, who waited for him to speak.

'Mrs King's sister's address might be in her handbag,' he said. 'Strange that she went to London without it. It's in her room.'

Christ! Lois managed not to say it aloud. God, how could she have been so careless?

'She has several handbags,' she said. 'She'd taken her best one to London.'

'Without her purse and her make-up things?' said Burton. 'Surely not. They're all in the one in her room.'

178

Lois fidgeted in her chair. Oh, for a drink! What could she say?

'She hasn't gone to her sister's,' she muttered. 'She ran off. We had an argument the other evening and I went up to bed, leaving her down here. In the morning she'd disappeared.'

'When was this, Mrs Reynard?' asked Rodway.

How they niggled at you, she thought: so many pettifogging questions.

'Wednesday,' she said. 'I mean, we had an argument on Wednesday evening and yesterday morning she'd disappeared.'

'Weren't you worried about her?'

'Not really. I thought she'd gone to that man,' said Lois.

'What man?'

'Some man she knew. I don't remember his name,' Lois said. 'I told that story about her sister to protect her reputation.'

'Why did you quarrel, Mrs Reynard?' Rodway asked.

'It was over this man. She wanted to go on holiday with him,' said Lois. It seemed odd to speak the truth.

'And you thought she shouldn't go?'

'Yes.'

'She must have been very upset to go off without her handbag,' Rodway suggested.

'Yes,' agreed Lois.

'Did she take a top coat?' Rodway asked.

'I suppose so,' Lois answered. 'I don't really know.'

'Let's have a look, shall we, and see what's missing,' Rodway proposed. 'And perhaps you've got a photograph of the lady?'

Lois hadn't. She'd avoided amateur photography. As they went upstairs, she wondered whether to invent a missing coat for Marcia, then decided not to, for she would not be wearing one if her body were found.

She described the clothes Marcia was wearing that final night, and in response to a direct request, allowed the superintendent to look through Marcia's desk. Lois knew that there was nothing there to give away her true identity, but they found her passport, which contained a rather poor photograph, and in which her name was given as Miss Marcia Felicity King.

They let her go. The uniformed officer took her back to the garden centre, but Rodway locked the garage and took both the keys, Lois's from her ring and the one from the kitchen. Rodway said he would close up the house when they left; he assumed she had no objection to their taking a final look around?

It would be folly to refuse.

The plastic sheeting Lois had used for wrapping the body was still in the van. When the constable had driven away, Lois took it out and put it in the rubbish bin at the centre.

Detective Sergeant Burton soon traced Andrew West. Rodway had sent him first to the antique shop, where he learned that Lois had telephoned the day before to say that Mary was unwell. The Paynes supplied the name and address of her man friend.

Half an hour later, Burton was interviewing first a puzzled and then an anxious Andrew, who had not seen Mary since Wednesday when they had had lunch together. He had expected her to call him yesterday, he said; he never rang her at home in the evening after her friend returned. When Burton asked why not, he replied that he had formed the opinion that Mrs Reynard was jealous and over-possessive.

'They quarrelled on Wednesday evening,' Burton said. 'Mrs King was missing the next day, and Mrs Reynard thought she had run to you.'

'She hadn't,' said Colonel West. 'Oh, my God! What's happened to her? I'd been going to ring her at the shop later this afternoon.'

'You'd expect her to get in touch with you, if she'd gone somewhere else?' Burton asked.

'Most certainly.'

'You'll let us know at once, if she does?'

'Of course. But where would she go, running off in the night?' Andrew asked. 'That place is right in the wilds.'

'She may be with friends in the village,' said Burton. 'She may have gone down there.'

'On foot?' Andrew had been told that she had not taken her car.

180

'If she was upset, she may have just dashed off,' said Burton.

Andrew could not conceive of Mary being too upset to snatch a coat and her car keys. He said so.

'If she's in the village, we'll soon know,' said Burton. 'We'll be asking at every house.'

By dusk that day the police had not only begun a door-to-door investigation in Witterton, but they had also started to examine Fir Tree House in the same painstaking way that, years before, Badger's End had been explored. Detectives had photographed the scuff marks on the garage floor and then it had been vacuumed, the dust sealed into plastic bags for the laboratory. They had looked for prints in the house, finding four clear sets.

The Assistant Chief Constable telephoned Frank later that day and told him that Mrs or Miss Mary King, who lived at Fir Tree House, Witterton, with Mrs Lois Reynard, could not at the moment be traced. There were puzzling factors about her disappearance, he said, whilst not telling Frank what these were. A full search was in progress and, when more was known, he would be informed.

The ACC did not reveal that the Home Office had been on the line.

Frank reported this conversation to Stephen.

'Well, will they find her this time?' said Stephen, with a wry laugh.

'I think they will,' said Frank. 'But perhaps not very quickly.'

'I'd better go home,' said Stephen.

'No,' said Frank. He was not going to spell out for Stephen that once the news broke, the media would be round him like bees round a hive. He'd soon work that out for himself. 'You need a bit of protection, old soul,' he said.

'It's sure to come out that I was down there. That it was I who telephoned,' said Stephen. 'Should we tell them?'

'Let's let them work it out for themselves,' said Frank, sure that the ACC had done this already.

'But there's Val,' Stephen protested. 'I don't want to make trouble between you.'

It was pointless to tell him that trouble existed already.

'You won't,' Frank said.

Val came back at half past three, before the children returned from school. She saw Frank's car outside, and a strange Mini. Very occasionally clients came to see him at home, but he had said nothing about such a possibility today. It was not her custom to interrupt him when he was in his study, so she was surprised when he asked her to join him and his visitor.

Val saw an ill-looking, grey-haired, bearded man sitting in one of the leather chairs. He stood up at once as she entered, and Frank introduced them.

'Val, this is one of my oldest friends,' he said. 'Stephen Dawes. He'll be staying here for a while.'

Stephen, in turn, saw a tall, well-built woman in her mid-thirties. She had rich brown hair, beautifully cut and brushed up on either side of her face, brown eyes, and a full, soft-looking mouth. She wore tight corduroy trousers tucked into high boots, and a padded jacket. She was very attractive.

Val was just about to smile in a welcoming manner whilst at the same time shooting a dagger glance at Frank for imposing a house guest upon her with no warning, when she realized who Stephen was.

'But – ' she began, and looked appalled.

Frank did not give her time to object.

'Stephen has just discovered that his wife did not die all those years ago. She's been living in the West Country under an assumed name. Unfortunately, she's now disappeared again.'

'What?' Val stared first at him, then at Stephen, and looked back at her husband. 'That can't be true,' she said.

'It is,' said Frank. 'We don't yet know what really happened – the police are still investigating. But Stephen will be hounded by the press as soon as the story gets out, so we've got to take care of him.'

'I thought he – you – were still in prison,' said Val.

'I was released on parole a month ago,' Stephen said. His voice was slightly hoarse, as if rarely used.

'Are you sure about this, Frank?' Val demanded. 'About – about – about her, I mean?'

182

'I've always been sure Stephen never killed her,' said Frank. 'And I've told you so, dozens of times. But I thought she was dead.'

'I hope the police will find her quickly,' said Val coldly. 'I'll go and see about the spare bedroom.'

'She's very annoyed,' said Stephen as she left the room. Frank grinned.

'She needs time to consider how to change her attitude to you,' he said. 'No one likes to be wrong, after all, and soon she'll want to boast about being among the first to be nice to you after your transformation from villain to victim.'

4

On Saturday morning, the nation was told by the press that a woman known as Mary King was missing from her home in Witterton. A grainy enlargement of Marcia's passport photograph appeared in most newspapers and was flashed across television screens during news bulletins. No reference was made to a puzzle about her identity, but it was mentioned that she lived at Witterton with Mrs Lois Reynard, who owned a garden centre.

Stephen had spent the night in the very comfortable spare bedroom at Dove House. He and Frank had sat up late, and both had had several brandies after an excellent dinner which Val had produced apparently by magic, but in fact from her well-stocked deep-freeze.

'It's going to take time,' Frank had warned. 'You remember what it was like before, Stephen. All those laboratory tests take ages. They may have found something in the garage.' But they needed to find Marcia, he thought: this time, there had to be a body.

During dinner, Val had been tight-lipped but civil. When the children came back from school, she had borne them off to their playroom lest, Stephen thought wryly, he contaminate them. They were nice-looking children, seven and five years old, who went to a private day school some eight miles away. Stephen would have liked to have talked to them, tried to make contact, but he felt shy. He'd had nothing to do with children in all those years in prison, and very little even before that.

He was awake early the next morning, and sat up in bed trying to read a book about Greece which was among the selection put in the room for visitors. He would like to go to Greece again. He and Marcia had been there once; she had found Athens noisy and dusty and hadn't liked the food, but she had enjoyed the Archaeological Museum. Stephen's attention wandered from the page. He remembered Marcia gracefully arranged as she sunbathed; he pictured her lazily swimming in the clear sea. If he had never become involved with Ruth, their lives would have continued tranquilly all this time, to all appearances a successful marriage, and Marcia would still be alive.

Faint sounds reached him from within the house. Stephen snapped the book shut and got out of bed. The sybaritic pleasures of Val's guest bathroom distracted him for a while; the towels here were thicker and softer than those at Ivy Lodge, and the pale yellow bath was not stained under the hot tap.

Marcia might never be found, or her body not discovered until she was unrecognizable and the cause of death impossible to establish. Even her teeth would be different: would the chart available all those years ago match in any respect the present state of her mouth? Had any earlier records been kept? Lois had been so infernally fiendish in her methods before, perhaps she had been as clever again and would once more outwit justice.

He was the only person, apart from her killer, who had seen the body, and he had turned and run. He should have faced it out – telephoned from Fir Tree House, stayed there till the police came, and confronted Lois if she had got there first. She wouldn't have been able to strangle him.

He was in a depressed mood when he came down to breakfast, wearing a clean shirt of Frank's and a pair of his socks.

A bright scene greeted him in the kitchen. Val, her face

innocent of make-up, was dishing out cereal to the children.
Frank was pouring fruit juice. Coffee percolated pleasantly
in the background, smelling delicious. The children, who
had barely seen the guest the previous evening, looked at
him with open curiosity. It was Saturday; they wouldn't be
going to school. Stephen wondered what explanation they
had been given for his presence. It seemed that Frank was
determined to see this through with Val, and, in a moment of
clarity, Stephen perceived that he might be the cause of this
other marriage foundering. He must, at least, do his best to
get on with her, show her that he could remember the
common courtesies and was grateful. She obviously had a lot
of physical energy; Frank had told him that she played tennis
throughout the year, and squash, and was involved with a
number of local activities, a very different sort of person from
Marcia; she was much more positive, Stephen thought, but
both were proud.

Stephen had had little contact with women for years.
Some of the prison tutors were female, and he had met
female librarians. When he was in the open prison and on
working parties he had come across others, but this and his
meeting with Mrs Henshaw and the Wainwrights were his
first real social contacts since his release.

And this time his hostess knew who he was.

He sat down at the kitchen table, accepted a bowl of
muesli and a large cup of strong coffee, and asked Fiona what
she had done at school yesterday, the only conversational
approach he could think of.

She was not a shy child, and she told him she had learned
about the body.

'The body?' Val repeated after her, raising one well-
trimmed eyebrow. Could it be that sex education at seven
had crept on to the curriculum at that carefully chosen
school?

'Mm, yes. Me and Jenny lay on the floor and was drawed
round,' said Fiona. 'Then we was cut out and put on the wall
to show what's inside. Lungs and things. We had to take our
skirts off,' she added.

A sign of relief came from Val.

'Biology,' she said.

185

'No. Heart and stomach,' said Fiona, spooning up Cubs.

James said that he'd done colouring and band. He liked that. He then said that he could read Peter and Jane and began to recite an account of this pair's pedestrian activities, made familiar by repetition.

Val cut him short, telling the children to hurry with their breakfast. They were going off for a riding lesson afterwards.

After they left, Frank produced the newspaper, which he had hidden in a drawer, and silently handed it to Stephen, who had a sense of *déjà vu* as he looked at Marcia's photograph and read that Mrs or Miss Mary or Marcia King was missing. But this time she really was dead; this time there was a killer who, surely, must have left some clues, and who certainly knew what she had done with the body.

The police had taken a statement from Lois. She stuck to her story about Mary, as she remembered still to call her, disappearing after their quarrel on Wednesday evening.

Meanwhile, some of the distinct sets of fingerprints found in Fir Tree House had been identified. One set was that of Andrew West, who had willingly allowed his to be taken for comparison, as he had been at the house so recently. Another set was Lois's. A third set, found on silver hairbrushes and toilet things in the missing woman's bedroom, could be presumed to be her own.

A fourth set remained.

Meanwhile high-level telephone conversations had taken place between the Home Office and the police, and old files had been opened. Top priority was to find Mary or Marcia King, alive or dead, and make sure of her identity.

Early on Saturday morning, a jogger on the beach below Watch Point saw something on the foreshore, a bundle of what looked like sodden rags, lapped by the tide. He paused to glance at it, and saw that it was the body of a woman.

Andrew West identified Marcia, or Mary, as she was to him. He had seen many dead men in his life, but he was profoundly shocked as he looked at the still, purplish face.

The police surgeon had been summoned to the body as it lay on the beach, and the pathologist, too, had seen her as she lay just above the tide mark. She had not drowned. There were petechial spots not only in the whites of her eyes but in her scalp: sure sign of asphyxiation.

Some limbs were broken; the pathologist thought that he would be able to show this had happened after death and that the fractures had been caused by the body's fall from the cliff.

Detective Superintendent Rodway had ordered the dead woman's hands to be bagged; scrapings from under her nails might yield useful matter.

Her fingerprints matched those found in Fir Tree House and attributed to Mrs King. Moreover, they matched others assumed, years before, to belong to Marcia Dawes. And the fourth set of prints had now been identified as those of Marcia Dawes's husband, Stephen, recently released from prison.

Frank played briefly with the idea of taking Stephen up to the golf club on Saturday morning, but without booking they were unlikely to get on the course, and were anyway not in a calm enough state of mind to enjoy a game. Instead, Frank got out his long ladder and said he must clean the gutters. Stephen helped with the job, and after that they set about sweeping up leaves. They were still doing this when Val returned, having left the children with some friends for the rest of the day.

She had bought the *Daily Mirror*, which gave a speculative report of the search for the missing woman. Val read it carefully. Then she went into Frank's study, and opened his big flat-topped desk. She knew where he kept the elder Mrs Dawes's volume of press-cuttings about Stephen's trial. At the time of her death Frank had said he could not leave them at Ivy Lodge, even locked in the attic; they must be kept safely in case one day Stephen wanted them.

Val compared photographs. She made allowance for the passage of time and for poor photography.

It was possible.

Over lunch – leek soup and cold ham and salad – Val told Stephen that she would put some more shirts, socks and underclothes of Frank's in his room and would he please leave his washing in the bin in his bathroom.

Stephen protested.

'It's an awful imposition, my being here,' he said. 'I'll be off home tomorrow.'

'No.' Val spoke before Frank could. 'Frank's right – the press will soon get hold of your connection with it all.' The words came out painfully. 'You do need help,' she said.

'I did see that body, Val, and she was my wife,' said Stephen, and he spoke so sadly that Val's last doubts vanished. 'I can't expect you to take me on trust, like Frank does,' Stephen went on. 'He and my mother were the only two people who really believed I hadn't killed her.' Even counsel had been unconvinced, but his job was to get Stephen off by his skill, guilty or not. 'Why should I have wanted her to die?' he asked, and wondered if Frank had ever been unfaithful to Val. Surely not: she was lovely, a warm woman, one who would feel deeply both love and hate; and there were the two lively children.

Val managed a smile. She was feeling ashamed and, seldom at a loss, was unsure how far to go by way of apology.

'Well, that's all past, now,' she said. 'Let's hope it won't take too long to sort things out.'

Val had gone to fetch the children, and Frank and Stephen were watching the sports programme on television, when the doorbell rang later that afternoon.

Frank went to answer it.

When he returned to the study, he was accompanied by two men whom Stephen knew at once, despite their plain clothes, to be policemen.

'They've found her,' Frank said. 'And they're satisfied it's Marcia. She was found on the shore near Watch Point and they know she didn't drown.'

He introduced them all by name.

Detective Chief Superintendent Rodway had come all the way to Surrey himself, with Detective Sergeant Burton, to question Stephen. He knew where to find him because Frank, in a further conversation with the Assistant Chief

Constable, had now said that Stephen was staying w
for the present.

'Mr Rodway, let me say that Mr Dawes appreciate
the earlier case in which he was wrongfully convicted i
your province, except in so far as it concerns what happe
at Witterton,' said Frank. 'Now, let's all sit down, shall we

He seemed very much in control of things, thoug
Stephen gratefully. He tried to master his instinctive fear o
the men before him; years ago, Stephen would have considered a policeman a friend, but not now.

'Mr Dawes, you entered Fir Tree House, Witterton, the
home of Mrs Lois Reynard, formerly Carter, and a woman
known as Mary King but now identified as Marcia Dawes,
née King, recently,' Rodway stated. He spoke in neutral tones.
'Your fingerprints were found,' he added as an explanation.

'I did,' said Stephen. He spoke firmly and looked the chief
superintendent in the eye. 'On Thursday, in fact.'

'You found your wife there?'

'No. The place was empty. I went in – ' For a moment
Stephen's voice wavered: he was guilty of breaking and
entering. 'I found my wife in the garage, dead. She was
wrapped in black polythene.'

'I see,' said Rodway. 'So what did you do?'

'Nothing, for quite a time,' said Stephen. 'What would
you have done, Mr Rodway, if you'd just been released on
parole for a murder you never committed, and then found
that the person you were supposed to have killed wasn't dead
at all?'

'Why did you go to Witterton?' Rodway asked.

'I'd found out that Lois was living there – Lois Carter. She
and Marcia were close friends and I wanted to get her to
admit that Marcia had framed me while killing herself, as I'd
thought she'd done.'

'You say you found the dead body and did nothing for
some time,' said Rodway. 'What did you do, eventually?'

'Left the place,' said Stephen.

'Why didn't you go back into the house – you admit you
entered it – and telephone the police?'

'I wish I had,' said Stephen. 'But I needed to collect
myself. I couldn't take it in.'

189

'Well?'

'I drove down the road, away from the garden centre – I didn't want to meet Lois then – not till I'd sorted things out in my mind. I stopped at a lay-by for quite some time. Then I telephoned the police from a call box.'

'You gave no name.'

'No.'

'Why not?'

'Come, Chief Superintendent, where is all this leading?' Frank asked. 'You received the call.'

'We received the call,' Rodway acknowledged. 'And when a constable reached Fir Tree House, there was no body in the garage. Why do you think that was, Mr Dawes?'

'Because Lois had come back and removed it,' said Stephen.

'I suggest that you had removed it, Mr Dawes,' said Rodway. 'I suggest that you called at Fir Tree House late on Wednesday night after Mrs Reynard had gone to bed, found your wife there and killed her in a fit of rage, then went to Watch Point and dumped the body over the cliff. The next day you made the telephone call to direct attention away from you, knowing that when the body was found, we would discover you had been to the house. You went to the garden centre, too, didn't you, and spoke to Mr Harris?'

'I spoke to a man there, yes,' said Stephen. 'But that's not what happened, Mr Rodway.' He laughed, a harsh, mirthless sound in the room where the crackle of the log fire formed a faint background noise; he could hear a clock ticking, measuring life as it passed.

'Stephen, you don't have to answer any of the chief superintendent's questions,' said Frank. He was appalled at the direction the interview was taking.

'I can't be charged with the same murder twice, Frank,' Stephen said in a weary voice. 'Mr Rodway can't send me down for this one.'

'Oh – now you've put it into words yourself,' said Rodway. 'That was what you thought, when you saw her – your wife. You were understandably angry, and strangled her. We know that was how she died – we have had a preliminary report. The post mortem's going on now.'

190

He let that sink in, pausing to allow Stephen to imagine Marcia's body stretched out in the mortuary, its secrets disclosed to the probe of the pathologist.

'Lois killed her,' Stephen said.

'Mrs Reynard clearly has questions to answer about the earlier indictment,' replied Rodway. 'But she had no motive to kill her friend. She'd already inherited all her money. She was devoted to Mrs King. You, on the other hand, could well have become mentally disturbed on seeing your wife still alive.'

'Chief Superintendent, Mr Dawes telephoned me early yesterday, when he returned from Witterton,' said Frank. 'He told me what had happened. Would he have done that if he had just killed his wife? Would he have telephoned you? Wouldn't he have disposed of the body and left it to look as though she had disappeared?'

'Not at all. He'd want her found, in order to clear himself of the earlier charge,' said Rodway.

Rodway had come to Surrey with every intention of taking Stephen back with him to help with his inquiries – that useful ritual which often leads to confession. In every murder case, the spouse had first to be eliminated before other suspects were considered, and Stephen was the spouse, even though, as he had said, he could not be tried again for the same murder. But if the police were seen to make the least error over the handling of this case, added to what had gone before, the officer responsible would be crucified.

There would be scientific evidence to connect whoever had killed Mary King, or Marcia Dawes, with the victim. There would be fibres of clothing, hairs, some proof. Stephen Dawes might say that such matter could have been transferred when he found the body; Lois Reynard, or Carter, could protest that in the normal course of daily life contact between her and the dead woman could be explained. But Rodway pinned his faith on the bagged hands. Marcia might have clutched at her killer. Stephen Dawes bore no scratches on his face, but he was bearded; a hair from his beard might be lodged under one of those rather long, varnished nails. Or some other substance, to be identified by patient examination.

Because he wanted to guard his rear, Rodway decided to

191

go back without Stephen, making Frank Jeffries responsible for producing him if and when required.

Lois Reynard also had some explaining to do. Detective Inspector Cave was interrogating her at this moment and might come up with something useful while they waited for the evidence from the mortuary.

5

Lois had spent Friday night in a cell, a most unpleasant experience. She was brought some breakfast on Saturday morning, and then the questions began again.

She repeated the story she had already told – how she had, at first, invented the sister to protect Mary's good name because she was making a fool of herself over some man. It was established that Mrs King had not made a habit of brief disappearances.

Nobody mentioned the Dawes murder case.

Lois wondered if she should insist on calling a solicitor, but she did not want to do anything that might be construed as indicating guilt; besides, since Marcia's affairs were settled and she had bought the garden centre, she had had no dealings with any solicitor and would have a problem about whom to consult; it could be no one from the past.

She must keep her nerve.

She described her own movements on Wednesday. She had borrowed Fred Harris's car to go to the dentist. In the evening, she had been rather late arriving home, making up for time lost during the day. Mary had been full of this man and some plan they had for going on holiday together, and there had been a quarrel. Lois had gone to bed, and in the morning Mary had gone.

They went over it all again and again, but she stuck to what she had said.

At last they told her that the missing woman's body had been found, and her true identity was known.

There would be no escape from facing the consequences of that early deception, Lois saw, but she could pin almost all the blame on Marcia, implying that she had been the most reluctant of accomplices. She would be sent to prison; Lois accepted that, and reflected that it was lucky her mother noticed her visits so little that she would not miss them when they ceased. Because life without Marcia was going to be bleak indeed, the thought of prison was not totally dismaying; she wondered if she would be forced to surrender the garden centre. Would the law make her return Marcia's money to Stephen?

If only she knew whether he had been released! Who else could have come asking for Mr Reynard? Who else could have found the body?

She had so much to lose that Lois decided she must take the risk of assuming it was Stephen. She had successfully incriminated him before, and she could do it again: the police must be made to believe that he had killed Marcia.

'It didn't happen like that,' she said. 'I made it up to stop you finding out what happened before. But now you know, so there's no point in going on.' She gave a most effective, genuine sigh. 'It was Stephen Dawes who killed her. Her husband. He'd somehow traced us when he came out of prison.' Fleetingly she wondered how he'd done it: there were holes in the trail, of course; she couldn't block them all. 'He was looking for revenge because she'd tricked him all those years ago. He'd been sentenced for murdering her. It was me that he came looking for – he wanted revenge against me. After all, he thought she was really dead and I'd inherited her money.' She paused.

'Well?' asked Detective Inspector Cave. 'What happened?'

'He came to the house,' said Lois.

'When?'

'On Thursday.'

'What time?'

What time had that telephone call been made to the police? 'About six,' she said. 'I didn't look at the clock.'

'What happened?' asked Cave.

'The doorbell rang,' said Lois.

'I see. And who answered the door?'

193

'I did. It was Stephen. He burst into the house before I could stop him,' said Lois. 'He said "I've found you – " – something like that.' Lois frowned, as if trying to remember the exact words while she invented what came next. What would have happened if it had really been like that? Would Marcia have stayed in the drawing-room? Would she have recognized Stephen's voice and shrunk back in fear, or come forward?

'I took him into the dining-room,' said Lois. 'We talked for a bit. He said he hadn't killed Marcia and why had I helped her to set him up. Marcia must have got curious. She came into the room.' Lois was pleased with this part of the story. It would explain any evidence there might be in the room that Marcia had died there. 'Of course he recognized her straight away, even though he last saw her eleven years ago, and besides looking older, her hair is darker and done another way.' Cave noticed Lois referred to the dead woman as Marcia, and in the present tense. 'He went mad,' said Lois. 'He grabbed her by the throat and shook her and in a few seconds she collapsed. She was dead. There was nothing I could have done to save her, it was so quick. Like a terrier with a rat.' As she spoke, her eyes filled with tears. It had been quick, just as she said.

'Well?'

'I thought she'd had a heart attack, so I tried the kiss of life,' said Lois. 'But it wasn't any good. Then we had a few drinks and thought of a plan. Or he did. He'd calmed down by this time. We struck a deal. He said he couldn't be tried for the same crime twice, and he'd forget about the past if I forgot about that night. I fetched some polythene sheeting from the shed and we wrapped her up and Stephen put her in the boot of his car and drove off.'

'And the telephone call?'

'He must have made that after he left. I suppose he thought he could get away with it – get away with having just killed Marcia, and clear himself from the past.'

She made a fresh statement, and after that, because she had already been in police custody for some time and there was no firm case for keeping her, Cave let her go.

'I'm surprised they didn't take me back with them, down to the scene of the crime,' said Stephen when Rodway and Burton had gone.

So was Frank, though he wouldn't have agreed to it without making a great many difficulties.

'They've nothing to hold you on,' he said.

'They hadn't before, at first, but they found it,' said Stephen.

'The trouble is, however it happened, their tests take some time to produce results, and coppers always want an arrest,' said Frank. 'While they wait for evidence, the trail goes cold. Give it time – there'll be something to show what happened. After all, there is a body this time.'

'Frank!' This protest was from Val, who had joined them in the study while the children watched television in their playroom, where they had a separate small set.

'They work very deliberately, you know,' Stephen said to her. 'They go from step to step – no flashes of intuition. Marcia and Lois were too smart for them last time. Maybe they will be – or Lois will be – again.'

'Oh no!'

'We don't know what she's said to them. She could have said that I'd strangled Marcia in front of her, and that she'd made the telephone call, anonymously, hoping to get me caught,' said Stephen.

'Waiting is awful, isn't it?' said Val. 'I'm sure it will be all right in the end, Stephen.' Then she looked at Frank and said, rather like a child wanting consolation, 'Won't it?'

'It will,' said Frank grimly. 'If I have to go and get hold of the Home Secretary myself and kidnap him while he reads the files.'

'We need a good dinner,' said Val, and went off to prepare it.

Oddly enough, in spite of his anxiety, Stephen was hungry. Val produced spinach soup and braised ham and he enjoyed the meal, although he had a horrible feeling of its being the condemned man's last one.

He went up to bed at ten o'clock, hoping that by making an early move his host and hostess would soon retire too. Frank, he had noticed, though concerned about him, was

195

otherwise much more relaxed, and Stephen knew this was due to Val's changed attitude. She had stuck to it, in spite of the visit from Rodway. He heard them come up later.

Stephen had a plan. He intended to accomplish what he had earlier failed to do at Witterton, and when the house was quiet, he crept downstairs in his socks, holding his shoes in his hand.

It was after twelve. A light still burned in the main bedroom, but he hoped that Frank and Val were too much engrossed with each other to hear stray sounds, if he made any as he let himself out of the kitchen door.

The Mini was parked on the sweep in front of the house. It was very light, quite easy to push round in a circle and along the drive into the road, where he judged it safe to start the engine.

He made good time to Witterton.

Fir Tree House, he feared, might still be under police guard, but there was no sign of that as he turned in at the gate. He thought about breaking in again. It would be easy to do so, to go up to Lois's bedroom and really terrify her, but the sight of her in bed, no doubt in schoolgirl pyjamas, was not one he wished to see. He decided to play it straight, and rang the doorbell, pealing it hard and thumping the knocker.

In the end, when there was no answer, he unlocked the window again, but this time he wore gloves. If only he'd done that the other night! He'd had a pair in the car, and it would have saved him so much trouble.

Lois's bedroom was empty. Her bed had not been disturbed at all.

Was she in police custody? She should be, for she was guilty, Stephen knew, but the police would want to blame him, if they could: it would make the earlier prosecution seem less heinous for it would show that he was capable of murder.

Perhaps he was.

He let himself out of the house and went round to the garage. The doors were pushed to but not locked, and only the Mini was there. Stephen thought the police might have taken it off for inspection. If Lois was being questioned, would she have gone to the police station in her own van? He

196

remembered being collected by a police car on some of the occasions when he was taken in, and sometimes being taken by Frank. Of course, his own car had been impounded.

Where could she be?

He went back into the house and looked around. There were the remains of a meal in the kitchen: a plate, knife and fork and frying pan piled into the sink, and a glass on the side. He sniffed at it and smelled whisky.

Wearing his gloves, he looked round the house again, this time with more care, as if the inanimate objects could tell him where Lois was. In the drawing-room, the cushions in one of the chairs were crushed as if someone had sat there, and beside it, on a small table, stood an empty glass. He sniffed that: whisky again.

A phrase he had spoken earlier that day recurred to him. He remembered, too, the alleged previous pattern of events which had been repeated in fact.

Stephen got into his car and consulted the map. Then he set off for Watch Point. He had to keep stopping, looking at signposts and the map again, but at last he came to a pointer which said *To the Beach*. The track led through a farm gate. Stephen opened it and drove through, closing the gate behind him. He drove carefully on, down the rutted path, his headlights picking up the shapes of cows in the darkness. He went through another gate and the track began to climb. After some distance it branched, one lane leading on upwards to the cliffs, the other dwindling into a footpath that went to the beach. Stephen took the cliff track and soon came to another gate. He went through it and drove on over short turf. Then he saw the van. It was parked some fifty yards ahead of him, near some gorse bushes. He doused his lights and drove closer to it, then got out of the Mini and approached on foot. He opened the van door, but it was empty.

Blood surged in his temples. He had found Lois, unless it was already too late and in a fit of guilt she had flung herself over the cliff, denying him the chance of a confrontation.

But she hadn't.

Stephen walked along the headland towards Watch Point, over which Marcia's cold, stiff body had been cast to the beach below. The night was clear, and there was a crescent moon. His eyes had adapted to the darkness and he could make out the rough terrain over which he walked. There were odd outcrops of rock and scrubby gorse bushes here and there. All the time he could hear the plash and sigh of the sea.

And then he saw her.

She was standing with her back to him, looking down at the shore below, a foot or two from the edge of the cliff, so intent on her thoughts that she had not noticed the lights of his car as he approached, nor heard its engine. One push would do it, thought Stephen. But a push was too good for Lois.

He called to her.

'Lois. I want to talk to you,' he said. His voice, pitched to carry above the sound of the sea, sounded loud in the night air.

He had to call her twice more before her head turned. She moved it about, like a hound pointing.

'Lois, you know who it is,' said Stephen. 'Come away from there. We have to talk.'

'Who are you to tell me what to do?' said Lois. Her voice was slurred.

'It's Stephen. You know that. You owe me an explanation.'

'Of what?'

'Of how you and Marcia came to do that to me, eleven years ago.'

There was a silence. Then Lois spoke, her voice sing-song now.

'You had to be punished. You sinned against her,' she said.

'But such a punishment!' said Stephen. She was still turned away from him and he had moved closer.

'I only helped,' said Lois, remembering what she had told the police. The more she repeated her story, the easier it would be the next time, and she was going to have to convince a lot of people that the idea was entirely Marcia's.

'Marcia never thought all that up on her own. She couldn't have done it. She hadn't the energy,' said Stephen. Nor the invention.

'You can think what you like,' said Lois.

'Why did you kill her, Lois?' asked Stephen. 'I know you did and the police will be able to prove it.'

'They won't. They think you did it. I told them I saw you do it, and that I helped you wrap up the body and put it in the boot of your car. Then you drove off, I told them. They believed me.'

Now Lois took some steps towards him. She wore an anorak jacket and her arms were folded across her chest. Her head was bare, the wiry grey curls stirred by the breeze from the sea.

'Why did you do it, Lois?' Stephen asked again. 'Why did any of it happen?'

'Why does the world go round?' asked Lois. She unclasped her arms and put her hands on her sides. 'They can't try you a second time, Stephen,' she went on. 'I may be charged with what happened before – I don't know – but I wouldn't get a long sentence. I'd survive. I've got a good business. You could run it for me – I'd need someone to keep it going while I was away and I don't suppose you've got a job, have you? I'd pay you an annuity for the rest of your life, after I came out and took the reins over again.'

'Lois, really! I thought I'd heard it all – but you – there's no end to what you think you can manipulate, is there? First Marcia, and now me. Oh, you put her up to it. I know that. My God, but you're grotesque!' He laughed, a bitter sound in the night.

It was the laughter that turned Lois. She ran suddenly past him in the direction of the van, showing quite a turn of speed. Her flight took Stephen by surprise and gave her a good start. He went after her, but his leather shoes slipped on the dewy headland, and she reached the van before he caught up with her, jumping in, turning the headlights on and starting the engine while he was still some distance away.

Lois swung the van round and drove straight at him, the lights blinding him and the engine roaring.

Stephen put up an arm instinctively as he jumped to one side. The van's wing caught him on the thigh and he fell to the ground, feeling a sharp pain in his wrist, but he rolled away from the path of the van and got to his feet, ready to dodge if she turned the van and came after him again.

She tried to swing the van round, but she left it too late and, unable to make the circle, it careened at the edge of the cliff for seconds before it went over.

6

It was after eight o'clock on Sunday morning when Stephen turned the Mini in at the entrance to Dove House. He had stood at the top of the cliff for several minutes, looking down, after Lois tipped the van over the edge. Its lights had gone out and there was no sound except the sigh of the sea. There was no more to be done.

He limped back to the Mini, nursing his left arm. His hand didn't seem to be working and he could not move his wrist. Very slowly and carefully, because of the pain and the difficulty he had with the gear lever – he had to reach across and move it with his right hand – Stephen drove back across the clifftop and along the tracks, through the various gateways and so to the main road. As he pointed the car eastwards, easing up into top gear and hoping he would be able to remain there, it began to rain.

If the rain had started sooner, he would have left tyre marks on the cliff. As it was, there would be no sign that another car had stood there beside the van.

The pain in his wrist forced him to concentrate simply on driving. He pushed on, helped by the fact that so early on a Sunday morning at this time of the year there was almost no traffic. He passed close to Anderton, stopping once for petrol at an all-night self-service station.

He parked the car on the spot where he had left it on Friday and went round to the kitchen door of Dove House, which he had left unlocked. Surely they would be up?

But there was no sign of life. He went into the kitchen, taking off his damp shoes and locking the back door. Then he slipped up the stairs and along to his room. He slid into it silently, able to do so because the passage was thickly carpeted and the door opened and closed smoothly. He leaned against the closed door, giddy with exhaustion, and fairly sure by now that he had broken a bone or bones in his wrist.

A bath would revive him. He managed to get his clothes off, and was soon lying in hot water soaking the stiffness from his body. But for the pain in his wrist, he would have dozed off. As it was, the cooling water stirred him into getting out and drying himself on one of Val's expensive towels. Luckily it was not his right hand which was injured; he shaved, brushed his teeth, and dressed again in some of the clean clothes which Val had produced for him. Now he was hungry, and longing for some coffee. What time did Val and Frank get up on a Sunday? Wouldn't the children be wanting their breakfast? Would it be all right if he went downstairs and helped himself?

There were Panadol tablets in the medicine cupboard in the guest's bathroom. He swallowed three. That should help the wrist.

He could hear Frank whistling as he entered the kitchen. The coffee was on and the children were eating their cereal; it seemed they had been up for some time. Val, in a quilted dressing-gown, her hair in attractive disarray, was sitting at the table while Frank cut bread and put it in the toaster. Val's eyes were soft and she seemed to glow: absorbed though he was with the task of trying to behave as if he had spent the night safely asleep, Stephen noticed and he understood.

Luckily the children's chatter masked Stephen's silence. He felt better after two cups of coffee, but he could not hold his toast to butter it, and Fiona noticed his left arm hanging at his side.

'I use two hands to do mine,' she said. 'One to hold and one to spread.'

'Would you like to spread mine for me?' Stephen asked. 'I've hurt my wrist, that's why I can't do it.'

Filled with importance, Fiona got down from her place and came to Stephen's side. Elaborately, she carved a piece of butter from the dish and spread it thickly, then consulted him about his preference for marmalade or honey. A strand of her hair tickled his face as she stretched across him to reach the honeypot. Two days ago, Val would have snatched her back from such contaminating contact.

'What did you do? Fall in the bathroom?' asked Val.

'No – I – er – I couldn't sleep – I went for a stroll in the garden and slipped and fell. Silly, wasn't it?' said Stephen.

Val poured the coffee, and concentrated on the children, coaxing them to eat up quickly, and she sent them off as soon as they had finished.

'Your wrist's bad, isn't it?' she said.

'It is, rather,' Stephen admitted. 'Sorry, Val. I think I've broken something.'

'Falling in the garden?' said Frank. 'How could you do such damage like that?'

'Easily – putting out a hand to save yourself,' said Val. 'Frank will take you in to the hospital, Stephen. It's the quickest way to get you fixed.'

Stephen didn't protest. It would have to be done, and best get on with it in the lull before Lois was found.

'You'd be better with it in a sling,' said Val. She stood up, a warm scent coming from her body as she rose. 'I'll find something and fix you one,' she added, going from the room. She returned with a large silk handkerchief with which she fastened his hand and arm across his chest; it felt better with the weight supported.

Frank took him to the casualty department of the hospital.

'You're limping a bit,' Val said as they left the house. 'I should show the doctor whatever it is you've done to your leg, too.'

'It's only a bruise,' said Stephen.

'All the same, let him see it,' Val insisted.

Stephen did so.

Detective Inspector Cave and a detective sergeant went to Fir Tree House early on Sunday morning to take Lois in for further questioning.

Cave had found himself in trouble with Detective Chief Superintendent Rodway for letting her go at all. After his

202

return from seeing Stephen, Rodway had gone straight to his headquarters where the pathologist's report was waiting.

'You let Mrs Reynard go before seeing this,' Rodway stated, and Cave agreed.

'We can always get her back,' he said, defensively. 'She'd been here for more than twenty-four hours. I didn't think we wanted some lawyer insisting that we let her go later, when we really need her.'

'Hm.' Rodway tapped the report. 'You've read this?'

'Yes.'

Rodway was running his eye quickly over the pathologist's conclusions. He glanced again at Lois's new statement, where she said that Stephen Dawes had called at Fir Tree House at approximately six o'clock and then killed his former wife.

'She's lying,' he snapped. 'The woman was killed immediately after eating a substantial meal. I don't think those two ladies were given to eating high tea, do you, Cave?'

Cave shook his head.

Rodway read through the rest of the pathologist's report. Mrs King, or Dawes, had drunk some wine; there was chicken in the stomach; also grapes, rice and carrots. The doctor was certain, too, that death had taken place on Wednesday, and the cause was manual strangulation. There were nailmarks pitted in the neck, and the hyoid bone was broken.

'So Stephen Dawes put the body in the boot of his car, did he?' he said grimly. 'That'd be a tricky operation. How'd you like to ram a five-foot-eight-inch woman into the boot of a hired Mini, eh, Cave? That's what Dawes was driving. Think it could be done?'

'No,' said Cave.

'She weighed ten and a half stone, too,' said Rodway.

'Mrs Reynard isn't going to run away,' said Cave.

'No, she isn't,' Rodway agreed. 'But I'd like her back again, first thing in the morning. Say six o'clock. And her clothes, though no doubt she'll have a plausible excuse if we find the deceased's hairs on her jumper.' He thought about bringing Lois straight back now, and looked again at the pathologist's report. There were fibres underneath the fingernails; once analysed, they might match something that the killer had been wearing. Rodway sifted through the statements taken by his officers. Staff at the garden centre had been interviewed and asked about Thursday's activities. Fred Harris had stated that Mrs Reynard had visited a customer to advise about her garden, an appointment postponed from the day before because Mrs Reynard had had bad toothache and had gone to the dentist on the Wednesday, borrowing his, Fred's, car, so that the van could be used for some deliveries, a simple switch.

There had been a visitor for Mrs Reynard on the Thursday, Fred had said; a man, middle-aged, with grey hair and a beard: Stephen Dawes, without a doubt.

But Mary King, or Marcia Dawes, was already dead on Thursday, the pathologist was certain.

The chicken meal that Mrs King, or Dawes, had eaten just before her death might have been her midday meal, but Colonel West had said that they had spent the afternoon together, so that seemed most unlikely unless he had been the killer. He must be asked what they had had for lunch, and it could be checked with the Three Horseshoes. An officer must make inquiries, and the dentist who had dealt with Mrs Reynard's toothache must be found.

It would be simple to ask her who her dentist was, then check with him.

Rodway thought again about sending Cave to fetch the woman Reynard right away; she would be tired, and so less guarded in her answers. But in the morning there would be more fuel for their interrogation, after seeing Colonel West and the staff at the Three Horseshoes. A few hours' sleep for himself, and less for Cave, would make them more efficient. They'd have to trace the dentist to his home, but that would not be difficult. An officer arriving at eight o'clock on Sunday morning would be received with less displeasure than one calling in the middle of the night.

On balance, he decided it could wait a few more hours.

When Cave and a woman police officer reached Fir Tree House at six o'clock on Sunday morning, they found that Lois Reynard was not there. They looked for her at the garden centre, but it was all locked up. The van was missing, so it seemed that she had skipped, though the centre and the house and grounds would have to be thoroughly searched.

Cave did not know how to break the news to Rodway.

The same jogger who had found Marcia's body saw the green van at the base of the high cliffs that morning. There was a dead woman inside, wedged behind the steering wheel, her face lacerated by the shattered windscreen. He did not run on the beach again until the following spring.

Saturday evening's local radio and television news programmes had the story about the discovery of Mrs Mary King's body. Her death was being treated as a case of murder. Only one reporter, however, picked up the bigger story in time to give it to a Sunday paper. He was a freelance journalist who had gone along to Fir Tree House and found it empty.

He had a contact at police headquarters who had tipped him off before when something big was under wraps, and now he learned that a woman had been helping police with their inquiries. By inference, the woman had to be Mrs Reynard, but the reporter learned that there was some query about the victim's true identity. The name of Marcia Dawes was mentioned; it linked up with an earlier investigation, but his informant knew no more at present.

The name rang a bell in the reporter's mind. He made some inquiries in Witterton and soon found out about Fred Harris, who had worked for Mrs Reynard all these years. The reporter tracked Fred down at his home, and asked him a number of innocent-seeming questions about Mrs Reynard and her friend. Fred respected his employer, even liked her, and would never have set out to be disloyal, but he had no idea that she was in any sort of trouble. He had seen the police take her off, and when he was questioned himself about Thursday's activities, he had assumed she was helping them to look for Mrs King. When the reporter told him that Mrs King was dead, he was shocked and horrified.

'Oh, poor Mrs Reynard!' he exclaimed. 'She thought the world of Mrs King. However did it happen?'

He talked a lot, then. He told the reporter about the man

who had been inquiring for Mr Reynard, and who then had asked the whereabouts of Fir Tree House. When asked, he described the man. He described Mrs King, who was an artistic sort of lady.

'Where had they come from?' asked the journalist.

Fred didn't know.

'And both widows?'

'Seemingly,' said Fred.

Had Fred known their maiden names, by any chance?

He racked his brains, thinking aloud, muttering that he'd heard Mrs Reynard sometimes call Mrs King Marcia, though her name was Mary. He'd thought it odd, but folk had strange nicknames. Then he remembered that the nursing home where Mrs Reynard's mother lived had once telephoned, when the old lady was ill with pneumonia. Fred had taken the call when Mrs Reynard was out, and had noticed the old lady's name because it was the same as his sister's married name – Carter. Mrs Reynard's first name was Lois.

On his way home to write up the story, the reporter called on another of his contacts, an old woman now, but still a murder buff who studied every big case. She kept files of cuttings and had an excellent memory. She'd come up with gold before, and she did so again. There had been the unusual case of Stephen Dawes, sentenced some ten or eleven years ago for the murder of his wife, whose body had never been found. She produced the file and the reporter read what had happened then.

He borrowed the files and showed the old newspaper photographs to Fred Harris, who, shocked almost speechless, said that, yes, allowing for age, that could be Mrs Reynard, though the other lady wasn't very like Mrs King, who was dark and had curly hair.

He wasn't at all sure about Thursday's visitor. Stephen Dawes, in the newspaper photographs, had dark hair and was clean-shaven. Thursday's caller was grey-haired and had a beard.

The reporter made some telephone calls. He learned that Stephen Dawes had been released on parole about a month before, when he had grey hair and wore a beard.

He rang London with his story, and an editor who did not

hold his job because he lacked nerve cleared the front page of his tabloid.

So the story broke before the police were ready to release the facts.

BODY ON BEACH. ELEVEN-YEAR-OLD MYSTERY SOLVED? ran the headline, and below, WAS MARY REALLY MARCIA? The paper dug out old photographs, and one of Stephen, taken at the time of his arrest, appeared above the caption WRONGED HUSBAND?

7

Ruth Mansfield and her husband did not take the tabloid paper which posed the possible connection between the woman dead in Somerset and the case eleven years before, but their neighbours did, and it was on the table when the Mansfields went next door for a drink to celebrate their host's fortieth birthday.

Edward Mansfield noticed it.

'At forty you should be past reading that stuff,' he teased. 'What's all that about? Don't they mean Martha, not Marcia?'

This biblical reference did not click with their host. He gave a straight answer.

'Some woman who's been found dead on a beach. Seems she wasn't who people thought she was,' he said. 'Seems people thought her husband killed her years ago, and the poor guy's been in clink all this time for doing her in, when all the time she was alive.'

'Is that right?' asked Edward.

'Sounds like it. Marcia something or other, her real name was. Set her husband up properly, she did, poor bugger. Here, read it.'

Edward wasn't really interested. He'd made his joky point with his friend. Edward never found it easy to seem light-hearted and to quip, though he worked at it, off duty.

But Ruth had heard. Slowly, she put her hand out and pulled the paper forward. Her head swam as she saw the photograph and the lead-in to the story. It was continued on an inside page, and she turned to it. Several other couples were also in the house to celebrate, and at first nobody noticed that she was not joining in the party. Then Edward, who was never unaware for very long of where she was, missed her.

'Why Ruth! What are you doing?' he asked in his rallying domestic voice. 'You're not reading about that old murder, are you? You hate things like that.'

She did; in all the time that he had known her, she had avoided anything that dealt with violence – films, books, television programmes, and newspaper reports about contemporary crimes. He had heard her express sympathy for the victims in notorious cases, but no interest at all in what the criminals had done, how they were caught, or why it had happened. Edward fondly thought her super-sensitive; and he was right.

Now she was reading avidly.

Ruth pulled herself together.

'Oh – it's nothing special – it just seemed rather odd,' she said, trying to smile.

'You've gone quite pale. Silly duck, reading about something that gives you the creeps,' said Edward, giving her a gentle hug.

Ruth went up to the paper shop that afternoon, while Edward took the children out for a walk. Usually, on fine Sundays, they all went off to the downs together, but today she pleaded a headache. The paper shop closed at three o'clock on Sundays. She got there just in time, and they had one copy left of the tabloid.

She cut the story out of the paper and put the clipping in a drawer in her bedroom, under some sweaters.

When Stephen came back from hospital with his arm in plaster, the morning was almost over. He had a broken wrist and severe bruising, and he looked exhausted.

'Shock,' said Val, and made him go to bed after lunch.

She had glanced through the *Sunday Times*, where a small paragraph referred to a woman missing from her home near Witterton having been found dead on the beach below Watch Point, and nothing more.

The children wanted to sign their names on his plaster. Fiona drew some circles and two pointed ears and fanning whiskers, making a cat.

'Leave him alone now, children,' Val said firmly. 'Stephen, you look awful. Get right into bed and put the electric blanket on.'

Stephen did as she advised. Exhaustion and the doctor's painkillers worked. He slept.

At five o'clock the sound of the door being quietly opened snapped him awake and he sat up, pulse racing, mouth dry.

A small person peered round the door and a high voice spoke.

'Are you awake? I brought you a cup of tea. I made it,' announced Fiona, and entered the room carrying a tray on which was a large, steaming mug and a huge slice of chocolate cake on a china plate.

'Oh, how lovely! Thank you, Fiona,' said Stephen, struggling to adjust himself to the present as he pushed away nightmare dreams. He smiled at the little girl, in her blue jeans and thick Arran sweater.

'Mummy said we ought to let you sleep, but Daddy and me think you won't go to sleep tonight if you don't wake up now,' said Fiona.

'I think you're right,' said Stephen. He felt the waves of sleep trying to claim him again, and pushed himself up in the bed. 'I'll just drink this, and then I'll come downstairs,' he said. 'Thank you.'

He had stiffened up. His leg ached quite badly. The doctor had noted the bruises and thought that he might have pulled a muscle.

'If you hadn't told me how this happened, I'd have said you'd been hit by a car,' he said, and added, 'Were you?'

Stephen looked at the concerned young face. Doctors were supposed to keep your secrets.

'Yes,' he said.

'I see,' said the doctor, and made no further comment.

Stephen found the family playing children's Scrabble. Fiona was almost ready to play the advanced game, but Jamie still needed help. Stephen watched them finish the contest, and then Frank said the sun was over the yardarm and they could have a drink.

Val took the children upstairs. It was school tomorrow and they must have baths and their toenails cut; also, it was hair-wash night.

'Rodway rang, while you were asleep,' Frank told Stephen. 'Lois is dead.'

'Oh!' Stephen did his best to look surprised.

'Drove her van over the cliff, it seems, at Watch Point – that place where they found Marcia,' Frank related.

'Oh,' said Stephen again.

'Suicide, they think. The inquest is on Tuesday.' Frank paused. 'They're satisfied that she killed Marcia. It seems there was a diamond-and-emerald ring in her pocket. Marcia had a boyfriend whom she planned to marry. He identified it – said she always wore it – said she'd certainly had it on when they met last Wednesday.'

'I gave Marcia an emerald-and-diamond ring when we were engaged,' said Stephen.

'I know, and it was among the things missing from Badger's End,' said Frank. 'It shouldn't be too hard to prove that it's the same ring. I expect you remember where you bought it.'

Stephen did.

'There will be two inquests,' said Frank. 'Both will probably be adjourned to give the police time to prepare their cases. They'll be just to identify the – the women,' he hesitated, about to say 'the bodies'. After all, one of them was Stephen's wife. 'So that the funerals can be arranged, you see,' he added. There hadn't been that problem last time.

'Oh,' said Stephen, yet again. 'Who'll see to that?' he asked. 'Isn't it up to us?'

'I thought you'd feel like that,' said Frank. 'It seems that Mrs Carter isn't *compos mentis*, so she can't be consulted. I expect there'll be a firm of solicitors somewhere in the background, once the police look through Lois's papers, but no

210

one knows of any other relatives. I'll find some undertakers down there in the morning.'

Rodway had said that orange fibres had been found beneath Marcia's fingernails; they matched a sweater Lois owned. The case was clear-cut, though the motive was obscure unless she had been jealous over Marcia's friendship with Colonel West.

In time, Stephen would receive what was left of Marcia's estate, and further compensation for wrongful conviction, but that could all be gone into later. Settling everything would be complicated, but the announcement that his conviction had been quashed would be made without delay.

'You can sleep soundly now,' Frank told Stephen.

On a bleak, grey day, with the rain pouring down, the funerals of both women were held. In a short service at Shawton crematorium, Marcia's remains were committed to the furnace. Apart from the undertaker's men and the crematorium chaplain, the only people there were Stephen and Frank, and Andrew West, a spare, controlled figure in his dark suit and black tie. Twenty minutes later, Lois was dispatched. Andrew did not attend the second service; he waited outside the chapel until the others emerged, then had a short chat with Stephen.

He was leaving the area, he said, selling up and going to live in Boston, near his daughter. He said that he was grateful for the interlude with Marcia, and that he thought it had made her happy too, during all the years that they had known each other.

His dignity impressed Stephen.

Ruth had followed every report in the papers. Old photographs and film of Stephen's trial were shown on television; the quashing of his conviction was a *cause célèbre*. Reporters found out about Ivy Lodge and went there, but the house was empty, with a constable outside, for Frank had foreseen this news escaping, tempting thieves, and had insisted that the place should be protected.

A fleeting shot of Stephen leaving the crematorium with his arm in plaster appeared on television, but he gave no interviews.

This will pass, Ruth thought as she lay awake at night, haunted by remorse. She grew pale, and had to tell Edward she thought she'd got flu.

Then, one Thursday afternoon, her doorbell rang, and there on the doorstep was Stephen. She knew him at once, despite the grey hair and the beard, which anyway she'd seen on television.

'You'd better come in,' she said.

'Is it convenient?' Stephen asked. 'You're alone?' He'd picked a weekday, making sure it was neither half-term nor a school holiday, so that there was every chance that none of her family was at home with Ruth.

'Yes, I'm quite alone,' said Ruth. She led him into a large sitting-room with a big picture window opening on to the neat garden and a view beyond it to the downs. Modern prints hung on the walls; the furniture, too, was modern. It was a comfortable room. 'I thought you might come one day,' she told him. 'But I don't know how you found me. I thought it would take you longer.'

'I didn't put spies on to you, Ruth,' said Stephen. 'But long ago my mother traced you. She was anxious about Susannah and she knew I would be when I got out. She's dead now.' He paused. 'I had your Oxford address. Someone there told me you were married, and I found you.'

'I've been lucky,' said Ruth. 'Edward's a good, kind man.'

'You've got a son,' said Stephen.

'Yes,' said Ruth. 'Two of them. Tommy and Bill.'

Stephen saw photographs on a shelf.

'Are those the boys?' he asked.

'Yes. And Susannah,' said Ruth. She got up and brought the photographs to him. The boys had round, smiling faces and fair hair. The girl whom he had seen in Anderton and here, going to the bus, was indeed his daughter. He saw again, in the photograph, how her hair flopped forward exactly like his own. 'She's like you, Stephen,' said Ruth. 'She always reminds me of you. I'm sorry. I should have known you hadn't done it.'

212

Stephen looked at her. For years he had dreamed of this moment, of asserting his rights to a part of his daughter's life. Now, he felt nothing. Ruth, whom he thought might arouse emotion of some sort in him – even bitterness – was just any middle-aged woman. She could have been a total stranger, yet once she had been a generous lover.

'You could have named me,' Ruth said in the silence between them.

'That wouldn't have helped,' said Stephen. 'I understood that you were protecting Susannah.'

'You've hurt your arm,' Ruth said.

'Yes.' With the plaster, Stephen was able to drive, but very cautiously. 'I broke my wrist,' he said. 'It's nothing. Does your husband know about Susannah?'

Ruth shook her head.

'No. He thinks I was engaged and that my fiancé was killed just before the wedding,' she answered.

'Shall you tell him the truth now?'

'I don't know. Are you going to force me to?'

'No.'

Ruth visibly relaxed.

'He'll never trust me if I do,' she said.

'If you don't, you may not trust yourself,' said Stephen, and added, because he could not help himself, 'Does Susannah ever ask about her father?'

'Sometimes. I've said I'll tell her more when she's older. I always thought I'd have to face it some day,' Ruth confessed.

'Well, I don't intend to upset things now,' said Stephen. 'My solicitor, Frank Jeffries, knows where you are, because of my will. Naturally, everything I have is left to Susannah, and one day she'll have to know the reason. Frank will always know where I am, too, in case you ever have an emergency and need some help. Have you got a piece of paper, so that I can write down his address?' He took a ballpoint from his pocket.

She found him a notepad. Holding it awkwardly, Stephen wrote down Frank's address and telephone number.

'You don't want to meet Susannah, then?' Ruth asked.

'I do. I want to get to know her. But not until or unless you're ready to let that happen. You – we – must think of

213

your husband and the other children – your whole family. There's been enough sorrow over all this. One day the time will be right to tell her, and your husband. You'll know when that is, and then you can get in touch with me, through Frank. Of course, that's only if Susannah wants to meet me. She may not be interested.'

She would be, Ruth knew. She'd asked to see a photograph and Ruth had said there were none.

'You're distressed,' said Stephen. 'This has upset you. There's nothing to be afraid of, Ruth. I won't do anything to cause you any harm.'

'You never did, did you?' she said, but she had harmed him by trying to trap him into leaving Marcia. As she began to weep, he turned from her and left the house.

He was going to spend the weekend with Mrs Henshaw and the Wainwrights. After the first clamour in the media when his conviction was quashed, he had written to Mrs Henshaw apologizing for masquerading as John Baxter. By return, the invitation had arrived.

His wrist would soon be healed; then he was going to give up his hired Mini and buy a car. He had long discussions with Jamie and Fiona about what he should get. They recommended a Porsche with lights that folded away, or at least a BMW like their father's, but Stephen explained he was not quite in that category of motorist. A Cavalier, he thought, or a Sierra; he didn't think he could wait until Austin Rover launched their new car after Christmas.

Val and Frank had insisted that he stay at Dove House until his plaster had been removed; Val planned to keep him even longer, saying he would need physiotherapy to strengthen his wrist.

He could get that at Fairbridge, Stephen had said.

She had taken him to Ivy Lodge to fetch some clothes while Frank was at the office.

'You went to Witterton, didn't you, the night Lois died?' she asked him. 'That was when you broke your wrist?'

Stephen nodded.

'How did you know?' he asked.

'I thought Frank was right – that you couldn't have done it in the garden, unless it was icy or something. But I pre-

tended otherwise,' said Val. 'When you'd both gone to the hospital, I went out to your car. It was still faintly warm. I guessed where you'd been because it's what I'd have done in your place. I thought maybe Lois had attacked you. Did she?'

'Sort of,' said Stephen. 'She wasn't at the house when I got there. I guessed she'd returned to what could be called the scene of the crime – the cliffs. I went there, and she drove her van at me. I jumped out of the way but she hit me and I fell.' He stared ahead through the windscreen. 'Then she tried to turn the van round to have another go, but she didn't make it.'

'I thought something like that must have happened,' said Val. The inquest on Lois had returned a verdict of death by misadventure: no one, it was said, could have been certain of her state of mind at the time. 'That was why I wanted you to make sure the doctor looked at your leg, as well as your wrist. In case you needed evidence that she'd provoked you,' she added, and went on, 'In case you'd killed her.'

'You thought I might have?'

'Only in self-defence,' said Val. 'I didn't tell Frank, just in case it was better for him not to know.'